THE DOG SIT AFFAIR

SEÁN KELLY

DEDICATION

To the many variety groups and troupes in Waterford and Tramore, whose company I've enjoyed over the years.

To Tramore writers group, and in particular the original facilitator, the talented John Hannigan who encouraged all to attempt that impossible dream-seeing your work in print!

To my dedicated Editor, Publisher and organiser Orla Kelly, under whose watchful and experienced eye, this project saw fruition.

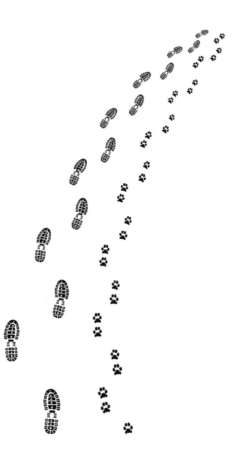

CONTENTS

CHAPTER ONE

~

May 2012, Dublin, Ireland

A minute before landing at Dublin airport, the plane banked at an angle, and from her passenger seat, Haley looked up at the sky. In the vastness above, there was nothing to see but a cold circle of blue and a flock of gulls. On the other side of the plane, the view was of sweeping roads, roofs of houses, and in the distance, a glimpse of the runway.

It was the first time she had flown on her own since her husband James had died in a helicopter crash, and a feeling of tension built in her chest. She had come to Dublin to help out her sister, but she had a plan of her own, to translate her grief into some form of adventure. The wheels crunched slightly on hitting the tarmac of the runway. She felt the sickening thump of solid ground as the plane rocked from side to side and then stabilised. The engines slackened speed, and the plane taxied towards the airport.

She eased herself from her seat and searched for some form of reassurance. She was met by a sea of jolly faces, raucous hen and stag parties that seem to have made the landing rockier than it should have been, arms flailing already to reach the overhead lockers. She was always fascinated by the immediate rush of passengers to the overhead luggage bins before the aircraft had even come to a stop. The scramble to collect hand luggage and duty-free bags and spend minutes standing, while the discharge steps were presented to the doors seemed pointless.

At least the two 'squawky', irritating spoiled brats three rows down from her were now quiet. Meanwhile, the dozen or so well-oiled Essex Girls had just completed the final chorus of Sisters Are Doing It For Themselves. Everyone within earshot was aware that their Hen-Night would be spent getting 'polluted' and 'laid', in Temple Bar. Haley suggested to the passenger beside her that this must be some wild, crazy pub, this Temple Bar! The elderly man smiled and explained that it was not just a pub, but a collection of bars, restaurants, night clubs and 'whatever-yur-havin-yur-self' area of enjoyment in Dublin city.

It was a magnet for stag and hen nights and for youth to have its fling. The area epitomised the excesses of the Celtic Tiger era, managed to survive the aftermath of the crash and still survived. Haley just returned the smile and added 'Look-out-Temple Bar!'

The impatient passengers had now moved to their new standing area - the luggage carousel - and the annoying wait continued. Eventually, Haley spotted her large maroon coloured suitcase appearing through the door flaps. As she moved and attempted to rescue her well-laden belongings, a tall well-built young man stepped in and said, 'Here, let me get that for you ma'am,' and planted the heavy case beside her. 'God! Have you got the kitchen sink in there, too?' he laughingly asked.

'Yup,' was the reply. 'It's right beside the hoover so let's hope the Customs don't need their washing or cleaning done.' Both laughed as Haley popped the release button on the top of the carry handle and began to wheel her two months' supply of clothing, shoes and other feminine requisites through the Blue EU Zone exit door.

For the first time in months, Haley felt as though she was coming up for air. She fumbled in her handbag, found a pair of sunglasses, and put them on.

One week previously, Berkshire, England
The fourth month of 2012 had not just been the thirty days of 'April-Showers' in Langton, Berkshire. It was a month of on and off downpours, with continuous road and rail disruptions and an array of flood warnings. The afternoon of the fifteenth saw severe thunderstorms, and at midnight Haley had been awakened to the sound of three feet of muddy water swirling around her detached dormer bungalow. She had feared the worst, but at least she had an upstairs to protect her from the mess.

Her house was at the bottom of their neatly manicured estate, which meant her home got the worst of this overflow from the nearby river. The consistent downpours and run-off could not be contained, so Oakland Crescent would suffer, with Haley's house being the recipient of Mother Nature's wetting.

The local Council quickly reacted to the situation and as the worst of the rains had passed, assured the residents that flood protection would be promptly put in place. Work crews immediately began the clean-up. However, the mess at number eighteen would mean that Haley's property would require substantial re-work. Drying out and relining all the downstairs walls and repainting and replacing everything except the upstairs. Her gardens (front and rear) also needed a total overhaul. The only bright side was that her Home Insurance policy would cover every penny, and this was confirmed by the polite assessor who had sloshed his way through the lower floors, on the day following the disaster.

Haley was widowed in 2011, when her husband, James died in a helicopter crash in Northern Russia. He was a senior Civil Servant who worked closely with all departments of the UK Foreign Office and Defence Forces, and his duties had taken both of them to the many outstations within the dwindling British Commonwealth. The thaw in the Cold-War meant that diplomatic relations with all the 'old enemies' were more open and viewed with less suspicion. She still did not know why or what this fatal visit was about, except that James was accompanied by a young IT specialist (Kerri), whom he had taken under his wing in Whitehall. He never spoke about work (not even in pillow-talk) as he felt the less his wife knew, the safer and better for her.

However, both her husband James and Kerri never came home. Russian sources confirmed all five on this flight died, including Conrad-Kremlin as he was known. He was the organiser of this trip, and James had trusted him. He even attended the Epsom Derby with families of various diplomats. Haley had found him to be very charming with his long flowing blond hair, and a liking for expensive food and wines.

She did her best to get on with her own life following the disaster and had taken a part-time job at an antiques shop in town. It was owned by good friends of theirs, Jake and Sally, and it got her mind off things for the three mornings a week she spent there. Jake did all the buying at various fairs and auctions as he had a good eye for detail and pricing, while Sally, with her charismatic personality, youthful looks and figure, was the specialist at clinching the sale.

When Sally heard of the flooding, she immediately insisted Haley move in with them until all was sorted and would not take no for an answer. Next day Haley was in the guest's room at their 'old-world' home on the edge of town. Their only son, Norman was an architect and was instructed by mum Sally, to ensure a qualified and competent builder would reconstruct her home to its former glory. Haley also used the opportunity to alter much of the ground floor area and change all the colour schemes, as it held too many memories.

Haley's mobile telephone had escaped the flood as it was on its charger on the kitchen worktop. It was annoyingly ringing, as she attempted to clear the dishes after the evening meal with her new landlords. Sally insisted this was her job, in her kitchen. 'So, go chat to your caller'.

It was Heather, particularly concerned for the wellbeing of her only sibling. God! Two calls in the one day; she is really getting paranoid!

'Hi Sis, AGAIN, can you talk freely? I need to run something by you,' inquired Heather.

'Ahh, no, - not really, but can you give it a few hours or so?'

'Great! I'll ring you at ten.'

Haley knew that Sally and Jake were going out to meet with some old school chums who had recently retired.

At 9.59 pm, Haley's phone rang. Dear God! talk about promptness, she thought. This sister has always had a being-on-time phobia. Hell, she was even prompt (five minutes early) for her own wedding!

'Hi Sis, it's me again. Can you talk freely now?'

'Yes, little H, I'm freeeeee (imitating the old line from 'Are You Being Served') so, fire away.'

'Well! A situation has developed here.'

Interrupting her, Haley exclaimed, 'Jeez, don't tell me your place is flooded as well!'

'No! Will you just please listen for a minute?

As you know, our only, 'demented' daughter Chloe is still out in Africa trying to save the planet and endangered apes and every other lame-duck situation that needs help. We get a 'crackly' short call every two weeks saying, "All good here, ye don't realise how well-off you are at home, talk soon, byeeeee!" Now, we hear from her travelling pal, who is home having contracted some crazy shit bug, and has been quarantined here, that Chloe is moving to some field hospital in the middle of a war-torn jungle in Angola!'

'Heather, please take a deep breath, settle down, speak slowly please! Is she getting hitched to some Tribal Chief out there? Because some of those 'loopers' can take eight or nine wives and father thirty or so kids with them, and a white-chick would be a special prize for the tribe.'

'Jeez Haley, you're a great fucking help, thank you so very fucking much,' Heather screamed.

Heather never used 'flowery' language, so Haley realised things were serious and this was NOT a joking conversation.

'Sorry Sis, I'm sorry, go on please. I won't interrupt, so tell me all.'

'Sorry about the outburst, but I'm at my wit's end with worry here.'

As it happened, Heather's husband, a high-ranking executive in the Irish Department of Foreign Affairs, was offered a three-month stint in Africa to cover for an ill colleague at the Embassy. Heather explained that she was allowed to travel with him, and they could then use the trip to check on where or what was actually going on with Chloe.

The problem was Cyprian and Tyson.

'Jeezz, Heather, after listening to that, how can your 19-year-old son and your dog be a problem? I thought he was the sensible child in your family.'

'Yes, sister dear, he IS, but he's taking the last exam of his two-year course at UCD in a month or so, and we want to make sure he attends classes and is 'minded', for want of a better phrase! Also, Tyson needs to be fed-walked and looked after.'

The penny had dropped with Haley. 'So, you want me to be a baby-sitter and a dog-sitter while you pair go on a fully paid, all expenses flea and mosquito-infested safari holiday to the far-flung wilds of some African wilderness? Brilliant, that's a pure fucking brilliant request to your big sister, recently widowed! Poor me, temporally shacked-up, thanks to the charity of my best friend, while my own home is a cross between a swamp, crocodile shit hole and a slurry pit!'

There was a shocked silence on the other end of the line before Haley burst out laughing. 'Of course, I'll do it. Sally is driving me bananas here, fussing over everything, even small insignificant detail of no consequence. Plus, I have to work with her six days a week now. I feel obliged because there is nothing else for me to do, except wait for the dryers to do their job before the builders can move in to commence refurbishment.'

'Anyway, Norman has taken charge of the repairs (under pain of the wrath of mummy) so it will certainly be completed properly, eventually. I love Sally and Jake to bits. They have been such a comfort and support, and always there for me. I hate being a burden on them, so it suits me to be away for a while. I actually haven't seen Cyprian since the funeral two years ago, so it'll be a change of scenery.'

James had been his godfather and really liked the boy. Cyprian thought of him as some James Bond type of character, even after being told umpteen times that his career was purely administration.

CHAPTER TWO

Exactly seven days later, Haley dragged her overladen suitcase, surrounded by Essex hens who had started into "Sisters Are Doing It For Themselves" for the fourth or fifth time. As they wobbled past her, she realised the relevance of that particular song. They were all dressed (rather scantily) as nuns with the presumed bride in a white veil and tiara festooned with small imitation penises. The front dick, having a small set of dentures gripping it. The two Customs Officers just smiled as the crew weaved past. 'Anything to declare, ladies?' one asked with a wry grin. 'I declare we intend to enjoy ourselves,' the bride slurred back in return.

Haley had latched herself onto the back end of the troupe, as there was no way any sane Customs Official would attempt to intervene in the march of a well-stewed hen-party. As she passed the officers, Haley cheekily asked, 'Well boys, will we be seeing you in Temple Bar later?' The older one grinned, 'If I was thirty years younger, perhaps.' The other calmly remarked, 'Well, I might have to, as I think Grandad needs his false-teeth returned.' The three of them burst into hysterical laughter. Great Irish repartee, she thought to herself.

It was easy to spot the minibus driver for the party girls. He was the one wearing the rooster cap!

Suddenly Haley was gripped in a bear-hug by her brother-in-law, Trevor. 'How is my favourite sister in-law?' he said beaming. 'I am glad to see you and thanks so very much for agreeing to this,' he added, without giving Haley a second to reply. 'Your sister is up to ninety over the past few weeks and is on the verge of a breakdown with worry, so we need a safe pair hands in charge while we are away,' he blurted out.

'And great to see you too Trev,' Haley replied. 'Glad to help my dearest and now only, relatives. So, when are Tarzan and Jane off to their jungle hideaway?' she enquired with a cheeky smile.

'Not funny Haley,' was the curt reply. 'But we fly to Madrid tomorrow evening, thanks to our government minister moving things forward for me. Then we connect to Lusaka where one of our Consular staff will take us to our rooms at the Embassy.'

'Trevor, even I know Lusaka is in Namibia, NOT Angola.'

'Well, it's our nearest consular office to Angola and the last contact area we had for Chloe was only 300 km north of the Namibian border. So, we'll be able to manage that, right?' he asked as a re-assuring request rather than a question.

'Trevor, I thought 'Florence Chloe Nightingale' was only going on this adventure for three or four months to 'find-herself'. What's with these youngsters urge' to 'find themselves' shite'?

'Haley, it's a reason to leave the constraints of home, take-off to some far-flung remote camp and do-your-own-thing. Another horse's ass phrase that means whatever the hell you want it to mean,' he replied with a mixture of anger, regret and disbelief. 'It's almost fifteen months since she took-off and whatever security there is in a recognised charity compound, moving with some disorganised collection of do-gooders is recklessly dangerous.'

'I'm afraid I made some stupid jokes to Heather about all this when she rang, and I hope she has settled down since. Is she packing at the moment?'

'She's at the beauty parlour having her hair or whatever else women get done there,' he sheepishly replied.

'Yup, that IS my little sister for sure. Off to forty degrees of mosquitoes, scorpions, snakes, crocodiles and whatever else can either burn, eat or poison a human and she is in the midst of beautification.'

'Is she not aware it's in three months time, that she'll need all that?'

Both laughed as they emerged into a misty Dublin air and the noise of flights heading off to wherever. 'Have we far to walk to the car park?' she asked.

'Nope, we're here outside the front door. It's one of the perks, being able to park the official government taxi wherever is convenient. Plus, I told the guard on foot patrol, that you were related to the British ambassador,' he said and winked at her.

The driver took the case from Trevor and grunted as he heaved the luggage into the car trunk. She kept a firm grip of the duty-free bag which housed two bottles of Grey Goose vodka and two cartons of Marlboro Light. It was actually twice the official limit but slotting in with the "Sisters Who Were Doing It For Themselves" ensured an uninterrupted passage through the Customs zone. 'I presume Chloe is aware of this impending visit?' Haley asked.

The raised eyebrows and four seconds delay in answering should have been enough, but she asked again.

'She doesn't know, we haven't told her,' stuttered Trevor. 'And how precisely, do you think she will react when you both arrive on Planet Chloe without HER permission or a Visa to enter? Can he hear us?' asked Haley, pointing to the glass partition between the driver's seat and theirs in the back?

'No, only when I press this blue button.'

'Well!' continued his sister in law. 'She will shit-a-brick for starters and blast you both for attempting to drag her home.'

'No,' was the calm reply.

'WHAT?'

'We first want to find her and see that she is in a healthy state of body and mind.'

'Then,' interrupted Haley, 'drag her into the Jeep and get the hell out of there pronto!'

'Quite the opposite,' replied Trevor.

'NOW I am certainly confused,' bellowed Haley.

Trevor gently took her hand and said 'If there's anything I learned in twenty years of rearing and watching her grow-up was, I had to suggest the opposite. Yes, we gave her the 'find-myself / need my space' opportunity, but this is a reality-boot-up-the-ass situation for us all.

'I, we, intend to reassure her that her family and all her friends are so proud of her wonderful commitment to this most worthy cause. We are out there to support and encourage her hopes and dreams of a better and safer planet for mankind and all her wildlife projects. And as she has NOT visited home in fifteen months or so, has obviously put down her long-term roots out there to help all less fortunate cases. It IS a noble cause and life career she has chosen, by herself and for herself, and we would not dare interfere. I'll tell her that I'm thinking about taking early retirement, as all this air travel has triggered tinnitus and that her mothers' knee is playing-up, so long-haul travel is out of the question into the future. We also intend to convert the guest's bedroom into an office where we can do some part-time work from home.

'It's ingenious,' said Haley with a laugh. 'It's like something James would have concocted many years ago and most likely will work. Well done, you two. And there was I thinking Little H was about to implode. I take it was you dreamed up all this?'

Trevor gave her hand an extra squeeze as he nodded. 'The implosion is Heather worrying about the possibility of me taking retirement and being under her feet all day.'

A thin drizzle settled over the streets as they drove through the city, turning everything miserable and dank. They passed a public park. With its leafy trees, it resembled an island in a sea of grey concrete. There were beech and poplar trees bursting with green buds and cherry trees loaded with pink blossoms. The park's aura of peace was soothing after the raucous flight.

'Which house, Mr. Parkinson?' asked the driver, via the intercom as they approached Fernpark Drive.

'Number fifteen, up ahead on the left,' replied Trevor as the BMW X5 slowed down. The driver grunted even more heavily as he heaved the luggage case from the car trunk. Trevor then grabbed the handle and wheeled it easily towards the gate. 'So, it's 3 pm tomorrow then, to the airport Mr. Parkinson?' the driver asked for confirmation. 'Perfect,' replied Trevor. By now Haley had reached the last of the five steps to be greeted in another bear-hug.

'Great to see you again Aunt Haley,' beamed Cyprian.

'And look at you, handsome man, boy, have you grown in two years!'

'And the hair and face fungus,' she said, tugging the 'attempted' wispy beard.

'Tell me,' she inquired, 'did you hurt yourself badly when you tripped and fell?' She pointed to the open slitted knees on his baggy jeans.

'Oh God! Don't you start as well,' said Cyprian with a laugh.

'I'm just kidding,' re-assured Haley. 'It's your house, your town and your era, so you do your own thing. You should have seen how your mother dressed when she was your age. See, it didn't help, her being the younger sister, she got what I had grown out of, while I got the new stuff.' Trevor was blowing hard as he reached the door and handed the case to his son.

'To the special guest's quarters in the East Wing, Jeeves,' he joked.

'That's his way of saying the spare room, which Dansie has cleaned out and hoovered up all the dead bluebottles, wasps and bugs,' replied Cyprian.

'What about the mice?' Haley quipped.

'Tyson sorted them out for you, so all's good,' he said and laughed back. Having heard his name, Tyson came bounding from the kitchen to greet the new guest and slobbered all over Haley as she bent down to rub the boxer's head.

'You remembered,' she said. 'Well, good, because I'm your new minder, walker and 'dooh-dooh picker-upper' for the next few months.'

Trevor gave her a reassuring 'thanks-wink' as Cyprian bounced the luggage case upstairs to the guests' room. 'Would you like a nice strong cuppa?' asked Cyprian. 'Not at the moment, thanks. I'll unpack this lot before it gets too wrinkled and might have a little nap as I believe we're going for some 'posh-nosh' later this evening when your mother has completed the 'beautification'.'

By eight that evening, all four had been escorted to their table and presented with menus by a beautiful, petite girl with long blonde hair. She looked like a young Brigette Bardot with a Dolly Parton bosom. As she handed each a large leather-bound piece, Heather spied Trevor 'eyeing' the attractive figure before him.

'Eyes on the menu, please,' she whispered to him.

'Cyps is that you?' the waitress asked. It was the first time his parents had heard his nickname. Trevor said to Heather, 'I'll view the menu here, but prefer my meals at home,' with a cheeky wink.

'Oh, hi Kaitlin. I haven't seen you since secondary school,' Cyprian replied. 'So, how are things? You look as great as ever.'

'Oh fine,' came her casual reply. 'I'm here full time now and luckily, we are rushed-off our feet almost every day. And you?'

'Just finishing-up college in a few weeks,' he answered.

She leaned over his shoulder, brushing a well-developed breast against his cheek and suggesting that the Dover sole had just arrived into the kitchen from the dockside.

Taking the opportunity to avail of the full view, he announced, 'Kaitlin says the sole is freshly in and recommends it,' with a slight blush inside his wispy beard. Eventually all orders were taken. Having been quizzed by his mother, Cyprian explained, 'She didn't finish secondary having been offered a modelling contract in London at only sixteen. Her parents were fuming and tried everything to stop her, even though she had the figure and personality to succeed. She was certainly the most popular girl in the class, especially with the boys and was the envy of most girls, with all her curves.'

He added, 'She had curves in places, where other girls didn't even have places.' This was a great laugh to all, but then an abrupt silence fell, as the waitress delivered their starters.

'So, why is she waitressing when she looks that amazing?' asked Heather.

'Seemingly, at five foot six, you are not tall enough to be a fashion model. Designers require six foot two, skinny mobile clothes hangers, to display their creations. She did some beachwear and underwear stuff, and it was in many of the women's magazines. Some of the lads actually saw it and brought it into class for us all to 'inspect.' Then her agents wanted her to perform in adult movies.'

'You mean porn,' interrupted Heather.

'Yeah, but Kaitlin is not, and never was that kind of person. Just because she is a gorgeous girl with a stunning figure does not necessarily mean she has to totally undress to earn a living, especially in that sleazy environment. And she genuinely has a super personality and is great company. Anyway, she is back home. And for the record, her Dad owns this gaffe and is the head chef. So, she will eventually be the proud owner of all this.'

That finished my pretentious sermon, thought Heather.

The meal was first class with Trevor being ignored in both sets of conversations at their table. Cyprian and Haley admired the array of artwork and silverware and attempted to value them. Haley suggested possible alterations to the décor, her being an interior designer.

'Can we please park-up the day-jobs or I will bore you all with a load of political bull-shit?' joked Trevor.

They had just finished their Baked-Alaska desserts when Kaitlin appeared with a try of Irish Coffees. 'Compliments of the house,' she said, smiling, and placed a glass in front of each customer.

Using the opportunity to stand directly behind Cyprian with her bosom resting discreetly on his head, she said, 'We always take care of old pals.'

'Good job Shakeera is not here,' smiled Heather, 'as she would be crazy jealous.'

'MAM! Please,' warned her blushing son.

Next day at 2.55 pm, the State taxi arrived and three huge luggage cases were stuffed into the trunk. After much fussing, tears and kissing goodbye, Trevor and Heather departed on their excursion.

Cyprian released a huge sigh.

'At last! Mam has been like a coiled spring for the past month and especially the last week. I thought she was going to implode with panic anxiety or whatever the official medical term is.'

'Don't worry,' Haley reassured him. 'She'll ring from the airport with another list of do's and don'ts before the plane even leaves.' She placed her comforting hand around his shoulder at the door. 'From now on kiddo,' she said in a fake gangster accent. 'You look after your studies and the exams. I'll look after the dog. Dansie looks after the housework and Tyson looks after us all.'

'Sounds like a good plan Aunt Haley,' was the reply. 'So, what can possibly go wrong.'

'Now one other thing please. From now on, I am Haley, so let's drop the Aunt bit as it makes me feel old.

And don't worry, I'll stay out of your hair, all of it,' she said rubbing the ends falling onto his shoulders. 'Now let me make us a nice toastie and strong cuppa, and you can tell me all about this part-time job at the antiques shop and perhaps any other special young lady in your love life.'

'Aunt Haley, I have lots of friends, boys and girls, mostly from college, but if you are expecting a wedding invite soon, no holding of breath please, as you might burst,' he said, laughing in reply.

She interrupted, 'Again, LESS of the Aunt Haley, please.'

He explained that dad wanted him to get into the Civil Service and secure a safe job good for life with good holidays and a pension.

Mam just wanted him to be happy as long as it was in Ireland and not some mosquito-infested corner of the globe with different traditions, cultures and lifestyles.

'I certainly wouldn't inflict what Chloe has put my parents through,' he said. 'Anyway, Dublin is a European Capital City with much going on, and thousands are queueing up to get in here so why would I want to 'up sticks' from this nice house where I'm fed and watered daily?' he joked?

'Clever boy, Cyprian, so you just get through these exams and decide later on a plan when YOU are ready.'

'Oh! I'll be leaving earlier than usual tomorrow morning, as I'm helping a pal to finish off a project that's slightly behind its completion date, so it's you and Tyson on your own all day, as Dansie isn't due 'till Thursday morning. Enjoy the 'quietness' while you can.'

'Is she as talkative as ever?' asked Haley.

'No,' was the quick reply. 'She's even worse,' he said laughingly. 'But hey, she has a heart of gold and mam trusts her one hundred percent.'

CHAPTER THREE

First night in a strange bed always made for an uneasy night's sleep with Haley. She was fully awakened by the shutting of the front door at dawn.

Quickly hopping out of bed and peering through the curtains, she saw her nephew hurry down the steps armed with his large back-pack of schoolbooks. It's six am, she thought, so may as well get up and get into day one. As she entered the kitchen, Tyson was already chewing through his morning food which Cyprian had put out for him. A strong Americano, topped up with additional coffee granules and a slice of toast would kick-start her morning. Cyprian had switched on the internet radio which was tuned into 'Hits of the sixties and seventies.' Great choice she mused as the Beatles sang one of her favourites - 'A Day In The Life'. Tyson was now looking at his lead which hung on the kitchen door, so it was obviously his way of saying 'walkies'! Dressed and well wrapped for a murky Dublin early summer morning, she clipped on the lead, collected a dooh-dooh bag and set out into the quiet dawn. They strolled down the narrow street of houses and headed into the main adjoining thoroughfare that would bring them into the green pastures and playgrounds of the park.

Like all dogs, Tyson sniffed his way along the path he knew so well and 'watered' many of the lampposts on the route. As he was in the process of a particularly long sniff near the adjoining ditch, Haley noticed a very slow-moving car coming in their direction from behind. Haley and Tyson moved on, and the car eventually passed them, at a 'walking-rate' speed, which was most unusual. There was very little traffic of any description except the odd delivery van or cyclist, all in a hurry. Haley noticed the driver was sitting back in the car, staring straight ahead. Jokingly she thought 'a bit early for kerb-crawling' or maybe a bit too late! The car had moved on at the same very slow rate but then stopped, as the front wheels had run against the high footpath. With the engine still running, the driver sat propped upright, staring ahead. Haley peeped through the passenger window as she passed the stationary vehicle. Tyson had also stopped and emptied the remainder of his bladder against the lamppost nearby. The driver was still motionless as Haley tapped on the passenger window and asked. 'Hey! Are you OK in there?'

There was no response and not a single person on either side of the street. Again, she asked, without any reply from the heavy-set man in his fifties. Opening the door, she asked again and, leaning in, prodded him in his left arm. She jumped back in horror as the driver fell forward motionless, against the steering wheel. 'Sweet

Jesus in Heaven, this guy is in a bad way,' she muttered, as she leaned forward to check his neck for a pulse. There was no pulse. He was dead! It must have been a massive heart attack. As the car had an automatic transmission, was in the drive mode and his foot was not on the accelerator, it would just roll on until it hit something solid. He was an ugly brute, probably East European, by his looks. There was certainly no blood stain, and he had a very pale pallor and purple lips; Haley deduced major heart failure. With the car door open, Tyson had jumped into the car and taken up position on the green hold-all on the passenger floor. As she quickly ushered Tyson off the hold-all, it became tangled in the dog-lead and fell onto the footpath. Haley froze when she saw it was partially open and stuffed with fifty euro notes.

Another look, up and down the deserted street. There was nobody she could flag down for help. What help? she thought. This guy is stone dead and do I need all the hassle of form filling from officialdom, especially as he has a bag full of cash that is most likely gangster related? She quietly closed the car door, wiping any possible fingerprints she left behind. Picking up the bag, she headed a hundred meters or so to the park entrance. Oh God, what have I just done she thought to herself shaking herself back to reality as Tyson headed into a grassy corner to complete his toilet duties. She dropped the hold-all, reached into her jacket pocket for the small bag to collect the 'dog dump'. Panicking she hid the hold-all in the adjoining thick hedge which would camouflage it perfectly. The only other people in the park were some early morning joggers at the far end, 'glued-into' their earphones, but the traffic was now beginning to increase. It was time to high-tail it back towards home before somebody would notice the stalled car and driver dead at the wheel.

The walk home was brisk, and a hundred crazy thoughts ran through her mind. The sight of the money and the dead driver sparked a fugitive image in her head, something to do with what James had been working on in the months before his death. She tried to corner the image, but it scurried along the fringes of her consciousness. Meanwhile, she kept walking, without veering, straight in the direction of her sister's home.

Who was the dead John Do? Was he some dangerous crook? Had he been bumped-off? Was he being watched? Who owned all the cash? Would someone come looking for it? Had she been seen? The questions piled in her mind: what if this, what if that? Why the fuck did I even open that goddamn car door, she ranted, as she slid into the safety of her sister's home. In her heart, she could not but help feel the sinister workings of fate. If something strange was underway, it could not have come at a worse time in her life. Recovering from grief, relocated by a house flood, adrift in a new and strange city, she felt the irresistible lure of danger.

Peeping out between the front room curtains, she surveyed the outside street for any suspicious activity or surveillance on the house. By now Tyson had curled up onto his comfortable bean-bag and would sleep, blissfully unaware of Haley's paranoia.

It's way too early for a large vodka, she thought until that silent inner voice, screamed at her: 'Get a fucking grip woman and settle down, you demented idiot. YOU did NOT cause this. You just 'parked' the loot out of harms-way.' Just like the famous line from the Fr. Ted comedy show - the money was just 'resting' in my account, she reassured herself.

She then went upstairs, undressed and dumped the jacket, T-shirt, jeans and socks into the wash basket and had a long hot relaxing shower. It was as if she wanted to cleanse whatever sin had been committed. Then she put the clothes into the washing machine and switched it on. Feeling refreshed and relieved that the earlier crazy emotion rush had passed, she lay down and slept for a couple of hours.

When she roused herself from sleep, she decided that sufficient time had elapsed to safely revisit the scene, from the opposite side of the road. Dublin traffic was in full flow, with the infamous car cordoned off with Garda cones and fluorescent tape. She also noted the street did not have outside monitoring CCTV, so no visuals, she happily thought.

The early morning coffee shop directly opposite the car was open for business. An ambulance with flashing lights, and redirection traffic signs with the usual collection of gawpers armed with their phone cameras added to the chaos.

As Haley took a seat near the window, the young Polish lady brought her the pot of tea and heated scone which she had ordered. 'Anyone die in the crash?' enquired Haley.

In broken English, the lady explained; 'No, not crash. Man, he die in car of heart sickness. On his own. Police asking all of shops on this street, if we see somethings or have we outside camera. But no, we only have inside security camera near till. This must happen late last night and car was there with police, when we open up. My partner, Joseph, he say this is like person from Russia, so police will call their Embassy to find name, as he had no papers. Looks like he just die. Not murder or somethings bad like that.'

Haley remained patient. She kept on asking questions. She needed more clues about the Russian man, but the waitress was unable to give her any. Another customer arrived, and the waitress left Haley.

It'll be interesting to see what appears on the news programmes today; she thought as she made her way home. Strangely, there was no reference on either local radio or national news stations during that day or the evening TV news. If the dead man had no ID, it would have been normal for the police to seek help from the public in tracing his movements or family members, but it was as if it never happened.

In spite of having had a better night's sleep, Haley was still woken by the shutting of the front door at 6 am.

She checked through the bedroom curtains and saw her nephew lug his heavy backpack into the early dawn gloom. I suppose we best take the morning walk and check to see if that hold-all is 'safe,' she thought. Tyson was already at the front door, lead in his mouth.

Haley decided to take a larger carry bag into which the 'money-bag' would fit, assuming it was still there. Heather's large gym hold-all was ideal, and they both headed off on the same route as the previous morning.

The same lampposts were visited by the boxer and traffic was almost non-existent except for the odd delivery van and truck. Four speedy cyclists passed as if they were late for the Tour de France. She could now recall seeing them twenty-four hours earlier. Early birds seemed to have the same routines. No cars passed in her direction as she regularly glanced to check. They came to the first gate at the park where they had entered the previous morning, and Tyson made his way to almost the same spot to relieve himself. Haley could feel herself tensing up as she bagged the 'dog-dooh.' There were just a couple of early morning joggers at the far end of the park. She peered into the hedging. Well, fuck-me, it's gone she muttered. Someone must have found it or seen me hide it there. Then it dawned on her. She had hidden it well. She parted some more of the greenery, and there was the well-camouflaged green hold-all. With her foot on the dog lead, so Tyson would not decide to have a run-about, she dragged case from its hiding spot, placed it into the larger bag.

Zipping it up completely she took a brisker walk home to the safety of 15, Fernpark Drive. Tyson had finished off the remains of his food, then slobbered the fresh water from his dish and arranged himself in a comfortable position for his long morning nap. Hayley placed her sister's expensive gym bag on the kitchen table. 'I'll need to fumigate this before I return it to her wardrobe,' she muttered. Taking the damp hold all out and unzipping the top she was surprised to discover how many fifty euro notes it contained.

The money was in neatly packed 'blocks', four in length, three across and four deep. There was ten thousand in each pack, held together by a strong elastic band. A quick calculation showed that would amount to four hundred and eighty thousand euro. All the irritating paranoid questions suddenly cluttered her mind. Is it marked? Is it fake? Has the bag a tracking device?

Peeling some notes from all the top bundles, she checked for any strange markings, against a fifty she had taken from her purse. There were no unusual markings of any description, and all were previously used, so it looked like genuine cash. If there was a tracking bug, surely someone would have traced it by now she thought.

Still, best to dump this hold-all as quickly as possible. As she began emptying the piles of cash packs, she was stopped in her tracks. At the bottom lay a pistol.

It was a Glock 22. She had seen and handled one, many years earlier. Following the butchery of 911 and then the later terrorist attacks in England, many personnel involved in the 'intelligence gathering' and security sections of government were supplied and trained with firearms for self-protection. James was such, and as Haley was his wife, she could avail of similar training in the event of hostage situations. She initially was not keen to complete the course, but as she witnessed a police officer and a brave 'have-a-go' bystander being stabbed, she decided to complete the training course.

She checked the clip. It was loaded, but the safety device was on. Dumping the bag would be easy, but how to safely dispose of a loaded weapon was a completely different proposition. As she attempted to cure her 'parodied-bone', she examined the bag thoroughly to see if it had any small attachment. She noticed the thick cardboard support at the bottom was slightly higher in the mid-section than at both ends.

'Oh, holy shit!' she screamed. 'Is it bugged?' She quietly lifted the support piece. To her extreme relief, it was not a transmitting device, but a white padded sock that joggers wear for foot comfort. It felt rough like it contained pebbles. To her utter shock, she poured out the contents on to kitchen table. Diamonds fell on to the table; sixty large diamonds, like she had never seen before in her life.

That little re-assuring voice of common sense inside her head said, 'OK, this is MAJOR, so figure it all out calmly, and do what needs to be done QUICKLY.'

A sharp intake of air and a slow exhale later, Haley decided to (1) dump the hold-all (2) find a way to check if those fifties were genuine (3) hide the diamonds until it could be confirmed if they were real or fakes and GET A MOVE ON, as Dansie was due in an hour.

She put the sock of diamonds inside the cover of Tyson's bean bag and placed the cash into the bottom of her own travel case, which still had some of her clothes. Looking out the front window, she noticed that some of her neighbours had their refuse bins out for collection but was unsure which day Heather's bin was due to be emptied. She checked. It was almost empty, so that must have happened a few days ago. She wrapped the green hold-all into a large brown paper shopping bag and headed down the road to find a suitable receptacle and hopefully not be seen in the act. It was easier than she thought, and anyway who would mind a caring citizen disposing of some piece of litter. Before she had closed her front door, the refuse truck had buzzed its noisy way on the street, emptied that particular bin and hurried off to the next collection area.

Perfect timing. She allowed herself a smile. Now, let's figure if this cash is genuine currency. She could buy one of those marker pens used in supermarkets, but it would take forever testing all nine hundred and sixty of them. All that can wait, she thought, as I need to sit down, draw breath and gather myself.

The 9 am news headlines had no mention of a police enquiry for information or reports of diamond robberies. She was startled from her thoughts by the sound of the doorbell ringing.

Dansie was her punctual self. She greeted Haley with an outstretched hand and a warm smile. 'Great to see you, Mrs. Harrington and so sorry to hear about your handsome husband, so sad indeed. He was always so polite when ye stayed here four or five years ago, yes, I remember.'

'Thank you so much, Dansie, and PLEASE, my name is Haley, so no more Missus for the next three months.'

'Ok then,' said Dansie with a smile. 'But I insist on calling your sister Mrs. Parkinson even though she gets on to me every now and then. I know my place and her and Mr. Parkinson have been very loyal to me.'

'Dansie, you are here seven years or so, which makes you part of her family.'

'I hope they talk some sense into Chloe and get her back here quickly,' said Dansie.

'There's enough here in this Country for do-gooders, without shaggin' off half-way around the world to do it. And doing it for FREE!'

'Well! That's the plan,' re-assured Haley as she switched on the kettle and invited Dansie to tell her all the local news. Heather had been very selective on what was what and only revealed morsels of information.

'Hopefully all yours are well and must be all grown up by now?'

'Mesef and Danno is in great order, but his auld back is at him since he fell in the old garage, they use to work outa. Aldo, me eldest, twenty five he is, now runs the place and they have a nice little business goin' between them, even though he's still livin' with us. He's like the bad weather,' she said with a laugh. 'We can't get rid of him. The youngest, Wayne, was a bit of a hand-full, but he's now in the Army and training for electrical engineering.'

'Great news, Dansie, and I see you are as sprightly as ever.'

'Sure, why wouldn't I?' she replied. 'Isn't Nanno still livin' with us?'

'Nanno?' asked Haley.

'Yeah, Danno's Ma. She'll be eighty five in a few weeks and as it was her original house, she insists on doin' all the housework and most of the cooking. Only all the handy and easy stuff. But we let her off, and it allows me to get out four mornings a week for me own little nixers. Two days with your sister and another two with her friend Mrs. Donoghue, and that suits us all fine.'

'It's great that your family business is thriving and you are all in good health, and living happily together,' Haley said as she put on her fleece jacket. 'I'll get out of your way here and I'll be back before you leave. Tyson has been walked so he'll probably stay put.'

'Don't worry,' she replied. 'He can always have poolie out the back if he needs to.'

Haley arrived back at 1.15 and saw that Dansie had cleaned, mopped and dusted most of the living areas.

'C'mon,' Haley called. 'I have two full salad sandwiches here that need to be 'polished'-off.' The attempted pun was lost on Dansie, as she topped up the kettle. It suddenly dawned on Haley that her sister, in her panicky exit, had never mentioned wages for the housework. It wasn't as if she was now cash strapped, thinking of her suitcase stuffed with fifties.

'Oh, I had a text from Heather. They eventually arrived into the Embassy and are trying to adapt to the intense heat,' said Haley

'It's not the heat will be the problem out there, but dem snakes, flies and other crawly yokes to poison you,' Dansie replied with a cheeky grin.

Haley laughed. 'I already bounced that off my sister, and she nearly had a seizure on the spot.'

'Sorry for making bad jokes, but I would never make fun of Mrs or Mrs Parkinson,' said Dansie. Adding that she had been paid in advance for the next three months. This sorted that particular sticky question for Haley.

Dansie munched her way through the sandwich, while in full chat mode, and insisted on washing up after their lunch. She bade farewell 'till next Tuesday and instructed the sleeping Tyson "to look after Mrs. Parkinson's sister now, won't ya," in her best broad Dublin accent.

CHAPTER FOUR

It had been a long morning, so Haley decided to have a lie-down, having checked her luggage case which had not been disturbed. She even quietly scolded herself for even thinking Dansie would dare. The housekeeper had just vacuumed the two bedrooms that were being occupied.

Her sleep was broken by the sound of the front door closing and the barking of Tyson. 'Sweet holy shit, they're here. I've been tracked,' she thought as she quietly opened her bedroom door. It was Cyprian, being followed up the stairs by Tyson. But it was the dishevelled demeanour of her nephew that shocked her.

'I'm fine,' he muttered.

'No! You're fucking not,' shouted Haley, observing his limping right leg, bleeding eyebrow and swollen jaw.

'What on earth happened to you? You look like you've been hit by a bus.'

'Aunty Haley, I don't want to talk about it.' 'Even if you don't, you need seeing to, and those cuts cleaning. Let me get an ice-pack for that jaw, and I have some 'decent' pain-killers that will soothe the aches.'

Three minutes later, she knocked on his bedroom door with an ice pack, some warm water and a couple of her prescription pain blocks. Ice applied, meds taken and cuts cleaned, she left the room. 'See,' she whispered, 'I'm not fussing or questioning, so get some rest. You won't be completely cured, but you WILL feel better in a few hours' time.' She ambled downstairs, hoping Heather would not ring and want a reassuring conversation with her son.

She had a strange gut-feeling about the cash, the pistol and the diamonds and the fact that the lady at the café had mentioned that as well as the police, some Russians had made enquiries about the car and the dead driver. Checking her phone, she found a number for Eddie Johnson who was a former close associate of both her husband James and Kerri Callaghan who died together in the helicopter crash.

They had kept in touch for a while, but when Haley quit her admin position in the Government Foreign Office, the calls became less frequent, as Haley attempted to move-on with her life as a widow. Yes! The mobile number rang and was quickly answered with a surprised 'Hello Haley, is that you?'

'Hi Eddie, yup it's me, and at least you still have my number logged into your private phone.'

'Haley,' he whispered, 'it's not safe ringing me on this number from your own private phone.'

'Jeez, you are sounding like a 007 paranoid spook. What's up? We are all old mates or has all that been wiped?'

'No, no, no, not that at all,' he spluttered. 'Anyhow, where are you ringing from, as the number has an 'outside UK' showing.'

'I'm in Ireland at the moment. Remember! My sister lives here.'

'I believe there was some serious flooding down your way a few months back?'

'Yeh, that's it, but can you check a little something out for me on the Q T?'

'If I can, I certainly will H, but I am not high up the chain of command here.'

'Yeh,' she interrupted, 'but there is always 'the water-cooler-gossip- supply,' right?'

'OK, fire away, and I'll see what I can do.'

Haley told him part of the story of the dead-driver saga but left out the part about her finding and taking the holdall from the car. The Irish police claimed the 'John Do' had absolutely no ID. An elderly Polish café owner where she ate, reckoned the dead driver to be Russian and all the local shops had 'visits' from burly Russians claiming to be from the embassy, but never showing any ID. Always leaving in a hurry when requested to show official papers. Normally the cops would have photos and 'appeals' via the news channels, but there was total silence on this.

'Are you somehow involved in this as a witness or what?' asked Eddie.

'Good God, no,' she insisted. 'I actually passed by, saw his big ugly East European head, and was having breakfast in the café, when all the police, ambulance and news crews arrived. But there is no mention in any press bulletins and the part-owner was told by a reporter that he was not shot, stabbed or murdered. It was a heart attack. Perhaps you can check discreetly, with your lads in your Irish Embassy, to see if any high-ranking official snuffed it, two days ago.'

'Yeh, I'll have a quiet word with some of our crew and see if anything springs up,' he replied.

Quickly changing the topic, Haley inquired, 'So, have you found the love-of-your life yet, and prepared to make a genuine life-changing commitment? Or are you still footloose and fancy-free?'

'Jeez, is this a proposal as we haven't even kissed in over a year?' he laughingly whispered.

'Oh, you are the sly one,' she quickly replied. 'And if I recall, it was a slobbery grope at my last Christmas office party, with you crazy collection of drunks.'

'Yes, it was and I was bang-out-of-order, BUT I did grovel and apologise afterwards, so I do owe you a favour. I'll cast a fly, see what bites and will call back. As regards weddings, I'm attending a stag weekend in a couple of months' time, in Dublin. We've got a rugby match on the Friday night and a stag, for our full-back, lasting the rest of the weekend. So, if you're still there, we might catch up for a coffee? And just between you and the wall, yes, I intend to propose to a lovely Irish lass, Sinead, who works at the Dutch Embassy here. She is a cracker, and I know you and James would love her. So, now, you have all my news, and I'll ring you within the week on your P. I. stuff.'

At least, some little piece of good news, thought Haley as the Dublin afternoon filled with dark clouds that began to empty its contents in torrents. Where have I seen this before, she wondered, as she quietly made her way upstairs to check on her patient. Gently opening the door, she could see he was in a deep relaxing sleep with Tyson curled up at the end of the bed. She removed the ice pack as it was beginning to melt, and he would certainly need it later. Moving downstairs, she noticed the shadow of a person about to press the doorbell. She rushed to open it; in case the ringing would awaken Cyprian. On the step, stood the drenched figure of a young woman.

'Are you Cyprian's Aunt Haley?' she politely asked.

Shocked, Haley had never seen this person before, and the only two people to call her 'Aunt' were Cyprian and Chloe.

One was upstairs sleeping off an assault, and the other in some African jungle. Again, the multiple questions in the paranoid section of her brain kicked in.

'And you are?' Haley asked in the calmest voice she could muster.

'I apologise for just calling like this,' came the reply. 'I'm a good friend of Cyprian and I just need to know that he is OK, after what happened.'

'I'm sorry, love, please step inside. You are drenched. Here, give me your jacket, you are soaked through, and you'll catch pneumonia standing out there.'

The girl handed Haley her woollen jacket and beanie hat, which were both wringing wet.

'He's upstairs sleeping off the painkillers and ice pack, and I can safely predict he will survive this one even though he was not willing to disclose much to me about what happened,' Haley said with a sad smile.

'Oh, thank God,' the girl sobbed, as Haley hung the jacket and hat on the fireguard surrounding the lighted kitchen gas fire.

'Now let me get you a hot drink and some towels, and you can fill me in, as I only got the shortened version from my nephew.'

Haley boiled up the kettle. She hoped she would now get the full facts as to what exactly happened and why. The girl shivered and huddled herself as close to the fire as possible. Seeing her condition, Haley insisted she takes a hot shower. 'There are bath towels, shampoo and soaps in the shower room,' she said, as she handed her a towelling bathrobe. 'I'll find you some clean, dry clothes, while we dry out this lot.' Showing her to the shower room, Haley went back downstairs and waited for her new guest to return.

Meanwhile, she left clean underwear, T-shirt, cotton jeans, ankle socks and Heather's expensive training runners outside the bathroom door, as all seemed the correct size.

Ten minutes later the girl stepped into the kitchen and with a warm, polite, soft voice said, 'Thank you so very much, Mrs Haley, and my apologies again for interrupting your morning. I took the liberty of peeping into Cyprian's room, and both him and Tyson were in a deep sleep.'

Haley smiled and said, 'For the last time, I'm Haley, not Mrs. Anybody to any friends of my sister's family.

'Sorry,' the girl replied. 'I'm Shakeera, and we are the best of good friends, Cyprian and I. So, I'm shocked at what happened as it was not his fault at all.'

Releasing her hair from the head-towel, Haley asked if she required a hairdryer.

'No thank you,' she politely declined as she shook her long multi-coloured mane loose. 'It can dry out naturally.'

'Now love, it's vital that Cyprian's mam and dad know absolutely nothing about all this, as there is enough shite going-on elsewhere in their lives.'

'Yes,' she replied. 'I know all about Chloe. Anyway, they are just young thugs who bully anyone who attempts to stand up to them.'

'I made you a strong coffee. Now will you begin at the very start, so I can fully understand all this please?'

'They call themselves the Crew-Cut-Crew because their 'thing' is the old American fifties style crew cut,' she explained. 'There are probably four or five who spend most of their time at Flexo's Gym, downtown. It's a rough house and a small unlicensed bar at the back. We never go near that place, but last year my 'idiot' sister Edel got friendly with a member of theirs, Chalky. Again, he had a crew cut with blonde hair and blue eyes but is a much nicer type than his mates. He attended the same college as us and at least finished off his schooling. Cutting a long story short, she thought she was pregnant after only going out with him for three months. When she told him, he told her 'to go have an abortion and perhaps it was not even his!'

'Charming,' added Haley. 'And there was I still thinking the age of male chivalry was dead!'

'Perhaps the age of female stupidity is still alive,' joked Shakeera. 'Anyway, she was not pregnant, and it was just a case of her miscalculating, but it showed what a 'waster' Mr Chalky was. He never returned any of her texts, so she stayed well away from any of the regular haunts they hung around.'

'Do any of these clowns work at a job or trade?' asked Haley.

'Never' was the reply, 'but they always seem to have cash. It's thought they are into stealing cars to order, for larger gangs to carry-out their own dirty work.'

Shakeera recounted how three months previously the gang had attacked her and Edel. Cyprian had happened to be walking Tyson nearby, and hearing their shouts for help, came running over. Tyson had broken free from his lead and bit the assailants. He bit Mo on the hand and also Spike, who had tried to kick him.

The gang had realised Tyson was not going to back off, so they ran away swearing they would sort Cyprian and his friends out later.

'You DID report this the police, yes?' asked Haley.

'We were going to, but Edel would have had to explain about the false pregnancy, and our parents would go ballistic, absolutely, totally.'

Haley took another large swallow from her coffee and attempted to stay calm while she absorbed the facts.

'We all stayed out of their way, and Edel got a great job as a make-up artist with a large film company, in Wicklow.'

'By the way, has this anything to do with these six am exits from the house for this 'project completion' thing?' Haley asked.

'Well, ah, partly yes, as we get into college long before these shites even get out of bed,' was the reply.

'Classes finished early today', continued Shakeera, 'and we were walking along together when the gang pulled-up and got out of their big black BMW Jeep, grabbed me by the hair and asked where was my slapper sister. Spike began to lay into Cyprian, boasting, 'now you have no hairy mutt for support, so let's see what you've got."

'Did anybody stop to help, as there must have been students pouring out of the college?'

'No,' she sobbed. 'Nobody will ever get involved in situations like that.'

'Yeh, too true,' replied Haley angrily, 'they'll only take out their goddam mobile phone cameras for a cheap picture!'

'Anyway,' added Shakeera, 'I managed to get out a sharp pencil, and stick it into the back of Chalky's neck.'

'Well GOOD for you!' enthused Haley.

'I told him he had one hour to get to a hospital before he would be contaminated and die of lead poisoning. The three of them panicked and rushed off at speed with the pencil stuck above Chalky's collar line.'

Haley burst out laughing, 'Lead poisoning from a sharp pencil! What a collection of brain-deads, BUT,

Shakeera, they are very dangerous thugs, and I DO think the Irish Guards… what's the official name for them again?'

'Gardai plural' was the reply.

'Should be informed as these thugs will not just go away,' Haley advised.

The coffee mugs were now empty as Shakeera excused herself to visit the toilet. Haley was about to give directions, but the girl said she'd been here on quite a few occasions, as Cyprian and she really were the very best of friends.

'So, how long has this romance being going on,' Haley coyly asked?

'We're just great pals,' she replied.

'Seeing the disbelief on Haley's face, 'I'm not his type Haley,' was the polite reply, as she winked at her and headed for the loo.

You five-star stooge, Haley! You total moron! That little voice inside blasted at her. It was only now it dawned on her, that her nephew was gay. Shakeera returned and smilingly asked if she had figured it out?

'Do his parents know, as they have never mentioned anything to me?'

No', she replied. 'There was never the right moment for him to 'come-out,' especially with all this Chloe crap going on. Both his parents up to ninety with worry and having me, in at out, they just presumed we were boyfriend and girlfriend.'

'Well! It's NOT a problem for me,' Haley reassured her, 'and your secrets are safe here. I'm sure he will find the right time, and I KNOW both my sister and her husband WILL be OK. It may take Trevor a little longer - all this male macho bullshit stuff.' They both allowed each other a wry smile.

Tyson had now appeared at the bottom of the stairs which meant Cyprian was close behind. Staring at Shakeera, he announced in a surprised tone, 'Well, well, well, who is this new lady in our house,' as they hugged.

'You go have your chat,' said Haley. 'I have duties that require attending.' She heavily patted Tyson - 'Good boy you! Well done!'

She added, 'Oh, and I've checked your mother's freezer cabinet, so we will all be having Shepard's Pie BING - in exactly thirty minutes, so please be down by then.'

CHAPTER FIVE

~

'OK Grubs up!' called Haley from the kitchen door as the two friends made their way in. 'You're limping much better.' Haley flashed a smile at her nephew.

'Well done, Haley, you 'wormed' the whole story out of Shakeera,' he coyly replied.

'No.' She pretended to be busy at the cooker. 'I was able to put many of the two and two's together, but your lovely lady friend just joined up most of the missing dots for me.' 'And,' she added, 'it would take more than all that, to shock me. Your secret is safe, one hundred percent, until YOU pick YOUR own time to tell your parents. This is YOUR call and I, like Shakeera, am fully supportive.'

'Thank you so much, Aunt Haley.' He rushed towards her sobbing, planting a soft tender kiss on her cheek. 'Really, thanks, it means so much having your support!'

Quickly changing this awkward conversation, Shakeera chipped in, 'What's Shepard's pie, BING?'

Haley smiled back, and replied, 'It's when you stick the large holding dish into a microwave oven, wait, and when it goes BING, remove and devour.' Just then the microwave binged, and all three laughed loudly. We'll check to see if there is something else that does not require hard-chewing in that well-stuffed freezer, for tomorrow,' said Haley.

'Haley' asked Cyprian, 'are you embarrassed by this 'gay' thing? If so, just say it out, please. It won't annoy me.'

Haley smiled. 'Allow me to let you both in on a very, very personal girly secret. When I was at what you call secondary school, we had a gorgeous PE instructor, Miss Neilson. She was a stunning thirty-year-old, tall, leggy, beautiful Swedish lady. I was part of the school athletic team, and secretly we all (us girls) would love to develop into a copy of this 'Hollywood' beauty. She was the very first person we ever saw wearing tight lycra leggings, with never a bra and seemingly no undies. She worked us hard at physical education, which, I must say, stood to all of us in time. I was part of the school 100 meters relay team which was going for the All England Championships, so we had extra running as part of the 'school-honour' coaching. Not alone was she stunningly beautiful; she was also courteous, polite and treated us as adults. So, for sixteen-year-old, hormonal young girls, this was a very welcome first. After each extremely hard training session, she always finished by saying, ' Hit the showers ladies.'

'Our shower rooms were in two small lots, with four showerheads in each cubicle. After one particularly late evening and exhausting session, she undressed and surprisingly joined us teens for the usual wash-down. Normally she would have gone to the teacher's lockers, but she said they were closed. This meant four sweaty teens and a stunning thirty-year-old beauty, together in a very confined steamy shower area. I can still recall her perfect, naked body and seeing a 'Brazilian' for the first time.'

'I thought you said she was Swedish,' interrupted Cyprian.

Ignoring the joke, Haley continued, 'As it was cramped and there would always be the 'accidental' rub of body parts which was quietly exciting, especially when it was the full beautiful nakedness of Miss Neilson. It was the only time, ever, there was no giddy, giggly teen waffle amongst us, as we all were enraptured by being so close to such a mature nude beauty. She actually oiled-up and massaged my thigh in the shower, as I had complained of muscle cramp earlier. It was a private moment of teen pleasure we all shared and was never spoken about between ourselves, ever again. But we all took our secret thoughts home, and I personally relived it, many times. I believe if this happened today, she would be arrested and locked up by the PC brigade. We won the Championships, but Miss Neilson never returned for the new term. We think she went back home with her partner. We all had such a crazy crush her, but like her Brazilian, it was 'hair today, gone tomorrow.' This brought on huge laughter. 'So, yes, I do understand emotions and feelings, Cyprian. Its nature. How you love someone cannot be wrong, if it feels perfectly right.'

'You're a very witty, wise lady, and great company,' offered Shakeera.

'Isn't she just?' added Cyprian. 'Thanks again for taking time out, to be here.'

'Oops, pardon me,' burped Shakeera, 'I am so sorry.' Again, all three laughed.

Haley added, 'In certain parts of this lunatic planet, burping is considered a compliment to the host and the chef.' Trevor's phone whistled an incoming text message.

'It's from Mam,' he announced.

'You've got a crazy sense of humour,' said Shakeera with a laugh, as Cyprian tapped a reassuring reply to his parents.

'Shakeera, perhaps you should stay here tonight as it's still tipping down outside,' Cyprian suggested, while he took Tyson to the back yard for his nightly watering.

'Only, if that's OK with you Haley,' was the reply, as she sent a text to her mam, who quickly replied.

'She's used to me staying over and she knows I'm safe here,'

'You head to bed, and I'll be up later,' smiled Shakeera to her pal, as he wobbled up the stairs to his room.

'When did you know?' asked Haley after she heard the bedroom door slam, nodding to the upstairs

'There were six or seven of us in the same college class, and we all knocked around at the same gigs, films, parties, exhibitions or whatever. I always had a soft spot for Cyprian as he was warm, polite and most helpful to anyone who ever asked. It was after our graduation party, and he was staying over at our house. My parents went away for the weekend and fourteen or so of us had the place to ourselves. I was with Cyprian, and while we often kissed and cuddled together, nothing ever moved on. That night we eventually went to bed, and even though I was almost naked beside him, he was politely attentive, but never aroused to have sex. He gave me his warm, safe smile, kissed me goodnight and cuddled me to sleep, like a teddy bear. It was never spoken of, but we have been the very best of friends since. And before you ask, NO, he does not have a romantic boyfriend.'

'Now, I'm going to clear up this mess of plates, so you hit-the-hay,' announced Shakeera.

'I'll be in Cyprian's room, as I normally had the guest's quarters which I'm told are occupied,' she smiled.

'Thank you,' Haley replied as she headed upstairs. 'See you in the morning.'

Haley undressed and slid under the duvet to get some badly needed shut-eye.

Sleeping soundly, she was woken by a soft knock on her bedroom door. It was Cyprian, 'Breakfast is ready, whenever you are.'

'Morning all,' smiled Haley as Shakeera handed her a warm plate of bacon and egg, with toast on the side. 'Your favourite Americano with toppings is on the way,' Shakeera casually added. 'Our patient is much better following his good night's snore.' She laughed, rubbing Cyprian's jaw, which had reduced in size.

'We're giving classes a miss today, as it's Friday and many lecturers don't even bother as it's a half-day, anyway.' Shakeera placed her arm around Cyprian's shoulder. 'Edel texted to invite us to the film set she's working on. We have to call to Mr. Long first, Cyprian's part-time boss and advise that he won't be at work this evening or tomorrow. I'm sure his antiques-shop clients would not be impressed with all these bruises.'

Haley jumped in, 'No, I'll do that as I'd love to see what type of stuff he has on offer. Perhaps Sally and Jake, my own part-time bosses might like something he has on display.'

'I'm sure Cyprian will get you a decent family discount,' said Shakeera as she gently kissed the top of Cyprian's head.

'A change of scenery will be good for you all so, go and enjoy. Just make sure nobody dies of lead-poisoning out there.' Haley laughed as she headed upstairs.

By the time she dried and was fully dressed, the pair downstairs were giddily laughing and chatting like all youngsters should. Having reached the bottom step, there was a beeping of a car horn outside.

'She's here,' chirped Cyprian as they made for the front door.

Shakeera calmly turned and smiled. 'Lovely to have met you Haley and perhaps we'll all meet again before you leave.'

'Of course, we will,' piped-up Cyprian. 'She is here for another three months.' Both rushed out and into Edel's waiting car.

Now that she was on her own in her sister's house, Haley felt subdued. There was no lively conversation to distract her from her worries. She sat in silence over a cup of tea as the sound of the clock on the marble fireplace grew louder. She had thought that by coming to Dublin, she might escape loneliness, but now she realised the sense of isolation was even deeper here. There was so much danger associated with where the money had come from and the practical details of what she should do with it. She was frightened by the impulsiveness of her behaviour and her poor judgement in removing the money from the car in the first place.

She drank her cold tea, and her imagination began to supply more and more appalling possibilities to her predicament. She fought to regain her composure, and with an act of physical willpower, rose from her seat, pulled on her coat and hurried outside. She needed to keep her attention focused on Cyprian and his life.

Tyson was in his usual comfortable sleep position as Haley closed the front door to make the short walk to 'Times-Long-Past' and check out Cyprian's place of part-time employment.

After fifteen minutes or so, she saw the shop-sign over the antique store, and the 'closed' had just flipped to 'open' as she pressed the brass handle and stepped inside. She was immediately greeted by a very tall slim distinguished-looking gentleman in his mid sixties.

He had longish white hair with a well-groomed handlebars moustache. His green check shirt clashed with the tight red trousers and dark blue runners. However, his black leather waistcoat and brown bow-tie added a touch of eccentricity to his attire.

'Aah,' he enthused with open arms. 'My first customer of the day, which entitles you, lovely lady, to a cup of Albert Long's strong morning tea.'

'Why that would be lovely, thank you! Is it OK to browse?' asked Haley eyeing the well-stocked collection crammed onto every available shelf.

He nodded and asked, 'Sugar and milk?'

'Yes, and yes please.' She accepted the cup and saucer of morning brew. 'I'm Cyprian's aunt and unfortunately, he's feeling poorly so won't be able to fulfil his part-time duties this weekend.'

'How eloquently phrased,' he replied. 'May I assume you and his mum are sisters, as I can see a certain elegant likeness.'

'Most observant,' came her reply. 'It seems Cyprian really enjoys his employment here but says very little about it.'

'A very polite, well-mannered young man, whom I trust one hundred percent and has a wonderfully easy way with my clients,' added Albert. 'I actually have been trying to get him to come here full time as a career.'

Haley added, 'I believe his dad wants him in the safe, pensionable Civil Service.'

'And I can see the merit in that,' he replied.

'Certainly, my sister would love to have him nearby as her daughter is presently in some jungle out-post, trying to save the planet.'

'An admirable aspiration, but I don't think it pays too well,' he smiled. He added that many of these young impressionable 'wanna-help, must-do' kids were just fodder for some charity industries, who used their youthful enthusiasm to keep their own pious pot boiling.

After twenty uninterrupted minutes or so of browsing, Haley said, 'You have some really nice pieces. How is business?'

'Unpredictable but we are doing quite well,' he said. 'If you buy quality at the right price, you can sell at a handsome profit.'

'That's exactly what my part-time boss always preaches,' added Haley. She then explained her situation and told him about the part-time job and the types of items they sold, with Jake doing the buying at various fairs and auctions and Sally and her staff completing the sales.

Albert said, 'That's the way it was here until three years ago, I bought, and Cathy sold. Unfortunately, none of our two boys was interested. One is a dentist in New Zealand and the youngest an engineer for a mining company in Australia.'

'Jeez, they went far enough away,' quipped Haley, 'and to think they are both drilling, one into gums and the other into the earth.'

Albert burst out into a full and hearty belly-laugh. 'I never thought of it that way, but I could have done with their support here. Unfortunately, none have any interest in the business that paid for their good education and long-haul flights.' He sighed. 'You see my wife has bad dementia and needs full time care. She's been well looked after in a lovely rest home near Carlow, which is over an hour's drive from here. So, visiting can be a nuisance, with little cover in the shop and especially when she has no idea who I am, on most visits. Your nephew has been a lifesaver for me during the past two years. Working all through his holidays and almost every Friday afternoon and Saturday. He has even travelled with me to the rest home, and Cathy thinks that he is our youngest, but Cyprian plays along to humour her and never complains. He has seen my wife more often during the past two years, than most of our family members.'

'Well,' interrupted Haley, 'it's not easy for some people when they are unable to connect or communicate with such a disability. They feel embarrassed and unable to play-along.'

'As my sons have their own careers and no interest in antiques, I offered Cyprian a partnership and full-time position here with me.'

Haley was amazed at this, as nothing of that opportunity had been discussed at home.

But she surmised, with all the aggro in Africa and Cyprian's own sexuality issues, was it any wonder?

'Cyprian would not have the funds to buy into an established firm like yours.' she added. 'I need a safe pair of hands to ensure sales and proper records being kept. This was Cathy's department, as like your friend Jake, I did the buying.'

'I'm sure you could indeed find a buyer and give yourself more free time.

'No,' he sharply answered, 'and then be absorbed into some larger collection of carpet baggers who would just take only what they need. And the old name, which was my father's, disappear. No, not a chance.'

A well-dressed couple entered the showrooms, which allowed Haley her perfect exit opportunity.

'Of course, if he were to become a partner - shareholder in your well-established business, it would be vital that he brings something more to the table than 'youthful exuberance 'and new-fangled ideas,' she smiled.

'Let's see if we can work out something that is mutually satisfactory,' he reassured her, 'as I depend on all this to happen both for me, my family and our family business.'

Haley straightened herself up, shook both shoulders with an air of confidence and with an extended right hand said, 'I look forward to having another meaning chat with you, in the near future Mr. Long. Thank you so much for the time, your delicious morning tea and charming conversation. And do be assured everything discussed here, stays here.' Then she bid him goodbye.

'Good, so less of the Mr. Long. I'm Albert to my friends.' 'And I'm Haley to mine,' was the quick reply, as he opened the front door with the announcing ring of the bell overhead.

'I hear your bell has tolled for me,' said Haley with a smile.

'I see you are a Hemmingway fan,' replied Albert.

'Who isn't?' said Haley, 'but I prefer the Bee-Gees

old hit version.' Then she stepped into the crisp Dublin morning air.

OK, Tyson let's see if you are ready for a relaxing walk-in-the-park she thought, as she headed for home.

There was a confident stride in Haley's march home as it looked like Cyprian's future career had been mapped out for him by a reliable, sensitive employer.

CHAPTER SIX

Tyson was on the hall mat as Haley entered and the wagging tail was her cue to collect his lead. Setting off on the usual route to the park and his regular stops at the various 'watering-posts' Haley would regularly glance back to confirm she was not trailed by some slow-moving vehicle. It was the 'flash-back' to that money-bag situation, but Dublin traffic was back to its horn-honking usual, and there was a security in knowing that. Dog and handler entered the same entrance as before and passed the exact 'Aladdin-Cave' where the stash was hidden.

The nagging doubts chipped away inside her head: should I have just left it? Why have the authorities not issued some statement on the dead driver? Someone somewhere is out-of-pocket and obviously will be hunting for the lost loot. No CCTV footage thankfully, so no one could have seen me, so what's there to worry about? The re-assuring calm had presented the comforting cold facts and eased her anxiety.

Suddenly there was a rush from behind her, and a voice bellowed 'Now, you hairy mutt, here's one back for you.' A heavy iron bar walloped into Tyson's skull, and he fell instantly to the ground, blood streaming from his mouth. The voice shouted, 'Ya won't be bitin' anyone again,' in a broad Dublin accent. Haley turned in shock to see three youths all dressed in black quickly run through the park gate and down an adjoining side street.

'You fucking bastards,' shouted Haley as she dropped to her knees and gently raised Tyson's head. But it fell back, lifeless onto the pathway.

There was no one in the immediate vicinity, and apart from the outside traffic, the only sound was that of a lawnmower in the distance as Haley cradled the dogs head in her lap and wept uncontrollably. The noisy ride-on mower had stopped, and the driver in his well-worn high viz jacket approached the crouching figure on the walkway.

'Are you OK, missus?' he quietly asked.

'Those fucking thugs murdered my dog, so NO I'm not OK,' screamed Haley.

The attendant looked around. 'They seem to be gone, so should I call the Guards?'

'And what will we tell them, that some shower of animals killed my dog. That would get some laugh down in the station.'

'Here, let me help,' he offered.

'Nothing can help him, he's dead, look! D E A D,' she roared.

'Yes, he is gone, but let me help you anyway. Those scumbags shouldn't get away with that, and it could actually have been YOU that got a whack. Did they rob your handbag or hit you?'

Haley composed herself and realised that, yes, it could have been her who was battered.

'Sorry for snapping at you. It's just the shock of what happened. He isn't even my dog. He belongs to my sister's family, and I am minding him while she is away. Oh God!'

'Do you live far from here?'

'I, ah, just…' She pointed down the road they had just walked, unable to think straight. 'Just, oh God!' she stammered. 'Sorry, it's, ah, Fernpark Drive, number fifteen.'

'Know the area well,' he said. 'Sure, I pass it each morning on my way to the depot yard. Number fifteen, that would be the end house, with the side entrance, yes?'

'Yes, that's it. We hadn't gone far when all this…' She pointed to the stricken Tyson, 'happened.'

'Why would them gurriers do such a thing?' he asked.

'Well, he's my nephew's dog, and when his girlfriend was being jostled by a gang of thugs, Tyson jumped in and helped save the day.'

'So, your nephew can ID these thugs?'

'I'll speak to him when he returns home from college.'

'Do and be sure to go the Guards. These scums should be locked-up. If I had my way, I'd have them all put down, but like everything else, there are too many do-gooders, and nothing gets done, full stop. Now, why don't you head on home and I'll wrap up your dog and bring him over to your house, during my lunch break.'

We have a small van-truck for bringing away the grass and leaves, so I take him over in that as he produced a heavy-duty plastic bag. You'd never be able to carry him all that distance. It's no trouble' he reassured her as he helped her from the seat and pointed towards the exit gate. Three giddy teens had appeared and were staring down at the dead animal. 'Yuk! what happened here' asked one, as she pulled a piece of chewing gum from her painted black lips. 'Is he dead?' as she produced her mobile phone camera.

'Heh! Fuck-off, out of here, and get back to school you shower of scuts,' screamed the park attendant 'or I'll report ye! Scram,' he yelled again, as the girls took flight. Turning to Haley, he smiled, 'sorry about the language, as sometimes it's the only way to get understood around here. Typical - nobody will offer to help, but they all want a photo for their Booktube, Interface shite page or whatever. Now, I'll be over to your house shortly after one o clock, so you leave it to me from here.' Carefully, he removed the dog-collar and lead and handing them to her with a sincere smile, ushered her towards the exit gate.

Haley slowly retraced the walk home in complete shock, unable to comprehend what had happened. There was an unusually eerie silence in the hall as she slammed the front door closed. No sound of scratching paws on the hall floor and slobbering of water from Tyson's food dish.

Looking up at the ceiling, she cried out, Sweet

Jesus in Heaven, I am only here just two weeks or so and look at the mess I have gotten myself into. I have a shit load of cash/diamonds and a loaded gun, seen my nephew beaten-up, his friends harassed, and now his pet dog slaughtered before my very eyes. I'm supposed to be taking care of things here, so what the hell else can happen. It's a good job I wasn't carrying that gun an hour ago, or I certainly would have been tempted to blow one of them away!

Just then her phone 'beeped' an incoming call. Thankfully, it was just a text message from Sally.

'Hi, missing staff member:). Hope all is well over there in the Emerald Isle, and you are behaving yourself! We've had two weeks of sunshine with a drying east wind, so coupled with the heaters, your downstairs is almost ready for plastering. Norman says the place should be ready for painting, with your new kitchen units fitted in three to four weeks' time. The garden has dried out and is almost back to your fussy self's best. Will keep you posted. We both miss you and look forward to hearing all your news soon. Love Sally xxx.'

Haley couldn't even muster the enthusiasm to send a short thank you reply as she switched the phone to silent mode and flopped onto the couch. How am I going to explain this to Cyprian or to Heather and Trevor? The first time they've ever asked me to do a simple favour, and the whole thing goes 'tits up.' James would have called this a 'Royal-multi-cluster-fuck-up of the highest order! Eventually the concoction of negative thoughts, what-ifs, getting revenge, clouded her mind, and she drifted into an uneasy sleep.

The doorbell eventually woke her. It was five minutes past one and the park attendant informed her that he had reversed his van up the side entrance of the house, so nosey neighbours would be unaware of the sad circumstances. 'Oh, thank you so much,' blurted Haley. 'You are so very kind to do all this.'

They both walked through the kitchen and into the back yard. 'I have cleaned and nicely wrapped him up in a cloth sheet,' as he removed Tyson's body. Where will we put him? he politely asked. Haley opened the garden shed door and moved some old flower pots from a workbench. 'Here will be fine, thank you.' Picking up a shovel, 'I can dig a hole up the back if you want,' he asked.

'No, no thanks' she replied. 'It's my nephew's pet, so we'll allow him to sort that out, but thank you so very much for all your help.'

As he shook hands with Haley, she pressed a 50 Euro note into his palm. 'No, no, sorry missus, I cannot accept that, but thanks anyway.'

'With all that has happened this morning, I never even asked your name, young man.'

'I'm Jimmy,' he replied.

'Well, that was also my husband's name, and I'm Haley, and I INSIST, please. You have shown me kindness, and good deeds should always be rewarded.' She smiled.

'And bad deeds should always be punished.' he replied, pointing to the lifeless body of the pet dog.

'So please just humour me, take it and enjoy. Would

you like a coffee and sandwich?' she asked, pointing towards the kitchen.

'Now that would give the nosey neighbours something to gossip about,' he replied with a cheeky grin and wink. 'No thanks, I best be getting back to the job at hand. You really should report this to Guards,' he advised. 'What! It's only a fifty, and we never got inside the kitchen door.' she smiled.

It took a few seconds for the joke to register, but Jimmy laughed heartily as he closed up the back door of his vehicle. 'You take care of yourself and thanks again,' he said as he held up the Euro note. Haley shut the shed door, went inside and lying down again, closed her eyes, thinking that perhaps when she'd wake up, it would all have been just a bad dream.

She neither had an appetite for lunch or sleep and was dreading the thought of explaining the morning's disaster to Cyprian. He had exams in a week's time, was busy studying, had other personal issues and now his pet dog wrapped in a cloth shroud lay dead in the garden shed. As she lay on the sitting room sofa, her mind filled with all the possibilities of what might have happened had both she and Tyson had the opportunity of confronting those thugs. They had the advantage of surprise, and that's what won that particular battle for them. She still could hear the cold, sinister evil snarl from one of them as he gloated, "Ya won't be bitin' anyone again," Good old Tyson she thought, at least you got to tear a few lumps from some of them, but you paid dearly for it, my friend. Looking over at his empty bean-bag-bed, she wondered who was going to mind that stash of diamonds now? She decided to leave them where they were as nobody was going to move or disturb it in the immediate future. Those bloody things were bad luck, so perhaps I should unload them. But where, how, and to whom? Someone out there must be searching for their missing loot and Lord only knows if they are genuine or just costume jewellery fakes. The morning's aggravations had brought on a throbbing headache that required a strong chemical compound to be banished. This brought on a few hours of uneasy sleep, with the re-occurring flashes of the morning's horrors.

CHAPTER SEVEN

The slamming of the front door shook Haley from her slumber. She heard Cyprian's footsteps on the timber hall floor. She drowsily sat up on the sofa as Cyprian dropped his hold-all on the nearby table. Noticing the bothered look on her face, he sat down beside her, asking are you OK aunt Haley?

'Oh Cyprian, I'm so sorry,' she sobbed.

'Is mam OK?' he quickly asked.

'Yes, she's fine,' Haley replied.

'It's Dad or Chloe, then.'

'No, no, there are all fine, no problems out there at all, but it's Tyson; he's dead!'

Glancing over at the empty dog bed, he stood up with a look of disbelief. 'He got out and got knocked down then?'

'No, no, it's not like that at all. Here, sit down and I'll tell you exactly.'

Ten uninterrupted minutes later, she had spilled out the whole agonising event in full detail.

'Is he still in the garden shed?' asked Cyprian, quickly dashing through the kitchen. Haley allowed him the privacy to quietly sob over his canine pal who came to his rescue when needed. Emerging some minutes later, he sat next to his aunt and put a comforting right hand across her shoulders. He said, 'You are lucky it wasn't you as well, as these are complete nutters. I need to contact Shakeera and let her know. She will freak out but needs to be warned that these shites are looking for revenge. Then we'll decide where to bury Tyson.'

His text got an immediate reply, and they both regurgitated the story over and over as if it would somehow ease their pain.

'Now!' Haley sternly announced. 'Not a word of this to your parents. They are to know absolutely nothing of this horror story. They have enough to contend with as it as, so they will know soon enough when they return home. We will tell them Tyson had a brain haemorrhage and had to be put to sleep. He felt no pain, and it was quick. Got it? That's the story, or otherwise all these sordid recent events will come out!'

Cyprian hugged his aunt and openly wept, 'I suppose it's almost the truth, without all the gory details.'

'Good, we'll hold that line and what they don't know won't bother them.'

An incoming text and the slamming of two car doors announced the arrival of his pal. Haley felt the urge to dash upstairs to the safety of her bedroom and leave the youngsters to mull over what had happened.

'Oh, Cyps, my precious, how could shite like this happen in broad daylight?' They hugged in the hallway.

Haley noticed a well-dressed girl with very short well-groomed hairstyle standing uneasily behind Shakeera. She also joined the 'hug' and suddenly blurted, 'It's all my fault, everything, and now this. I'm to blame Cyprian, and I can never make it up to you both.'

'No, you're not,' he calmly said, but this made her more agitated. She raised her voice even louder screaming, 'YES! it's all MY fault, ME, ME and nobody….'

She was stopped in mid-sentence by Shakeera, grabbing both her shoulders and shaking her. 'Edel, get a fucking grip woman, you are getting completely hysterical.'

Haley, sensing an opportune time to intervene, stepped in saying, 'So I get to meet Edel. I had you pictured completely differently, glancing at her sisters' attire and NO, love, you are NOT to blame in any way. We are all connected to this, BUT the blame lies with these violent thugs. I do understand why the Guards were not called initially, and it's too late involving them now as it will just muddy the waters.'

'These are dangerous feral gangsters with no respect for anything or anybody, so you must all be on your guard to avoid them or their haunts. BUT if anyone is jostled or hassled or, God forbid attacked, the law must be contacted.'

'Now, we need to move on, and bury Tyson.' Haley suggested.

The pair had solemnly returned from the garden shed deep in conversation as to the exact burial area in the garden. 'Cyps may I make a suggestion here please,' Edel calmly announced. 'There is a pet crematorium outside the city. We can take him there, and within three to four days, he can be collected in an urn with his ashes. And perhaps a little plaque with his name on it. Then we just dig a small hole near the back wall and set him down there.'

'Edel, that's brilliant, absolutely the perfect solution' beamed Cyprian.

Haley watched as Cyprian carefully placed his precious pet into the car boot remarking, 'God I never realised he was this heavy!' The eight-year-old black Nissan drove slowly out from the side entrance and blended into the busy Dublin traffic. Trevor's wi-fi digital radio, permanently set on Golden-Oldies began playing the theme tune from "The Graduate". She knew every single word of the Simon & Garfunkel hit, but this was this very first time she heard the stillness, that was the sound-of-silence. It's lonely pang of sadness reverberated around the room, and the well-crafted lyrics only exacerbated her private grief.

Her immediate reaction was to drain the Grey Goose bottle of its potent contents but resisted the urge as the house phone landline began to ring.

'Number unknown' showed on the ID screen, but she pressed the answer button anyway.

'Hello big H, can you hear me OK?' came the hollowed sound.

Dear Jesus in Heaven, why now, thought Haley as she mustered every ouch of false courage to cheerfully reply. 'Hi little H, great to hear your voice again. Is everything going to plan out there?' she asked.

'It's slow but so-far-so-good,' came the reply. 'So, tell me how are things there since we left? You haven't flooded my house or sold off my only son?' she queried with hysterical laughter.

'No, not yet Heather, but I'm working on it. Your lad is a great kid. He has his head in the books and actually looking forward to his exams, spending much time working together with that lady friend of his. What's her name again?'

'Shakeera,' her sister quickly answered, but I wouldn't give high marks to her hairstylist or dress outfitter.' She laughed. 'No, I'm just kidding. She really is a sweet kid and she and Cyps, as she calls him, are as thick as thieves and really do watch out for each other.'

Quickly interrupting, Haley asked about their quest for Chloe, as that was the whole purpose of their trip.

'We have positive intel from the area that everyone at the particular camp is safe, and we're hoping to get up there next week. If she knew we were on her trail, she could well take off to some other outstation, being the cantankerous biddy that she is. Trevor says it's like being on a safari, stalking a dangerous wild animal; you must sneak up quietly and catch them by surprise.' Heather thought this description was hilarious, but Haley could only manage an uneasy 'Ha ha, good one!'

'At least our accommodation is bright, clean and secure.

The whole area here is a mass of contradictions; there is vulgar wealth beside appalling poverty;

incredibly beautiful scenery masking filthy slums. Everyone's extremely polite, but we are strongly advised not to go out alone at night, so that's the other side of this particular street. So, any news on your house repairs?'

Haley filled her in on the reports from Sally & son and kept talking for as long as possible, trying to avoid the dreaded question of dog-walking.

'Do you want me to bring you back anything special, as hopefully we won't be back here ever again and we certainly could not have done this without generous time-out for us?'

'No, just get yourselves, all three of you, home safely.'

'I thought perhaps something old or unusual that would fit into your antique shop,' Heather suggested. 'It may be some old piece of forgotten treasure that you could sell on if you don't lik...' Beep ...beep...beep...

The line had disconnected, and thankfully for Haley, there was no need for another lie to be added to her already depressing day. Replacing the receiver onto its cradle, she looked over at Tyson's old bean-bag-bed and wondered what type of treasure, if any, was tucked away there and how could she dispose of it. At least Heather and Trevor were making some progress, and when they returned, hopefully with their daughter, the joy of a united family would blot out the loss of their pet.

Haley felt completely drained and exhausted, having experienced a positive conversation with Albert, regarding his business plan, and the inclusion of her nephew as a pivotal player. Then the opposite emotion of that brutal attack in the park. It was just then she realised the expressions of concern were one hundred percent accurate; it could have been her at the receiving end. Fear or self-pity were emotions she always kept at arm's length, but she was also a realist. The frightening fact now was that these were dangerous thugs. Somehow this ongoing harassment had to be addressed. Perhaps the Guards should have been contacted day one and suffer the embarrassing consequences. She needed rest to unwind and attempt to address the manure-heap that had landed on her doorstep. Having snuggled down into a comfortable position on the couch, sleep eventually overcame all the negative thoughts, and she eventually nodded off.

The rattle of the mailbox woke her, and she wearily made her way to the front door. It was just an irritating ad flyer from the local shopping centre showing their wonderful sale offers. The recycle bin was immediately topped up. An early evening chill had indicated that she had managed a few hours' sleep. Checking her phone, Haley noticed a missed call from an unfamiliar local number. Before the negative thoughts had their chance to irritate her further, she had opened the text. It read: "Hi Haley, everything being taken take of with Tyson. Going for a meal/few drinks with the sis & Cyps. Tnx for paying. Rgds, Edel. PS, I'll mind the two lads for the night, so you try to get some sleep."

Beans on toast were the only item on Haley's dinner that night, and she found it difficult to finish that meagre meal. A hot soak with perfume scented bath salts helped ease her aching body later that night, and one of Heather's sleeping pills did precisely what it said on the tin.

Next morning the eerie silence was just as annoying. No scratchy paws on the hall floor, no slobbery face licking her nose to be allowed outside. As she put on her robe and opened the bedroom door, she was greeted by the aroma of bacon and strong coffee coming from the kitchen. 'Cyprian, is that you?' she called.

'Yup, I'm here and breakfast is almost ready. I was going to arrange a direct delivery. Seeing as you are awake, come-on-down.'

Making her way downstairs, she was wondering what condition her nephew would be in, bearing in mind all that had happened the previous day. She was greeted with a strong hug, kiss on the cheek and handed a glass of freshly squeezed orange juice.

'If I knew what your morning read was, it would be at hand for you,' he warmly announced.

'We got out of the habit of daily papers,' said Haley. 'James always said "the only difference each day was the date, death notices and sports results." So, he would buy two or three each Sunday, as most would be filled with the previous week's gossip anyway.' She laughed. Sipping the juice and looking at the plate of bacon and egg, her appetite was resurrected. 'Thank you, Jeeves.' She cheekily smiled.

'Oh, I'm sorry love. With all the goings-on, I forgot. Your Mam rang last evening. They are both settled in and are actually enjoying their stay. They hope to visit the area where Chloe was last stationed within a few days, so hopefully, we'll have good news from there.'

'You didn't mention about Tyson did you?' he interrupted.

'No, I just told her you were busy at your studies and all was well.'

His face warmed to a glowing smile as he took away the empties from the table, kissed her on the forehead and said, "Thanks again, Aunt Haley, as I don't know how we would have coped here without you.'

'Hell! That's what aged aunts are for, and family must stick together. Your Mam and Dad were very supportive when James passed away, so what goes around, come around.'

'I was going to give you the old family sticking together routine, but YOU just stole it on me,' he joked. 'Did I tell you Edel happened on Chalky, Spike and Tank last week?'

Haley's face dropped. 'What!' she shouted.

'She was with a few of the filming lads doing some 'walk-pasts' near Stephens Green when the Crew Cutters came against them. Chalky actually stared straight at the lads, but never recognised Edel - never! He obviously didn't recognise the new make-over.'

'Incredible,' agreed Haley. 'I cannot believe they were an item for a few weeks, slept in the same bed, and now he is unable to recognise her. Just goes to show the type of idiot she was with and isn't she the lucky lady to be well shut of that scum bucket. Knobheads like him only view a female from the shoulders to the shins and all parts in-between.'

Cyprian bust of laughing, 'Brilliant, where do you get all these sayings from?'

'It's fact, she added. 'I wonder is there a message in that particular event for Shakeera perhaps? I am allowed to call her Keera now?' She grinned.

'Yes of course. Actually, Edel decided to change her whole wardrobe approach the morning Keera came home dressed in your clothes. Which reminds me, she apologises for not returning them yet.' 'Well seeing as they worked wonders for her sister, tell her, it's a present and to please keep them.'

Haley jumped up from the table. 'Actually, I've just had a 'light-bulb' moment. Why don't we three go out shopping this evening, my treat and I insist. I believe there is a new shopping centre not far from here, so let's check it out.'

'I'll text Keera when my phone is ready. I know she'll be shy about going to expensive shops as her funds are low.' 'Like I said, MY treat and I am not taking no for an answer,' she sternly ordered.

The reply from Keera was prompt. "Great, Edel will collect you both @ 4.30 and drop us off to the Centre.'

CHAPTER EIGHT

At 4.20 that afternoon a car horn honked outside number 15, Fernpark Drive. Haley peered through the curtains and waved to a black Nissan outside. 'They're here,' she called to Cyprian, and both proceeded down the steps and into the back seat. 'So, what kind of shops are at this Mall?' inquired Haley.

'They've got everything to suit all tastes,' Keera remarked, 'but most of the purchases are way out of my budget.'

The car drew outside the main entrance. 'I'll give you all two hours then I'll be back exactly here to take you and the parcels home,' said Haley. 'Do I need to hitch-up the trailer?'

There were two floors of various shops, cafes, barbers and bars, with the lower circular part a large lounge-type waiting area. 'That's where the bored husbands and boyfriends hang out,' joked Keera, 'while us girls empty their wallets. 'Any ideas Haley as to where we should begin?' They all looked at the assortment of options.

Let's get the ball rolling here said Haley pointing to the large sign of "Hair Le Philippe."

'Ouch,' replied Keera. 'This place is very exclusive, expensive and I believe you need to make an appointment two weeks in advance.'

She felt a strong maternal and protective instinct towards Cyprian and Keera, and she decided to follow this instinct.

'You both leave all that to me and don't say a word,' she said as she marched them towards to glass doors. 'OK, lads stay right there and just ignore everything I say or do, and we'll get through this without a hitch.'

Both Cyprian and Keera, with raised eyebrows stood at the now open door as Haley strutted into the salon, removing her large sunglasses and pretending to fully inspect the premises.

'And what have we here?' came the over-the-top camp voice of a fifty-year-old man, dressed as a teenager. Pointing at two vacant chairs beside two sinks. 'We have a set of empty spaces which should be generating revenue for the proprietor,' Haley casually replied with a false posh Elizabethan accent. 'You are?' She looked at him quizzically.

'You, madam are in conversation with Philippe,' he replied in an equally false French dialect.

'Ah! At last,' she announced with an air of false excitement. 'Your artistry is well renowned but I'm unsure if this establishment can possibly achieve the high standards we require.' She waved her hands about. Cyprian and his pal were rooted at the entrance as they watched in wonder and amazement at the theatrics of Haley, in full flow.

'Now daahling, we have just disembarked from a boring flight from that ghastly Hollywood, and my two starlets are in need of immediate grooming. We've been involved in a remake of that old Woodstock era.' She gently squeezed his cheek. 'You are much too young to remember the decadency of that year. They now need modernising as there's a 'private' on its way to transport us to Pinewood Studios, pronto.'

Philippe stood in fixation as Haley called her nephew and Keera from the door and ushered them to the two empty chairs. 'Philippe, sweetie,' she cooed, 'you've got a pair of staff members giddily chatting about their weekend drinking plans, so can we please set the wheels in motion, with some degree of urgency?'

The three elderly ladies under the dryer hoods were oblivious to the histrionics unfolding on the salon floor. 'Tamara,' shouted the proprietor and clicked his fingers. 'Incoming stagecoach for transformation to Lear jet please!'

A beautiful Thai lady appeared wearing a tight top, mini skirt and bright green runners and made her way towards Cyprian. 'No, no, dearie, this one is mine, all mine,' he said and then pointing to Keera, added, 'Do take good care of this delicate creature I do so love a challenge.' He lowered his head to Cyprian's shoulder, peering into the mirror and extending the unkempt growth on his head and chin with both hands. He announced 'Goodness me; you look like you are bound for an Osama Bin laden fest!'

Looking at the fine print price chart on the wall, Haley knew it was going to be expensive, but she had a roll of fifties which some bad-ass dead crook had left behind, and she was going to make good use of it. Turning to Philippe, and raising her chin, she whispered, 'I will leave all this to your experienced eye and tasteful judgement. You can be assured your superior craftsmanship will be generously rewarded.' She stroked his tattooed arm.

Philippe was as much in shock and awe of the whole performance as were both his new clients. Pointing to the door, 'OK exit stage left,' he ordered. 'The maestro has a symphony to create.'

'Will ninety minutes suffice?' enquired Haley with an air of grandeur.

'Indeed, for you, one and a half hours, so please depart.'

'Oh, before I leave, can you recommend a suitable establishment whose couture can possibly complement your artistry?'

'Pointing to the ceiling, next floor, he said, 'Ask for Antoine proprietor of "Outfitters Inn" and tell him that Philippe requests, NO Philippe commands him to display only his most delicate finery to you.'

'OK,' said Haley, 'see you in eighty-eight minutes.' She winked at him.

By the time Haley left, Cyprian and Keera had been towelled up, heads leaning back into washbasins and unable to utter a word. She allowed herself a chuckle as she thought, yes, he is expensive, but you would pay good money to see a show like that. Now I need a large cool drink. She spied an open-doored bar opposite the salon.

It was only then she realised the number of stores in the plaza and the variety of offerings. A large food supermarket occupied most of the ground area, with a myriad of smaller units trying to extract the last remains of each wallet. She was surprised at the number of teenagers patrolling both floors, most of them with their heads stuck in expensive mobile phones. Those not peering into the screens were busy with 'selfies' and then dispatching the contents to their friends, sometimes only a few meters away. As she ambled towards the nearby bar, passing a brightly lit shoe store, her eyes were drawn to a bright pink pair of runners almost identical Heathers, which were now gifted to Keera. It was the opportune time to replace the stock as she stepped inside. There were two customers separately trying a variety on footwear that neither seemed completely satisfied with. A young lady with sleek jet-black hair brushed tightly back into a bun approached her. Haley thought, she could pass for a Spanish flamenco dancer. She just glanced at her potential customer as Haley asked about the footwear in the window display. 'Do you have those runners in size five?' She politely enquired.

'Trainers,' answered the young woman with an air of indifference. 'This establishment doesn't sell runners. We deal in quality trainers.'

Haley was taken aback by her rude, patronising reply. 'Oh, do pardon me,' she spouted in her recently acquired posh accent. 'Of course! Very few run these days. One must jog, mustn't one? The only thing that runs, this time of year is from a snotty arrogant Dublin nose!'

The assistant stood in shock at her reply as an older staff member intervened commanding, 'Tara, go take your break, NOW!'

'I do apologise for her lack of manners and decorum, so how may I assist you?' said the staff member.

Again, Haley enquired if the store had the pink shoes in size five. 'I believe we should, so just let's confirm that.' She swept aside a curtain into the stockroom. Loud voices from within suggested the 'flamenco' girl was sternly reprimanded. Reappearing with a box and producing what seemed an exact replica of her sister's shoes, she tried them on, and they were indeed a perfect fit and extremely comfortable wear.

'Ideal' Haley smiled. 'And would you possibly have them in a different colour?'

'Yes,' came the prompt reply, 'we have them in sky blue with a dark trim.' Another box was produced, quickly opened, and as Haley laced them up for size and strolled around the shop floor, she nodded at the new assistant. 'Perfect. I'll take these as well.'

She glanced around the store, 'I see you also have footwear for men.'

'Yes indeed.' She guided Haley to the opposite side.

'Size nine, comfortable, casual please,' said Haley. Five minutes later, an array of boxes was opened for Haley's inspection. She chose three different styles and colour which she hoped would meet with Cyprian's approval. 'I'll take these also.' Both moved to the counter.

The assistant smiled as she tapped the purchases into the cash register and handed her customer a bill for seven hundred and fifty euro. Haley reached into her handbag and produced fifteen fifties of her stash, and requested the ladies and gents purchases in separate bags, without the bulky boxes.

The sulky 'flamenco' head had appeared from behind the curtain, and her scowl indicated an annoyance at missing-out a sweet commission from that particular sale. The assistant handed Haley her cash receipt, thanked her for the welcomed custom and wished her well, as she exited the glass door and into the noisy mall.

Now, thought Haley, I do need that long cool drink. She made her way toward the part-opened doors of what seemed a comfortable lounge bar. It was a welcome change from the neon-lit exterior, and its array of modern, thump, thump, thump, thump, irritating music.

The lights were slightly dimmed, and the well-attended seating area was alive with a collection of well-dressed young people engaged in chat, laughter and obviously enjoying the array of cocktails and beverages provided by the two busy staff members. The violin sounds of "Four Seasons" were a welcome change as she spied an empty table near the door. Placing both bags of shoes on the seating bench, she marched almost in step with the music to the bar counter. Both waiters were serving and chatting to the clients and glancing around. Suddenly she realised she was much older than all other customers and could probably pass as their mother. Five smartly dressed handsome young men in their twenties were seated in the opposite corner to where she had dropped her purchases. Just for a split second, her glance tricked her into thinking one of them looked the image of a young James, her deceased husband when they first met. She looked over at the happy group, as they playfully teased each other about an upcoming rugby match, due on the telly in an hour or so. His side features and laugh ran a cold shudder down her spine. Then she recalled the counselling session provided by James' employers two years ago, about not believing ghosts and lookalike images as reality. When the young man spoke, it was a completely different dialect, and reality kicked in quickly. Not having the opportunity of seeing her dead husband in his coffin, she never had a sense of closure and this had always lingered in her subconscious mind. A smiling elderly bartender dressed in a white shirt, dark grey tie and light green tartan waistcoat interrupted her thought pattern 'And what may I get you?' he asked.

The classical composition was nearing its completion as Haley replied, 'Mr. Vivaldi I shall have a vodka, ice and slice with a dash of 7-up please.'

'At last, a client with a superior musical ear,' he returned with a slight nod of his head. 'And would your taste buds require any particular choice of distillation madam.'

'Grey Goose preferably,' answered Haley.

'A quality palette for a quality musical ear also.

You take a seat, and I'll drop it over to you.' The glass, wrapped in a small tissue to absorb the condensation, was promptly presented under a beer-mat and placed in front of his customer. She had removed her mobile phone and wedged her handbag between her two purchases.

'When it's my shift as manager, I make the call on CD choices here and looking around at the almost full room, I believe many come here to escape what masquerades out there as music,' he said with a smile. 'Isn't it strange that a classical piece like that, composed almost three hundred years ago has such incredible appeal in this era of plastic sounds?'?

Taking a large gulp from her purchase and picking up her phone, she suddenly realised she was now just like most others in the mall - staring into a small screen and checking if any of her contacts had sent her some messages. There was in fact a message in her inbox.

The short message from Sally made her realise she has not replied to the earlier report on the repairs at her flood-damaged home. She had best return a long confident reply or there would be a text or a call each day from her. She assured her all was well, absolutely no problems with the stay or her nephew. Had met lots of interesting people including Cyprian's boss and informed her of the type of articles for sale there, and the possibilities of co-operation between both houses. Thanked her for the progress on her own home and finished by promising to ring in a week or so. It was the longest message she had ever typed-up via text and then hit the 'send' button. The rotating icon revolved for about forty-five seconds, as she gulped down another swallow for her tasty mixture. 'Oh God, please go through as I cannot possibly retype all that again.' Short messages tend to pass rather quickly, but this was extra-long and eventually seemed to be fully transmitted. Her glass was now empty as 'Mr. Vivaldi' ghosted into her path. 'I'd like to settle my account, please,' she said with a polite smile. As he bent down to clear her table, Haley produced a twenty euro note onto his tray. 'That should cover my Grey Ganders,' she said and laughed. 'Have one yourself from whatever remains.'

'You, my dear lady are most welcome here anytime, and you take good care of yourself,' he emphasised.

She stepped out into the cacophony of sounds in the now much busier complex. The squeals of giddy teens mixed with the chatter of passing shoppers which intermingled with the guffaw laughs of male workers, glad their week-end frolics were in full swing. That, with the loud thumping beat from each shop wooing them, in an effort to lighten their wallets, reminded Haley that she actually had not been shopping, as such in over two years. Her only purchases in that time were a comfortable pair of walking shoes and underwear which was available at her local supermarket. She now had no need for any additions to her wardrobe, as invitations to parties and functions had decreased in the months following James' death and had now completely dried up. She certainly did not miss them, but it would have been nice to be asked. The large clock on the central wall indicated that she had used-up one hour of her allotted 'hair' time. Not wishing to pass the salon, she took the escalator to the first floor to inspect what 'fine-feathers' Antoine had on display in his boutique.

It was one of the largest units on that floor and the bright green neon sign displaying "Outfitters Inn" was unmissable. Haley decided it was best to continue with the aloof-posh accent as the proprietor would obviously discuss the theatrics with 'the demon-barber', later.

The shop was busy with many young people, mostly female browsing, comparing and 'oohing' at the price tags. Haley got that 'age' feeling again, as the array of clothing was aimed at the twenty - thirty age group with a deep purse. A tall well-built man in his forties approached her with a polite 'and may I be of assistance?'

Pointing to the floor, Haley announced that she had been directed by Philippe to ensure his finest couture were presented to her.

'At your service, dear lady,' came the swift reply. 'Oh, he is such a vixen, isn't he?' the attendant enthused. 'It's all an act, you know. The accent and everything. He began it over twenty years ago and it has overtaken him completely. But he is a sweet, caring person and doesn't deserve that bitch he is married to.'

'Married?' Haley asked quizzically. 'And with two wonderful children; William and Carmel. One is an airline pilot and the other a mechanical engineer.'

'Engineering is a most unusual career for a young woman,' said Haley.

'Oh, goodness no,' he replied. 'Carmel is the airline pilot and he is so proud of them, but he must keep up the 'camp' posture. All the old dears in particular just love his antics.' Haley almost dropped her guard as she smiled. 'Well he sure is good at it.'

'OK, so I have a 'him' and a 'her' to be clothed in full. Him, about your height, but not as well built and her...'

Antoine interrupted quickly, 'Let's begin with 'him' first.

What age group are discussing here?'

'Both nineteen,' she replied.

Taking a step back with both palms to his face in fake horror, 'Ouch!' he shrieked. 'That frightening end of teenage hissy fits. Are my boobs ever going to grow? Will these spots ever heal up? When will I shave a full growth? When are these Goddam hormones going to settle? Can Mam and Dad please get-off my case?' Haley laughed in agreement. 'Yup, you've nailed it.' Looking at Antoine, she imagined him a youthful Albert Long if he had a grey handlebar moustache. Admiring his dress sense, she added, 'Something along the lines of your attire should be perfect.'

'Let me take those bags and place them behind the counter, to make choosing easier for you. Rightyioh then, something slimmer than mine and neat casual rather than formal should be in order,' he whispered. Rummaging through the various racks of trousers and shirts, he produced his array for inspection. 'I'm trying to get things colour co-ordinated here,' he apologetically said as he moved the assorted garments into some form of order on the counter which was now full.'

'From what I've seen recently, the more of a colour-clash, the better,' she replied with a smile.

Eventually deciding on four sets of shirts and trousers, she said, 'I'll have all these please and what about a nice waist-coat similar to yours also?' A light blue sleeveless jacket with royal blue pinstripes was also added to the collection.

'And you also mentioned a 'her'?' he reminded Haley. Glancing towards the ladies' section, she noticed a tall slim young lady who was discretely trying to convince a potential client that the item she was holding against her largish frame was possibly not the appropriate choice for the function she was to attend. 'That lady with the auburn hair is the exact size required,' said Haley.

'Perhaps, we should wait until Melissa has sorted her client first, as it best I don't cross that gender line,' he joked. 'I'll just pack these away for you.'

'Can you remove the price tags also?' asked Haley

'You may require them in the event of a return,' advised Antoine.

'I trust your exquisite taste,' she replied, 'so I don't believe we will be travelling down that particular route.'

Eventually Melissa had completed her sale and was summoned by the owner. Haley smiled at the young lady and said, 'Something similar to your present attire. Just pick what you, yourself would like, if let loose here.' That was an open invite to wade through the variety of blouses, T-shirts and trousers on display. Antoine had moved back to his position and had placed the purchases under the counter, next to the bags of shoes. Admiring her attire, Haley said, 'You've got exemplary taste, so something along those lines, with variety, should be in order.'

Melissa produced an array of various items, suggesting she might model some to show exactly how they would wear. 'That would be excellent,' replied Haley, 'but I don't wish to use up all your time on just me.'

'Not a problem, as Dorina is due back from her break anytime now and we can always give the boss a visa to visit, if things get too busy,' she joked.

Taking two lots of blouses and trousers, she invited Haley to a large changing room. 'I'll need some help unzipping, so follow me.'

Her back-up had arrived as they both drew the curtain and Haley was asked to unzip the tight blouse she wore. 'I'll be outside,' replied Haley.

'No, do stay. Which combination would you like me to try first?' she said as she stood casually, in skimpy lace underwear, completely without a care. Picking two matching pieces, she said, 'Let's try these first and we'll view them outside where there's more light.' She exited the curtains with haste. No wonder Antoine was kept at bay she mused.

Five minutes later, Melissa paraded her choice and Haley was chuffed. 'Excellent,' she enthused. 'I will take the other three combinations as well. Oh, and if you were attending a special function, is there a particular formal dress here that takes your fancy?'

Melissa displayed three dresses, adding 'any of these are quality and class, suitable for most occasions.' One particular garment was a knee-length grey with a most unusual discreet pattern. 'This looks good and different,' said Haley holding it against her herself and viewing it in the adjacent mirror.

'That would have been my choice also,' said Melissa, smiling in agreement. 'Will I try it on, as I've been bursting to do so for weeks. Many customers immediately pick it out but replace it quickly when they view the price tag.'

'Quality and class come at a cost,' replied Haley, 'so yes, let's see it on parade.'

'Come on let's do so,' Melissa enthused, saying she would again require assistance in zipping' as it was rather tight fitting. Once inside with the curtain drawn, Melissa slowly peeled off the blouse and trousers, carefully draping them on separate hangers and invited Haley to drop the dress over her upstretched arms onto her perfectly shaped figure and then to be zipped up from the thong string to her neck. Haley stepped outside and waited as Melissa searched for an appropriate pair of shoes to accentuate her tight-fitting dress. As she stepped into the shop floor, a group of young ladies stopped their chatter to admire the stunning model who paraded down the floor to where Antoine was completing a sale. The young man who had just purchased also turned to stare with a 'Wow! All that sure looks good,' he gushed.

'Not your size,' joked the owner in reply as he complimented Melissa on her day's work. Strolling back to her client, she said, 'Was I right or what?'

'Young lady, you are a credit to this establishment,' said Haley, ensuring the boss was in earshot. 'You've got sublime taste and I will take the lot.'

I'll need help climbing out of this as I don't wish to damage your new purchase,' she said and smiled, inviting Haley into the changing room. Unzipping the garment, the assistant gently stepped out of her purchase and reassured Haley, 'The new owner will just adore this.'

Glancing at her watch, she realised her ninety minutes were almost up. Melissa then carefully folded all the pieces, without the price tags, as requested and proceed to the main counter where Antoine had completed a similar task. 'Shall we put the girlie pieces into a large pink carrier bag and the boy into a blue version, as it will be more identifiable?' he enquired. 'I've also included three leather belts to accompany the trousers, no charge,' he added.

'Excellent,' replied Haley and pop the smaller bags in there as well, so there is less to haul around. Their various price tags were totted-up and Antoine calmly said the total comes to one thousand six hundred and fifty euro. While he had been packing and totting, Haley had been discreetly peeling off fifty euro notes inside her handbag and stopped when she reached thirty-four. 'I've included a little extra for the efficient, courteous Melissa. She was such a help.' With her handbag extended and slung over her shoulder, Haley picked up both sets of large carriers and departed with a smug, 'Thank you all for your polite assistance.'

Antoine opened the door and with a warm smile returned the thanks and 'Not a word about Philippe's secret please,' he requested.

'Promise,' she replied and headed for the escalator in curious anticipation of what the 'maestro' had created. The mall was still buzzing with the variety of lookers, browsers and shoppers as she approached the salon entrance. The door was quickly opened by the proprietor with a bowing curtesy, saying 'Your punctuality is a credit to your charm.' Both Cyprian and Keera were both seated and about to be 'untowelled' as she placed her purchases on an empty chair in the waiting area. As she glanced towards the large front mirrored area, both stood up in unison. Haley stood transfixed as she stared at them, eyes wide open and unable to find the proper phrase to use. 'I am absolutely drained,' crowed Philippe in fake fainting voice.

'You both look absolutely stunning. I can't believe my eyes,' she stuttered, almost dropping the posh accent. 'No other word, stunning.'

'Now! what we did here,' announced Philippe, pointing to Shakeera, 'was to dismantle that mixed-up mane and cut back completely.' Shakeera now had a very short pink champagne coloured wavy cut with a high fringe. 'We needed that half-moon fringe to accentuate those incredible hazel pools, masquerading as eyes,' he cooed. 'I bet there are some deep mysteries hidden inside,' he added. Haley just glanced at her, smiling and thought if only you knew, my man, if only.

Turning to Cyprian who was brushing himself down. 'Here, I decided a modern young executive cut and that excuse for a beard was a must-go,' he explained.

Her nephew now had a short-back-and sides with much more on top and a 'tossed' look to the fringe.

'You look so handsome Cyprian; you really do,' was all Haley could manage.

Producing both carrier bags, she announced, 'I have some more appropriate apparel for both of you.' Turning to Philippe, she asked, 'Is it OK for them to change into something that complements your artistry?' Pointing to the large screen which accommodated the staff area, he announced, 'Enter stage right.' They both dashed off to examine the contents.

'Philippe, your choice of couture, pointing to the ceiling, is only matched by your exquisite artistry, which is only equalled by your personal charm and attention to detail, only to be surpassed by your exuberant eloquence,' said Haley with a sigh.

He sided up to her shoulder. 'Ooohhh, I love it when you talk dirty,' he replied with a false childish grin. The two emerged from behind the screen holding hands together and the carrier bags in the other.

'I could just cry,' moaned Philippe, as Haley, Tamara and an elderly customer gazed in wonder at the incredible transformation.

'You make such a beautiful couple and I wish you both well together,' said the customer with genuine sincerity. The two stared into a long mirror and giggled wildly as Shakeera's phone beeped an incoming text message. Turning to Philippe, Haley having glanced at the price list, reckoned the cost would be two hundred and fifty euro at least, adding 'Let's not speak of vulgar bills, as such.'

'OH God,' Shakeera interrupted, 'Edel is outside and the Yanks have landed, three days early.'

'Jesus, we're being invaded by the Americans,' the proprietor screamed in fake shock.

'Just some earlier than expected tourists,' replied Haley.

'Genius should receive appropriate remuneration as well as due recognition,' she said with an air of sanctimonious piety as she peeled off another bunch of fifties up to three hundred'. 'Here is also an additional one hundred for the immediate attention you generously provided,' she whispered. Pointing to the divide-screen, she said, 'Can you possibly find a suitable waste receptacle for that lot, as our props department certainly won't miss them.'

In their rush to the awaiting Edel, both had forgotten to collect their old clothes. Philippe politely held the door as Haley glided out and headed for the main exit adding 'Thank you so very much and please be assured your artistry will be mentioned in the appropriate surrounds.' 'Keep talking dirty,' said Philippe with a smile as he waved her goodbye.

Edel was in an argument with an overzealous security man. 'I'm NOT parked,' she barked at him. 'If I was parked, the engine would be switched off and the doors locked. The engine is running and all doors are open. I've already told you ten times - my friends are on the way out.' Spying Haley in the distance, she said, 'Now here they are.'

'And what are you two gawping at?' she barked at the pair beside the argumentative uniformed official, who said he would call the Guards. 'Call the Gestapo, you moron, because that's how you're behaving. I am waiting for my sister and her friends.'

'Hi sis,' smiled Shakeera. Edel had not recognised either of them.

'OH, MY, GOD!' she exclaimed, 'you are both stunning! See! I told you they were coming.

'Good! Now, MOVE!' barked the security man. The two youngsters piled into the back seat with their packages as Haley approached the Nissan. Turning to the security man and placing a note into the breast pocket of his uniform. 'Thank you for your kind understanding my good man, and please, do have a drink on me,' she calmly insisted, getting into the passenger seat. Edel asked, 'Did you give that knobhead cash for a drink?'

'Quick, quick get the hell out of here now,' shouted Haley.

'No, I gave him a tea-bag wrapped in pink tissue which I picked up from the café table, now MOVE!'

The car crew burst into hysterical laughter so much that she missed her exit lane and had to circle around a second time to get onto the main road.

'You are absolutely crazy, completely crazy,' Keera shouted through the laughter.

'And where did you learn to act like that? It was absolutely hilarious,' Cyprian agreed.

Looking into her rear-view mirror, Edel remarked, 'Seriously guys, you both look stunning, you really do!' 'Do you think Mam and Dad will like it?' Keera asked in an anxious tone.

'They will be chuffed to bits, trust me, I know they will.' It was obvious that Shakeera longed for a vote of approval from her parents on issues of dress code.

'So, when did the tourists arrive?' Haley enquired 'About two hours ago, and they are three days early,' came the reply. 'And boy! are they loud,' Edel added. They left Rome early because neither of the two Popes would see them for a selfie, left Venice because the roads were flooded, left Paris because the Mona Lisa looked exactly the same as all the pictures they'd seen in newspapers, left London because the only Queen they got to see was a Freddie Mercury tribute band, so they are in our house three days early. The hotel was booked for Tuesday next, so we're now stuck with them and they're in MY room, as it's cleaner than yours. So, we must double-up and that does NOT suit me, as you snore.'

'I most certainly do not,' snapped Keera.

Yes, you do, thought Haley to herself.

'Keera, you can come and stay with us for the weekend as we've got plenty of space, haven't we Aunt Haley,' offered Cyprian.

Haley certainly did not want to answer that particular question. The five second silence was broken when Keera quietly replied, 'I think it's best to stay at home and give Mam and Dad help with our visitors. Besides, I'd like them to get used to seeing the new me.' 'Haley,' she added, 'thank you so very much again for all this. I just can believe it.'

'Yes, Aunt Haley you've been way too generous.'

'Not at all lads, you are only young once, so enjoy it,' replied Haley. 'And if your own sister did not recognise you, there is little chance of that Crew-Cut-Crew ever knowing who you are.'

'Good point, I never thought of that,' mused Cyprian, 'but Keera if those visitors are too overpowering, we always have a spot for you, don't we Aunt Haley?'

Turning around to the passengers behind, she quietly reassured her nephew that any of his friends were always welcome at number fifteen, reminding him that she was also only a visitor. She caught a glimpse of Keera who was directly behind the driver give her a warm smile as if to say thanks for the support. 'Yur man and Dad are three-quarter ways through a litre bottle of Jameson and Mam has a leg of lamb in the oven, so it's all hands to the pump in our house' quipped Edel. 'Yeah! you're right sis' added Keera, 'but thanks a mill, Cyps and at least I know I have an escape hatch, laughed Keera. Jeez, I still can't stop laughing at that teabag prank, back there.'

'Well, I certainly can't ever go back there,' added Haley as all four were in hysterics, 'unless I am in complete disguise.' The Dublin traffic had slowed to a boring crawl, but this went unnoticed to both backseat passengers as they admired and teased each other lovingly.

'MOVE, your dozy bat,' yelled Edel at the driver who had delayed about seven seconds at the traffic lights. 'Are you waiting for any particular shade of green to appear'? Two fingers from his window was the reply, to much hilarity from Edel's passengers.

'Sorry Haley,' offered Edel as she changed gears and placed her hand on Haley's right arm. Casting her eyes backwards, she mouthed 'And big thanks for all that. Mam and Dad will be so pleased.'

Haley's return smile said a lot.

'OK! number fifteen approacheth,' announced the driver as she drew up to the only unlit house on their road. The backseat pair had kissed their goodbyes and Cyprian was already bouncing up the approach steps as the security light kicked on. Reaching onto Haley's shoulder, Keera thanked her again as she stepped from the passenger seat. 'Americans are mostly a friendly lot, and remember you both will have an address in the USA that you can visit,' she assured them. 'So, go help out your parents and enjoy the party.'

Edel sped away as Haley approached the opened front door. Cyprian, standing at the step, turned to her, 'Do you hear that?' he whispered.

'What!' answered his aunt. The only sound audible was Trevor's radio faintly emitting 'Elanor Rigby' from the kitchen. Again, she asked, 'What?'

'No scratchy paws on the timber floor, no big ugly slobbery head to greet me,' he sadly sighed.

'Cyps. I may call you Cyps,' she said with a smile. 'We've been over all this, and you and your friends have taken care of your old faithful pal. Yes! there is a gap, but you will get through all this.' She gently kissed him on the cheek. 'Wow!' she exclaimed. 'Much sweeter than that hairy head I had kissed last week.' That broke the ice as she directed him upstairs. 'Now put that lot on hangers to avoid creasing and get those pink trainers onto your mother's shoe rack.'

There was indeed a silence of 'something missing' and the slight smell of animal hung in the air. It was obviously from Tyson's old comfy bed, and there was no way Haley would dare touch it. That was her nephew's department, and he could eventually sort that in his own good time.

She still wondered what treasure, if any, was contained in the hidden sock there. Could it just be worthless costume stuff that would be used as props in a Christmas pantomime or were they real. Their bedfellows of cash and a Glock pistol suggested the latter, but she was in no mood to pursue that at the moment. Cyps had bounced down the stairs.

Pointing to the lounge, he said, 'Pray be seated, dear lady, you are being treated to dinner this evening.' He attempted to imitate Haley's earlier theatrics.

'What!' she feigned. 'One small peck on the cheek and now he wishes to woo her with dinner,' she gushed, in her most OTT snobby accent.

'Well! not as elegant as that' he laughed. 'We have a first-class chipper just three blocks down the street, and their stuff is really good.' Suddenly the phone rang, and she searched her bag until she realised it actually was the house landline. Heading across to the small table, she saw 'withheld number' on the screen.

An array of negative thoughts flashed through her mind: Shit, I been rumbled; I've spent too much cash in the one area; some of the notes were duds or marked; that bad-ass security guard could have traced the reg number of the Nissan; they could have picked up Cyprian. She was heading upstairs to get the Glock when the caller rang-off. Get a grip, woman, get a fucking grip you paranoid looper, the little voice of sensibility screamed inside her head. Taking another large slug from her glass, she returned to the kitchen and switched on the oven to ensure warm plates.

The digital radio was now wafting the incredible musical strains of 'Albatross' by Fleetwood Mac, and Haley was transported to her wedding day. That was their personal 'wedding-waltz'. It was a slow sexy tune to engage in a warm smooch, and their guests cheered and applauded loudly on the happiest day of her life. It brought a lump to her throat as she sipped again from her cool glass.

Her warm reminiscences were interrupted by the ringing of the phone. Again, it was 'withheld number' on the ID screen. She was much calmer now as she lifted the phone from its cradle, listened for a few seconds and quietly said, 'Hello.' There were no background noises, and after a few seconds, a voice whispered, 'Hi Haley, am I disturbing you? Its Keera here.'

With relief, Haley blurted, 'oh no not at all, sorry but Cyprian has gone to the chipper. We eating out tonight; Out of paper bags', she joked. 'Was that you earlier?

'Yes, it was. I'm ringing from our house phone, and I'm glad Cyps isn't there, as it's you I wish to speak to. I bet you are having cod, battered sausage and chips' she suggested. 'How did you know; have you this place bugged' she laughed. 'It's his favourite, and you will enjoy it as it's tasty' came the reply.

'I just wanted the opportunity, when you are alone to say a sincere thank you for everything, over the past few weeks. You've been a breath of fresh air in all our lives and mine in particular.

'No, thank you for everything you've done here, in supporting Cyprian.'

'By the way, my parents were almost in tears when I walked into our kitchen. Dad hugged me when he introduced me as his other princess. He's never said anything like that before. Maybe it was the Jameson talking, but I could see his expression, and he looked so proud.'

'Thanks, Keera for that and I know my nephew has a loyal, true friend in you.'

'I must dash was the reply, as the sherry trifle is being served here. They will all be absolutely hammered stupid, as Mam puts more sherry than trifle into it, so there'll be loud snoring upstairs tonight,' she said with a laugh. 'Enjoy Cyps' treat, and we'll see each other soon,' she whispered.

'Goodbye Keera and thanks again for the call,' said Haley, replacing the phone onto its cradle.

Two minutes later, her nephew came charging down the hall with his food parcel. 'Aunt Haley,' he beamed, 'you won't believe what happened.'

'Go on shock me,' replied Haley as right then she felt she was totally shock-proof. 'Gerry and Nicola who own the take-away did not recognise me. Nope, they served me and never even knew me. Isn't that the craziest thing ever.' 'Did you enlighten them?' asked Haley. 'No, the place was jammers. That's what delayed me.' Realising the relevance of her nephew's excitement, she replied, 'So the new Cyprian has emerged, handsome and now unrecognisable.'

'Do you think Mam and Dad will be pleased?' he asked in an invite of approval.

Have I just had this conversation a few minutes ago, Haley thought? 'Pleased! They will be chuffed to tiny pieces,' she assured him. 'Plates are there,' she said, pointing to grill. 'It certainly looks good,' she said, cutting a piece of the fish and confirming that what her nose had just inhaled, also tasted delicious.

The meal was thoroughly enjoyed as the empty plates testified. She smiled across at her nephew noticing how relaxed he had become. 'It's been a long day, and I'm beat,' she said as Cyprian cleared off the empties into the sink. 'I'll wash these, and you hit the sack' he smiled. 'Good night sweetie, I'll see you in the morning' was her parting reply.

CHAPTER NINE

Next morning Haley awoke in the exact same position she had curled into over nine hours earlier. The tiny shaft of morning light seeping through the curtains indicated it was much later than any other morning call since she arrived. Drawing them open, she saw a light blue Dublin sky, dappled with many small individual clouds spread across the rooftops. She noticed one particular member of altocumulus was shaped liked a map of Great Britain. She recalled how her late grandad would sit both her and Heather on his knees when babysitting and explain the various types of cloud formations. He would have a quiz to see who could recognise a unique formation that resembled something they knew. There would be a prize for the winner, which was always a shared bag of liquorice allsorts. He taught them the various names of every individual pattern and added that each had a silver lining, which was his way of saying 'always think positively'. However, she cursed the ugly collection that had dumped their contents on her quiet village, some months earlier.

She headed for the bathroom to find it sparkling, having been cleaned from door to window. Obviously, Cyprian had a head start on housework duties.

As she was exiting, the kitchen door was now open, and the sound of bacon crackled on the pan, wafted its delicious smell up to the landing where she stood. Hearing her on the move, Cyps stuck his head around the corner and announced, 'Breakfast is ready whenever you are.'

'Five minutes please,' came her reply.

'That looks delicious, thank you so much' offered Haley. 'Your coffee is on the way,' he replied.

'As it's the Sabbath, I presume you are going to Church,' she inquired with a smirk.

'I'm not in the mood for a sanctimonious sermon at the moment, so I'll pass for this week. I'm off to the Duffy's. Edel and her Dad are taking their tourists to see the film studios. Keera and her Mam are clearing out Edel's room to make more space for their visitors. I'm helping, and have been asked to stay for Sunday lunch if that's OK with you.'

'You don't need my approval, just fire away,' she replied as her phone beeped with an incoming message. Without looking and still chewing on the remainder of her food, she moaned, 'Oh! Please, Sally, not another long-winded report. Go to Church and pray.'

It was not from Sally.

It read, "H, ring me from a secure/safe line. Not your own phone or your home landline @ exactly 11.00 hrs to this number. Ed J."

It took a few seconds for her to realise it was Eddie, from whom she requested any information on the dead Russian. Cyps had reappeared in one of his newly acquired wardrobe pieces and new shoes, doing a twirl and inviting a compliment from his aunt. 'Stunning,' came the reply, 'absolutely stunning.'

'I hope Keera's Mam was pleased with her rig-out and maybe she won't even know me!'

Haley asked, 'Is there a public phone nearby or do people use them anymore?'

'This IS the twenty-first century, and most of Planet Earth are on mobiles now. There is one on the far side of the park, but it's hardly ever used, except to shelter from the rain,' he said with a laugh. 'I'm off,' he said with a spring in his step.

'Bye love,' answered his aunt in a faint voice, wondering what the hell Eddie was playing at, with his 'clean-phone' nonsense.

She had thirty-five minutes to spare but decided to check first and make sure it was in working order. So many public phones were regularly vandalised. She also needed coins. As of late, she was only dealing in fifty euro notes.

Luckily, she had a two euro coin and was hoping it would be sufficient to get through to the UK number Eddie had provided. It was a ten-minute walk to the kiosk, and Haley was relieved there was a dial tone when she lifted the receiver. The thought of trying to find another would be a major nuisance to her not being familiar with the geography of the area.

She strolled around the periphery of the well-manicured grounds, even taking a sad look at the area where Tyson had been killed. It still sent a shiver through her. She also recalled where she had hidden the infamous hold-all—the contents which she was now casually spending. The nagging suspicious doubt of 'am I being watched' was never far away, as obviously someone, somewhere had knowledge of the loot and certainly would be doing their best to recover it. It was 10.55 when she approached the kiosk and stepped inside in case someone else attempted to use it.

At exactly 11.00 she checked her own mobile phone and punched in the given digits, as provided. The number only gave two rings and was answered with a quick, "H, hang up immediately and I will call you straight back." She never got to say hello, as is it cut off, but placed her finger on the receiver button while holding the phone to her ear. It rang back in ten seconds.

'Haley?' the whispering voice said.

'Eddie, is that you?' replied Haley.

'Yeah! sorry about all the ringing-back stuff as I had to be certain we had a clear line.'

'Eddie you've seen too many OO7 films. What the hell is up with you?'

'Haley, please listen carefully as I should not be having this conversation with you.'

'Great! You remembered my full name and not just the first initial,' she snapped back.

'I didn't want to even mention your full name as you should know how things are around here.'

Haley then realised this was a serious conversation and not a friendly chat.

'Sorry, Moneypenny, fire away!'

'NOT funny,' he replied. 'Now, are you going to listen or trade Bond retorts?'

He had something important to say, so she apologised and invited him to continue.

'Please don't interrupt me as this is not fully verified, but our intel is fairly accurate. That dead Russian you inquired about, is Igor Jankonich. He was a small-time, tuppence worth in the KGB who went 'off-radar' two years ago. He was also a close colleague of Conrad Karnowski.'

'Is that the same Conrad....'

'Yes!' Eddie interrupted. 'We all knew him as Conrad Kremlin, because of his connections with officialdom in Moscow.'

'But he's dead. He died in the same helicopter crash with James and Kerri,' Haley said.

The four second silence at the other end of the line suggested otherwise.

'He's not, it looks like he's very much alive,' came the astonishing reply.

A shocked Haley asked, 'I thought all five on that flight had died.'

'That's what your department was officially told by Moscow.'

Again, that annoying four seconds of silence suggested to her that there was much more to this.

Eddie, clearing his throat, said, 'It is now very obvious he was never on that flight, and what's more, we have unconfirmed intel that Kerri somehow survived. It seems he is being 'cared-for' in some Siberian rest home, as the KGB would certainly want to get as much detail from him as possible.' He was trying to be as subtle as possible as this was the polite way of saying they would extract every ounce of intel they could from him. 'However, if he was seriously injured or concussed, they may not have achieved much.'

Haley leaned back against the perspex of the kiosk and tried desperately to make sense of this latest news. 'If this is the last piece of truth you are ever to speak again, please answer me honestly. The grave I regularly visit and the tombstone I speak to, please tell me that's where my James is resting.'

'Yes, Haley, yes, one hundred percent, yes, I can assure you. The DNA samples and dental records confirm this, without question. I'm sorry to resurrect all this right now, but ....'

Haley interrupted him in mid-sentence. 'What about Kerri's coffin? Were there DNA tests taken and how in fuck's name was that missed, if he is supposed to still be alive and who or what is buried in HIS grave?'

'I was not involved in all this when it happened and I'm just picking up bits and pieces. This is stuff I should not be sharing outside the department as it's highly classified.'

'Oh, spare me all this patronising horse-bollox-secret-crap and answer me, how did your geniuses miss on Kerri when they had a cast-iron ID on my husband?'

'Seemingly the body returned as Kerri was an appalling collection of ash and badly charred bones. But there was a tooth with a gold filling which had sufficient content to confirm it belonged to Kerri and his dentist also confirmed he had performed the filling some years earlier. So, they had proof and there was no need for further work. As you know, Kerri was an adopted child and both his new Mam and Dad had passed away some years ago. He had no immediate relations as both his parents were also from single families. If you recall his funeral was rather sparsely attended, apart from some work colleagues and near neighbours.'

'No, I don't actually,' Haley sadly replied. 'I'd attended one funeral too many that particular week.

So much for all your accurate intel over the past two years. My husband was not a killer or hit-man and neither was that other young man, so why did they have to die?'

'James had a wonderful ability to assess the information being shared by all our associates across the world and decipher what was fact from bullshit. His uncanny ability to co-ordinate this saved our country and the European mainland many atrocities that could have cost lives and untold damage. That's what he was good at, and he had the respect of all security sections right up the Prime Minister. He was the brains while others out in the field were the brawn. He kept a low profile for security reasons as well as his own and yours. Both he and Kerri had obviously 'stumbled' onto something that concerned security issues for the UK and Russia and that must have been what they were co-operating on. There's a lot …' Eddie's voice was just a jumble of faint words as Haley inhaled deeply, unable to absorb the contradictions presented to her over the previous two years.

'I need time to understand all this, as I never expected the hear stuff like that, never.'

He was in mid-sentence when Haley dropped the phone onto the receiver and opened the kiosk door to inhale some fresh air into her confused system. Thinking he might attempt to call back, she lifted the phone and placed it on top of its control unit. She was too upset and shocked to listen to any more of that saga. She thought, why wasn't it James who survived. Kerri had no family whatsoever and obviously had no grieving relatives. As she slowly ambled across the narrow path, she scolded herself for that unnecessary vulgar thought. If James had survived, what sorry condition would he be in, and how would she cope, having gone through the trauma of his funeral service and her attempts at 'getting-on' with her life.

Every collection of negative, nasty thoughts rushed through her brain as she quietly made her way across the park. In the distance, a referee's whistle blew, and a crowd cheered, kids laughed and squealed as parents pushed them on the playground swings. Sweaty joggers in tight lycra leggings trotted and attempted conversation. Elderly people walked their dogs. Young mums pushed their new-borns in expensive buggies. Teenagers playfully had a kick-around pretending to be Ronaldo, and an array of song-birds still continued the 'dawn-chorus'. It was a normal Sunday morning, but for Haley, it was like she had been kicked in the stomach.

The Russian whom her beloved, charming husband trusted and had shared sensitive notes with and probably saved atrocities in his own country, had left him on a doomed flight. Then somehow convinced even his own people that he himself was dead. As far as Haley was concerned, HE was a murderer and James one of his victims. She had come to terms with his death being another aircraft accident, as frequently happens. From what she had learned, it was cold-blooded murder, and her Government must take appropriate and immediate action. What took them so long to stumble on this? So much for co-operation between friendly security agency staff!

Her tormented brain was unable to cope, and without realising it, she was going in the opposite direction to home. A church bell peeled, calling the faithful to Sunday mass. As the sound grew louder, she suddenly recognised it as the church where Cyprian had made his Confirmation.

James, as his godfather, had insisted on taking time off to attend. He was officially the sponsor for that particular ceremony.

Neither Heather nor Trevor had expected his attendance, but James being the officious gent declared it was his duty. As with his job, when duty called, he would answer.

Such a call cost him his life. She sighed.

She was now at the church steps and vividly remembered the photo taken at the main doors with both parents, Cyprian and her husband alongside the

Bishop. She had only seen it recently when packing the downstairs belongings for higher ground.

The effort of attempting to stand in the exact spot where James was in that picture gave her a small sense of relief. Unintentionally, she joined the congregation as they moved through the vestibule and into the church proper. It was never her intention to attend Church that morning, recalling how she had teased her nephew about it earlier. She was now inside, and it seemed impolite to about-turn and leave, against the incoming flow of people. This morning the attendance was particularly sparse compared to Confirmation day. The last three pews to her right were completely vacant as most of the congregation had assembled down the centre aisles. She moved into the last pew, which only had a kneeler behind it, and felt secure in her isolation.

A portly priest accompanied by two altar boys appeared from a side door and up three steps to the main altar. His first words were, 'Good morning all.'

The congregation blandly replied, 'Good morning Father.' Haley sat with both feet on the padded kneeler, her two elbows perched onto both knees and her face staring blankly at the ceremony unfolding in front of her. The priest read from the open missal. Does he not know the words off by heart after all these years, she thought?

The congregation replied in an unconvincing voice.

They stood up and knelt down, then stood and eventually sat. Haley remained seated in the same position with a thousand mixed-up and jumbled thoughts gushing around her head. The priest moved from the altar to a lectern and proceeded to inflict a boring sermon in a patronising voice to his captive audience. His subject matter this morning was 'forgiveness' and he rambled on for what seemed an eternity, quoting various passages of Scripture to emphasise his message. By now Haley had dropped her head into her hands with both index fingers at her ears, to dull the monotone sound of his voice. Of all days, this was one piece of piety she had no wish to indulge.

He eventually finished. Everyone was still seated and the collection took place.

Good, there's no one near me, so perhaps I'll be bypassed. Eventually an elderly man stretched his arm with the 'plate' under her nose. Haley rummaged inside her bag and secured some small coins and placed them into the collection tray.

He most certainly wasn't going to get one of the 50s for an annoying effort like that. She also noticed there was no singing. Her Church of England service would be interspersed with various choral psalms sung by the willing congregation. Catholics did not get involved in communal hymns, just praying, kneeling, standing, sitting and collections, which also happen to be a central part of all religious services. The only section of the morning's offering which resonated with her was when the people stood for The Lord's Prayer. She did not have the energy or religious enthusiasm to partake in it, especially the line "as we forgive those who have trespassed against us".

It had a hollow ring to Haley's ears at that moment. The priest then invited his flock to "offer each other the sign of peace". Thankfully there was no one within touching distance, and they all shook hands and politely smiled at each other.

Eventually the praying and responses were finished, and the celebrant instructed the congregation, "Go in peace to love and serve the Lord". There was very little peace in her heart, but a gnawing burning hate. In fact, if she had her Glock and that ugly albino-headed Rooskie happened to be on the altar, she would calmly put two in his chest and one between his eyes, to be certain. She then felt annoyed with herself for having such feelings in a church, of all places, but that's was how it was, and she was never a hypocrite. The attendees had emptied their seats, and she was alone in the solemn quiet that's part and parcel of most old houses of prayer. Her knees were now sore from the weight of her pointed elbows. She raised her head to view the empty surrounds, through her moist and bloodshot eyes.

She suddenly felt the 'presence' of someone behind her. A hand lay gently on her left shoulder.

Haley froze in her seat, fearing the worst, as all her paranoid thoughts resumed their annoying activity.

With an uneasy casual glance, she saw an arthritic, wrinkled old hand resting easy on her uneasy shoulder.

A timid whisper said, 'I don't tink Sundays is always de best time to be prayin to Himself,' in a soft, unique Dublin dialect. Half turning around, she saw the wizened face of an old lady. Pinched mouth and wrinkled cheeks etched by at least ninety years of hardship. Her clothes reeked of smoke. Coal smoke, as that was most likely her only house heating. Pointing to the ceiling, she added, "How can He be listenin' to millions of prayers from millions of people in millions of chapels around the world, all at de wan time. Sometimes it's best to talk to someone you know. They may even be dead, but if they were good people, they are now in God's House and shur isn't dis one a God's Houses? Always talk to someone wise and trustworthy and they will listen, and isn't dat all anyone wants? No one seem to listen dees days. All too busy talkin and tryin to be heard. I'm not going to interfere, luv, but you look so sad, and it's not right being dat way in here.

I'm going over to my little pal in the corner, and I'll have a chat with him.'

Glancing at where the old lady was pointing, Haley noticed a statue of what seemed a Dominican Friar with a dark complexion.

'I knew him first, as Blessed Martin De Porres and he done me and mine many good turns. One of the Popes made him a Saint some time ago. Seemingly he pulled a good few rabbits out of the Miracle-Hat. I'd say he's much busier now, but he always listens to me. We go back a long way, him and me. So, I'll light a candle and ask him to help out whatever seems to be bothering you.'

The old lady used Haley's shoulder to ease her weary frame upright. She then crossed the church floor. Haley wanted to say something but her quivering lips, moist eyes and runny nose had put the handbrake on any words.

The lady stopped at the centre aisle, genuflected to the main altar and proceeded to the small shrine which surrounded the statue. By the time Haley moved from her stationary position and crossed to the shrine, a candle had been lit and placed in the centre of the holders. The old lady was dropping some small coins, mostly five cent pieces into the money box when she noticed Haley standing beside her.

'I'm afraid I left him a little short,' she said apologetically. 'I'll make it up to him when I get me pension. He'll understand and knows I'm good for it.' She knelt and prayed at the sculpted piece of plaster. Haley was in awe of her faith, devotion, and the genuine concern she'd shown to a complete stranger.

The old lady had not properly closed the handbag that hung on her right elbow. Haley peeled a fifty and gently slipped it inside. She placed her left hand on the lady's shoulder, pressed the clasp shut with the other and quietly whispered, 'Thank you so very much for your kind words and prayers.' It was as much as she could muster there and then, as any more would have reduced her to a blubbering heap. Taking some tissues to dry her eyes and nose, she took the five steps quickly to the brass handle on the large wooden exit door.

It took a strong effort to open, and she wondered, why, oh why are church doors so damned heavy? Was it to keep the sacred pious air inside, or to protect it from the vulgar sins of the outside world? All the congregation had dispersed as she turned up her collar, zipped up the jacket to her chin and headed home. She was completely confused at that very moment. Firstly, the earlier phone call. Then the sincerity of that old lady. She hoped a gentle soul like her would always remain safe. That frail, innocent figure would be vulnerable to some crazed thug seeking an easy victim. Obviously, her 'little friend' had been keeping her safe for many years. It had been another day of contradictions, but the burning hate she felt for Conrad Kremlin was now even more intense.

She headed home and unknowingly realised she was retracing the exact same steps that led her to morning Mass. She did not wish to pass by the phone box or be near the area where Tyson was brutalised. It was as if the whole park was her bad news depot. Contaminated with the ugliness and vulgarity she had recently experienced. She eventually found herself outside the café, opposite to where her saga had begun: that dead Russian, Igor whatever-his-name-was. The café was open. She ventured inside and took the exact same seat where she had viewed the squad cars and ambulance. Childlike, she wished her table was a time-machine, and could rewind to that fateful morning. She would never have intervened, and this whole manure-heap would not have evolved. Her thought pattern was interrupted by the same young Polish lady.

'Hello, again. Would you like the lunch menu?

Special today is stuffed pork steak - gravy -potatoes- mixed veg.'

'That sounds fine,' replied Haley.

'You like vino perhaps, as only have here licence for vino,' the lady explained in her best broken English.

'I could really do with something stronger, but yes I will have wine,' said Haley with a smile.

'Do you recall a few weeks ago, I sat here, and there was a commotion outside with a dead body?' Haley casually asked.

'Oh, yes,' she answered. 'He had heart problem; police say. Men from Russia Embassy they call here and ask if we see anything or anybody in car. Many mens call first but they were no official as they have ID paperwork and go quick when Joseph ask them. He no like these peoples as our parents had bad time when they rule in our country. But real Embassy mens have ID, with photo and stamp. They ask all shop peoples here. All this must happen in night, as car was there, as she pointed to the opposite side, when we all open in morning. They go and no come back, but Joseph he say they be no news on paper or television which he think in strange. Is not good have dead man outside our shop, as peoples could think he have lunch in here,' she laughed.

'I agree, and it's someone else's problem now,' replied Haley in her most uncaring accent; knowing damned well he was also a major part of her problems in many areas.

Somebody in authority and the crooks were obviously searching for clues as to what exactly happened and where than missing hold-all was destined. The thought sent another un-necessary shiver through her as she paid her bill and left.

The mixture of crazy thoughts and paranoia had been even more exacerbated following her conversation with the waitress. She needed the safety and tranquillity of number fifteen to relax-unwind and figure-out a plan that ensured both her and Cyprian's safety. It required immediate attention. It didn't take long to arrive at Fernpark Drive. She had been unaware of the various selection of Sunday joggers, cyclists and kids peering into their mobile phones, but conscious of any slow-moving cars.

As she was about to open the front gate, a well-dressed young woman wobbled in her direction. In a slurred eloquent voice, she enquired, 'Excuse me, but are you related to Chloe?'

'Yes, I am.' Before she could continue her sentence, the youngster said, 'Oh yes, I can see the resemblance to her mum. So, you must be Chloe's Nan.'

'NO!' barked Haley. 'I am her mother's sister which makes me her aunt,' and was about to add, 'you stupid twat,' but resisted. The explanation was lost, on the bleary-eyed youngster.

'Oh! Chloe is so wonderfully brave and dedicated,' she announced in an ever louder posher accent. 'We are in awe of her loyalty to all humanitarian causes. We were in college together and she had our full support on all efforts to correct the ills, that rot our living standards.'

'So, you accompanied her on the African expedition,' Haley asked in a louder voice.

'Oh! Goodness me, no, no, no. Mummy forbade me.

She said I was too precious to her, and all that stuff was way too primitive for my constitution. So, my sister and I went on a tour of the North Americas.' 'North Americas?' asked Haley with a tone of annoyance.

'Yes, firstly we went to New York and then down to Miami for a fab three weeks of sunbathing. Headed down to Cancun, just spending a few days there. It was rather tacky. Up to San Francisco, and later on to Vancouver. Have you ever been?' she asked.

'Not recently,' came the quick reply.

She continued, 'then on to Toronto for the remainder. That full six weeks went in a flash, but it was such fun.'

'I presume, in your glorious effort not to affect the delicate carbon footprint, you both sailed, cycled and walked to all those destinations' queried Haley with a look of mischievous annoyance.

The young woman burst into hysterical laughter saying, 'Oh! you are a hoot, absolutely. No, we flew, and luckily for us, it was business class all the way, as those long-hauls in cattle-class are so annoying and…' The expensive mobile phone in her hand rang, and she immediately answered. It was on-speaker so was audible to Haley.

'Portia, where exactly are we?' came an equally inebriated female voice.'

The reply was short and sharp, 'I'm almost home, so you leave, get a taxi and get-the-hell out.'

'Fine but where the hell are we, as I'm still well stewed? I've just woken up in a room of at least twelve naked people, and I see my thong on the head of some big black guy. What the fuck did we smoke, snort and drink last night, as I can't remember anything?' She said with a giggle.

'Get out and go home, NOW!' came the quick retort as she hung up.

Haley stood in absolute shock at what she had just heard. Just then, her own phone rang. 'I must dash,' she said, reaching into her handbag.

Her phone disconnected quickly before she had retrieved it. She watched Chloe's pal stagger away from the gate, only making it to the wall next door where she leaned over and got violently sick onto her neighbour's well-attended flowerbed.

Haley's phone showed 'unknown number', and another rush of panic took immediate hold. Had her phone been tapped? Was there a redial button on the payphone that someone could have used? Had the café owner squealed to the Embassy about her questions? Was she being trailed? She used the excuse of waving goodbye to the sick youngster and surveyed the surrounding streets, checking for strange cars or moving curtains. Beads of perspiration on her brow and torso only confirmed another anxiety attack. She quickly realised there was no one else around, and it was the same paranoia as before.

Watching her empty her stomach, Haley quietly whispered, 'Good girl. Get all that expensive shit you smoked, snorted and drank last night out of your 'delicate' constitution, you five-star, two-faced, dozy, stupid, fucking bimbo.'

With her stomach emptied, the girl was now squatting with knickers down around her ankles, at her neighbour's gate and discharging her bladder.

'I would offer you strong coffee and a lift home; only you bored my ass off with your gratuitous-snotty attitude. Wouldn't mummy just love to see her precious fanny-head of a daughter right now!'

As she unlocked her front door and entered, she realised that perhaps Heather had instilled better qualities into her kids. Maybe her unique way was the correct approach. Both of her children would never contemplate such atrocious acts of debauchery. She was genuinely horrified at the patronising comments and their lewd behaviour, especially as it seemed both came from obviously affluent families. She had placed her handbag on the bannister and was locking the door, securing the safety chain and adding the security bolt, when her phone rang again. She was most certainly not going to answer an unknown number, so she allowed it to ring for about twenty seconds. Taking it out carefully, as if it were a grenade, she hit the 'answer' button with relief.

'Hi, Aunt Haley,' came the happy voice of her nephew. 'Did you ring me just a few minutes ago?' she quickly enquired.

'No, we are just finished up rejigging things here, and you won't believe this! When I knocked on their door this morning Mrs Duffy answered and genuinely did not recognise me. Isn't that just absolutely mad? It was when Keera came down the hallway and called my name; she realised it was me.

'Her jaw nearly hit the ground, and she hugged and gave me a kiss - a big slobbery kiss. I don't think we even shook hands before, even though I've been over here for years. She said I look a million dollars. Isn't that the maddest thing ever?'

Haley found it difficult to share his youthful enthusiasm as she was more concerned with that recent phone call.

'Their visitors are on their way back home. Edel said they did not seem too impressed, as it wasn't a fraction the size of Hollywood and were disappointed Liam Neeson or someone famous wasn't there. They are taking us all to Sunday lunch at that fancy place we had dinner a few weeks ago. Remember that place where that gorgeous waitress 'ear-boobed' me, before Mam and Dad left for Africa? And you are also invited.'

'I just got back from a long walk, and I've already had lunch at that nice café opposite the park, so I'll pass. But please tell them I do appreciate the offer. I'm really glad the Duffy's are impressed with your change.'

'And Keera's new look has made a huge difference with her parents, so mega thanks Aunt Haley for all your generosity. I won't be too late, so see you later.'

'Bye, love and enjoy,' Haley quietly replied.

'Jeez, I better take all those locks off that door, as he would be unable to gain entrance to his own home,' she whispered.

That little voice of reason inside her head suggested she needed rest, and a clear head to figure out what course was necessary as she was turning into an uneasy mess and likely to make mistakes.

She switched off her phone and headed upstairs to the quiet of her bedroom. She dropped her shoes onto the bedside rug, turned the duvet over her weary body, craving for some peaceful, uninterrupted sleep.

Haley lapsed into a deep sleep without any annoying dreams or nightmares, and for a few short hours, all the problems of that depressing phone call had evaporated. She was the one who initiated the queries on the dead Russian and in fairness to Eddie, he was true to his word.

He had replied with facts, however unpalatable they were. She guessed that his information was second hand and unverified by 'officialdom' in Whitehall, but he had stuck his neck out for her on this. Whether it was an info call or a warning to her, remained to be seen. She was now hoping he would call back should he have more detail. Perhaps it was him earlier, ringing to check on her after dropping the huge bombshell into her lap.

The reality was, James had died and would never return to her. She tried to put the precise circumstances of his death to one side and decide what to with the cash and diamonds if they were worth anything. The Glock would be retained for protection, and she would use it if required. She really hoped it wouldn't come to that!

Taking a pen and paper, she wrote all the events which she knew were facts and one hundred per cent certainties:

She was not involved in the Russian's death.

She left no fingerprint traces.

No one saw her at the scene.

No one saw her hide the hold-all or retrieve it later.

There was no tracking bug.

The hold-all was safely disposed of long ago.

The Guards had not done house-to-house calls on it.

It was never mentioned on local TV or papers.

Her house was not under surveillance.

The cash was genuine.

So, she saw no immediate reason for anyone to come looking for her, be they crooks or officials. There was no paper trail, smoking gun or loose ends to link her to the missing money.

When she re-read her list three or four times, it re-assured her. All her negative thoughts and feelings were totally unfounded.

If she was to retain her sanity and find a route out of this quagmire, a calm, cool head was required. But one way or another, that rotten murdering Russian bastard would pay, and pay dearly for his crime.

CHAPTER TEN

Next morning, Cyprian had left by the time she had awoken, as was his normal departure schedule.

It would be a short week, as his exams commenced the following mid-week. He had turned on the digital radio in the kitchen, so that irritating silence was broken. Realising that Dansie was due the following day, she sent a text message to Cyps requesting her phone number. Haley did not feel up to explaining the gory details of the dog's demise. She had seen him healthy and would not have believed the story they would eventually spin to Heather and Trevor. An immediate reply told her to check Heather's small green book in the drawer of the phone table. Luckily it was a mobile number, so she sent a short text, rather than listen to a twenty-minute ramble from her. That could wait 'till Thursday. She needed a few days of quiet to figure things out, and perhaps Eddie may have received more concrete news, as it was obvious all efforts would be made to have this resolved at Whitehall, quickly and quietly. This was certainly the type of situation they would never condone or were complicit in, so wheels would be in motion to ascertain the facts.

A quick reply on her phone read, 'Thanks Haley, see you Thursday, D.'

Before Cyps left for college early on Tuesday, he had placed a 'sticky-pad' note on her table mat. It read, "Maybe home a bit late as we are collecting the ashes this afternoon. X". Even though she still glanced at the empty dog-bed and wondered what the contents were worth, if anything, she had completely overlooked the return of the dog's remains from the crematorium. Other, more pressing matters had overtaken recent home events.

However, the sadness of Tyson's homecoming had to be faced. Her nephew had more than enough emotional and personal issues in his life presently. She hoped the change of wardrobe and hairstyle that had lifted his spirits would ease his burden somewhat. He had his final exams due shortly and needed no distractions as youngsters were under sufficient pressure from all sides to achieve their goals.

The previous day was a boring drag at number 15, and Haley grew more anxious about the conversation she'd had on Sunday morning. The paranoia had evaporated, but she still had over four hundred and seventy-five thousand in cash hidden in her suitcase, a sock of what looked like expensive diamonds and a loaded pistol. It was more cash than most couples would save in a lifetime and she wondered should she just dump the lot and forget the annoying saga ever happened.

Her larder needed restocking, and she made a list of requirements. Glancing at Trevor's wine rack and liquor cabinet it also needed topping up but, off-licences only opened at 10.30 am.

The house phone rang. Hopefully it would not be another unknown number. It was a number she did not know, but she picked up the receiver this time without any panic fears.

'Hi, Haley, Trevor here, how are you?'

'Oh, Trev, it's great to hear from you. How are things with you both, out there? Wait, don't tell me, Heather has found an exotic new beauty parlour,' she said, laughing.

'Not just one, but two or three,' he replied. 'She's out with some of the other Embassy ladies at a charity gig. I'm ringing from a quiet office here, as I have some peace at the moment. Is everything OK at Fernpark? Hopefully Cyprian's still studying hard, and Tyson hasn't walked the legs off you.'

'Stop worrying Trevor, all's well and your boy is a model son. I guarantee he is also a Grade A student and the old widow has everything under control.' Wishing to avoid any more dog lies, she said, 'So any word on your quest for Chloe as Heather indicated last week you had made some progress.'

'It seems to be two steps forward and one step back. We know she moved a while ago and there is confirmation of no dangerous activity in that region. As we are moving under diplomatic visas, I thought it would make access easier, but it only seems to complicate things as we need bodyguards to escort us about. This draws attention from local militia who view such parties as potential bargaining chips, so it slows things down. They are all confident here that we should get up to that area within a week or so and are most co-operative. I'm glad I got to speak to you alone Haley and I can't thank you enough for your help on the home front. We couldn't or wouldn't have attempted this without you. At least we know our home, son and pet are safe and being cared f……. beep… beep… beep...'

Good! A giraffe has chewed the telegraph line, mused Haley, relieved the conversation had ended, happy that they were both well and seemed confident they would reach their daughter. She replaced the receiver and watched it for ten seconds or so to see if it would ring and praying it would not.

Her personal phone beeped an incoming text message.

It read, "Hi Haley, all going to plan here. House has dried out well, and plasterers will be here in two days. All your old wet stuff has been removed in three skips, and we have confirmed the kitchen units you picked will be ready when required. Your garden is springing back into bloom, and all should be OK here in three in three to four weeks.

Hope you haven't got a broad Irish accent yet :).

We miss you lots. Love Sally and Mr. Grumpy X X."

Two pieces of refreshingly good news brightened up Haley's day to some degree as she collected her bag to 'do the messages' as her late Gran called it.

She had placed her phone inside her handbag when it beeped in another text message.

It read, "Same again @ 11.00. Ed J."

Her shopping bag and list were discarded as she checked the time. She had twenty minutes to ensure the kiosk was empty and the phone was in working order. Approaching the perspex block, she could see a young man in an agitated state, shouting into the receiver. Two days earlier her paranoia would have sent her running away, but she was now more at ease. She calmly walked past him. She was just killing time and hoping he would run out of coins before 11 am. Not venturing far and keeping an eye on her watch as it ticked onto 10.54, he was still in an argumentative mood as she passed the box.

'And fuck you too,' he screamed, slamming down the receiver, exiting, and attempting to bang the door.

Don't bust-up the place, you moron, thought Haley. She entered the kiosk and checked for a dial tone. Thankfully all was in working order.

At 10.59 she dialled the given number.

It rang twice, and the voice again said, 'Hang up. I'll ring back.' With the phone to her ear and her finger on the receiver button, she waited. Ten seconds later, Eddie quietly asked her, 'How've you been since?'

Haley decided her replies would be much more measured and certainly no more smart-ass 'Bond' jokes.

She calmly explained there was much to digest. There were many contradictions to the official version of events. Some sections of Sunday's horror story did not add up.

It had taken three days for the crash, which was not a military trip, but a sightseeing tour, to be verified.

Another four days for the bodies to be repatriated to the British Embassy. Kerri, obviously, had a tooth extracted and placed into his body bag. It had been a full wasted week while the Russians 'manufactured' their story and sold it the London.

'Haley, you did ask, and I've promised to check and return your call,' said Eddie.

She did not respond, feeling there was much more 'coming-down-the-line.'

He explained how James and Kerri had accurate knowledge which implicated high ranking Moscow officials to Russian mobsters, who were supplying arms to various terrorist organisations. It was further complicated by the involvement of Nigerian crooks who were laundering diamonds by way of payment.

This sent a cold sweat through Haley's fragile body with the thought of what was hidden in Tyson's beanbag. Eddie added that all this may never have been unearthed, but for a casual conversation with Sinead. She had overheard a discussion at her Embassy when Europol investigators visited their London offices.

It transpired the Dutch authorities had permanent surveillance on some Nigerian crooks. Holland, being a major diamond trading centre, attracted criminal elements apart from genuine traders. A small country with a large cosmopolitan population has a constant flow of personnel, and their security authorities are always on the alert. There had been recent terrorist atrocities on their soil which necessitated surveillance on an array of 'undesirables' and monitoring such movements within their borders. A tall Russian with long blonde hair had been on their radar for the past year. They noted he was in contact with the Africans they had under surveillance. His passport seemed authentic but showed no exit from his homeland and a check on a similar individual, matching his description, verified he had died a year earlier in a plane crash.

Eddie seemed certain that James and Kerri had evidence that would have caused a major diplomatic storm and were quietly assessing the situation, before taking their findings to the appropriate section in Government. Conrad or whatever new name he was now trading as was a major go-between in the arms smuggling racket. He would have had a free run to travel abroad regularly, and his former employers would not have been aware of his extracurricular activities. By keeping the injured Kerri under wraps for so long indicated the authorities suspected something irregular within their own ranks.

The tall Russian with the long flowing blonde locks had faked his own death, managed to disappear and lie low for many months without a trace. His mob pals would have provided a new identity, but his size and demeanour would always make him stand-out. A recent transaction had gone badly wrong as Conrad and his crew got greedy. Diamonds were the preferred currency in most of these deals - less cumbersome than gold bars. Cash was becoming more difficult to launder due to stricter banking regulations. The hardest precious gem - the diamond - was valuable, easy to transport and, when cut, impossible to trace.

Not being content with his commission on these illicit transactions, he was skimming off the top for himself.

He now found himself hunted by Africans who were short-changed - Russian mobsters demanding their slice of the deal and KGB officers who were trying to tie up loose ends at their side.

'Haley, are you still there?' he asked.

'Yeah! I'm trying to digest all the various connections in this saga,' came her reply. Knowing the implications of bumping off British Government officials, she couldn't understand why they would have 'detained' Kerri for so long. Did they think he was just any ordinary citizen, like the many other dissenting voices who go missing out there? Perhaps he was badly concussed and unable to 'co-operate' with his interrogators.

'Eddie,' she calmly said, 'the only genuine fact in all this convoluted conversation is: my husband was returned to me as a bag of charred ash, with his damaged watch and wedding ring.'

He was not expecting such a graphic reply and wasn't able to respond with any words of comfort.

'Are your lot sure this IS actually Kerri?' she asked.

Again, the four seconds silence indicated not.

'We're almost certain as it came from Mossad,' he replied.

'The Israelis were also involved,' she shouted in disbelief.

'No, Haley, no but they had intel from inside Russia that an English citizen was under house-arrest somewhere in Siberia. It would have seemed strange as there were no noises emanating from British Diplomatic sources or from his relatives. Normally the internet sites would be blasting this out, day after day.

But there was complete silence from the West. Their field-agents thought it most unusual, and a description fitted that of Kerri. He was not on their radar or wanted by them. They already had their hands full with security worries of their own and never pursued it. It was mentioned casually in a report to the CIA with whom they work closely on such matters, and it was the Americans who provided an accurate visual, which identified Kerri.

'They are regularly 'trading' captured KGB spies for US citizens who are arrested under dubious conditions.'

'Dear Jesus, Eddie you have mentioned almost every spy family on the planet except China or North Korea.'

'Haley, those two are out there in the high grass, waiting for their opportunity,' came his quick reply. 'If you want accurate information, Mossad is your first port of call. They are vulnerable on all sides, given their geographic location, as all their immediate neighbours would nuke them off the plant, given the opportunity. It's a must for them to know what's going on, especially with the constant rocket attacks into their territories.'

'Eddie, you have given me a truckload of specialized, detail on surveillances. I may not be the brightest bulb in the chandelier, but I think these calls were not to inform - but to warn me!'

Once again, there was that irritating silence that said much. Haley had already put together many of the nuts and bolts of this dangerous machine. Her husband was murdered; his colleague was quietly incarcerated, and the Russian thug who planned the killings was on the run. If his henchman was in Dublin with a chunk of misappropriated diamonds, Conrad must also be in the vicinity or on his way here. There were three vicious organisations on his trail, all baying for revenge. A cornered rat is an extremely dangerous animal, but she was the only person who knew precisely where the loot was.

'Haley, if Igor was in Ireland, so must Conrad. You would not recognise him if he was standing outside the phone box right now. His long hair has been shaved, and he now has a droopy moustache like a Mexican bandit from an old Western film. He is also slimmed down, having shed at least four stone weight. The Dutch police ID'd him on a technical photo camera as he boarded a flight to Dublin, even without the hair and weight. They were glad to see the back of him and hoped he would never return. He was not on the radar of the Irish authorities as they have enough crap of their own to deal with between paramilitaries and organised crime gangs. Like I said, you would not recognise him, BUT he could certainly remember you from all the many events you had attended. If he suspected you had any idea of his double-dealing, then you would be a target. He does not like leaving loose-ends to chance and is definitely a cold-hearted bastard.'

It was just as Haley had already surmised. She calmly suggested, 'I best leave off my make-up and not wear my posh frock.'

Eddie tried his best to sound relaxed, as he attempted to warn, yet reassure her.

She assured him she just happened to be in Dublin because her house had been flooded. He again pleaded that she keep all his conversations to herself, as only a handful of people were privy to what was happening. There was always the danger of some gossip journalist creating a monster out of the existing mess that existed. It was vital that a lid be kept on everything as they also had Kerri to consider.

Haley re-assured the agitated Eddie that her lips were sealed and she was 'secret-proof.'

'We need an accurate visual and to be one hundred per cent certain this is Kerri, as we don't want to go off half-cocked and create a further mess,' he added.

'Hell! We had a funeral service and lodged the death insurance to his bank account. Having no immediate family, he had bequeathed everything to the local animal rescue shelter. A home for dumped dogs, stray cats, neglected donkeys and goats got an unexpected gift, a barrow full of cash. His old dog 'Bondie' was a rescue mutt from there, but luckily some elderly neighbours adopted him.

Thinking back, they were the only people who actually fucking cried at the service.'

This time the awkward silence was at Haley's end. She realised there was much more involved than her own personal grief. Composing herself, she calmly asked, 'Eddie may I ask you what probably seems a crazy question?'

'Fire away,' he replied. 'I have told you everything I know, and would not dare bull-shit you with a load of pious political waffle. You do NOT deserve that.'

'Of all the three hounds that are chasing Conrad's ass, which would give him the most painful death?' was her query.

His reply was quick. 'The Nigerians would behead him live on some internet site to scare off others; the Russian mob would immediately put a bullet in his head to silence him; the KGB would torture him within an inch of his life to extract every ounce of info, then leave him to rot in some filthy gulag until he eventually passed away. And he would die, wishing any of the other two would have gotten to him first.'

'Nice people you're all dealing with,' was her retort. 'But why would they be in Ireland?'

'Like I said Haley, he wasn't on the Irish list of undesirables and most certainly had to leave Holland quickly when he was found with his hand in the cookie jar.' Eddie was unaware the missing loot was in Dublin and was attempting to put two and two together as to what Conrad's exit plans would be. Wanted in Holland, UK, Nigeria and Russia, the obvious get-away would be South America. A ferry from Ireland to France - a train to Lisbon or Madrid and a direct flight to any South American country, then blend in with whatever collection of other crooks were hiding out down there.

'He would have had sufficient funds to live an easy, comfortable life as long as he didn't piss in some other crook's pot.'

Haley was the only person who knew that was NOT going to happen. She had a chunk of his spending money safely stashed, and under no circumstance would that murdering scum see a cent of it.

'Haley, remember I mentioned we were coming over to Dublin soon, to place a match and enjoy a stag-night? It should be in a few weeks' time, but it depends on the Dublin team we play, and availability of their facilities. I would love to meet up for a coffee and chat if you are still there?'

'We'll see Eddie, as my house may be refurbished and ready for me. Thanks for the heads-up on all this as I know you have stuck your neck out to keep me informed. You can be assured I am not going to broadcast this.'

'You can contact me anytime, Haley, but do NOT ring this phone. Just send a cryptic text, and I will eventually reply. You know how things are here, and no one is aware of our conversations, so you take care.'

'Thanks again, and don't you break that lovely Sinead's heart, as only for her, we would still be in the dark on most of this.' Haley replaced the receiver, with the agitated previous user pacing up and down outside the kiosk. As she exited, he grabbed the door's edge, barking, 'About fucking time.' She immediately slammed it back, crunching his fingers as she screamed, 'Watch your language, you knobheaded.' Pointing her mobile at him and poking an index finger into his chest, 'I've got your ugly mug in print, and I'm reporting you for assault and criminal damage to this phone box.'

The yob took a step back in fright, and holding his painful hand, stuttered, sorry, as he entered the safety of the kiosk.

'Don't be sorry. Be more fucking polite,' shouted Haley and strode out of the park.

An elderly couple wheeling a buggy had witnessed the whole episode. As they passed the lady remarked, 'Well done missus. Some of them scuts think they own the place.' Haley nodded her thanks. She had never stood up for herself in such an aggressive manner before. She decided she would never listen to, or take shite from anyone, ever again.

The conversations with Eddie had clarified many of the hazy question marks that had haunted her over the previous three days. The currency involved in Conrad's skimming operation was diamonds. There was never any mention of cash, and that gave her a strange feeling of comfort. Perhaps the actual scam involved switching fake for real diamonds. None of the security agencies really knew or probably didn't care. The bottom line was, arms were being supplied to terrorists, funded by diamonds supplied by Nigerian smugglers with the Russian mob being providers and Conrad as an accepted go-between.

She needed to ascertain if the contents inside Tyson's beanbag were the real deal or not. If they were the genuine article, then some Russian crooks would be on the prowl looking for their booty.

Four hundred and seventy-five grand could buy a lot of firepower but would also generate a lot of hassle. Why would she bother, when she had a loaded Glock and knew how to use it? The constant nagging doubt was the actual value of the contents in that jogging sock.

She most certainly couldn't and wouldn't dare walk into a pawn shop, deposit a shiny piece of stone on the counter and enquire, 'How much will you gimme for this?'

Jake and Sally steered clear from dealing in precious stones. Old jewellery pieces were a different proposition and easy to value. However, Haley's collection was for a specialist and would most definitely attract many questions.

It was vital to somehow evaluate the haul, but how and where, and who could she trust? There was a vicious, callous killer and his hench-men, who may well be in her city searching for a missing cargo. Even if the stash was just costume jewellery, there was a considerable quantity of cash that she was hell-bent on using to her advantage.

CHAPTER ELEVEN

It had taken Haley twenty minutes to walk from the kiosk to elegant building that housed "Times Long Past."

A young couple leaving the premises held the door open for her. She stepped inside as a pregnant young lady, who she presumed was Anna, was busy with an abundance of stock sheets. With a smile, Haley asked, 'Mr. Long please.' Anna, pointing to the small office area, said, 'Hiding somewhere over there.'

Haley approached the small counter as a series of swears emanated from below its mahogany top.

'Please, pardon me!' said Albert with a frown as he stood up from beneath. 'Oh! Haley, it's you. So good to see you again. Do you know anything about computers?' he asked, pointing to the bulky antiquated contraption on his desk. 'I'm a pencil and paper man myself, and these hideous machines are way out of my league.'

'Well,' replied Haley, 'I do know they are expensive, useful, troublesome, intent of sending you annoying 'spam' which surprisingly fed armies some years ago and 'cookies' which are an excuse to sell on your personal details to some other dealer but can be most helpful in business if used properly.'

'By Jove, she's gottit,' he laughed back in his Rex Harrison accent.

Your nephew has been advising me to upgrade this, set up a web site and do some of our trading online as he calls it. Do you know you can actually finalise a deal from the comfort of this old swivel chair?'

Haley had a mirror version of this at her own employment rooms, as both Jake and Sally reluctantly refused to engage in the modern era of online dealing. She could understand both sides of this debate, but she was also aware that if these businesses were to flourish, they needed to keep ahead of the opposition. Youth with its knowledge of technology, coupled with years of experienced graft, should be a perfect union.

'Mr. Long, could I have a private chat with you, please?' she asked.

'When a sentence begins with, Mr. Long, it generally means a 'business' conversation,' he joked.

Haley wished to 'flesh out' the contents of her previous visit and was unsure how best to approach the topic. However, recent events during her Dublin stay had changed her attitude and outlook. Her own life might be in danger if that Russian crook ever met her face to face, but she now realised the chances of that were remote.

Vigilance was still a must, but there were other issues that were beginning to have an influence in her life.

Albert had expressed his desire to sell his present home in the Dublin suburbs. His plan was to then live in the upstairs apartment when it had been vacated by his renters. The profit generated by this would ensure sufficient funds to cover all medical and care costs at the nursing home where his wife was now a permanent resident. He had explained how Cathy was still in great health apart from her dementia. Her medical staff indicated that she could possibly live another fifteen years or so unless some unforeseen terminal ailment took its toll.

It was still vital for Albert's thriving business to continue. If he enjoyed such longevity, he might also require care similar to his wife. His funds would be greatly diminished, and this was weighing heavy on his mind. Hence his plan to introduce a young, reliable co-worker to ease the burden.

'Do you still wish to offer my nephew a 'partnership' in your thriving business?' Haley asked in her most polite voice.

'Absolutely,' came the immediate positive reply.

Albert required a permanent partner whom he could trust implicitly. Having seen Cyprian in action, both at work and on their joint visits to the Care Home, he was in no doubt that this was a perfect answer to his concerns. By offering a 'piece-of-the-pie,' he would ensure the unwavering commitment of his new employee and guarantee dedication to the job.

In any business transaction, securing such a directorship, would certainly require a 'buy-in' or be earned after many years of hard graft.

'Could I ask what type of remuneration or deal you had in mind on the partnership issue?' asked Haley, slightly embarrassed to be so 'up-front' on a matter that should be of no concern to her. After all, she was only his aunt, and this was just her second conversation with Mr. Long.

She was about to apologise for being so forward when he immediately voiced concern.

'You're not going to attempt to talk him out of this, are you?'

'Heavens, NO!' replied Haley. 'Quite the opposite. I would encourage him, as you obviously hold him in high regard. He would learn much from your years of experience. Something that is old now becomes an antique in a few years and there will always be a market for such.

This will be my nephew's choice and his alone. And I would not dare interfere. I know he enjoys being in your company and is thoroughly at ease working in your establishment. But he will make the decision.'

'Oh good. I feared I had muddied the waters with all my ramblings and attempted planning.

I should not have been so presumptuous here, but I had mentioned much of this to him some months ago. We had never discussed salary or a buy-in as his studies, and upcoming exams are the priority right now.'

'The only reason for asking was that he would not have the financial resources to buy into a thriving business,' replied Haley. 'I was hoping a thirty per cent shareholding would cement the agreement,' said Albert.

'Absolutely NOT,' answered Haley.

Albert was visibly shocked by her retort, even thinking he should increase his offer to a 50/50 working arrangement. He was banking on a reliable partner to share the workload, as Anna would soon be taking maternity leave and only returning on a part-time basis. He had made it clear on his first conversation with Haley that he never would sell and insisted on retaining the old family name over his shop. It seemed she now had become aggressive in her negotiations.

'Goodness me, that is far too generous,' she added to a now confused, slightly relieved Albert.

'He's just a boy - wet behind the ears and straight out of college. He must learn to walk before he can run.'

Haley wanted the best for her nephew, but also recognised he must 'earn-his-stripes'.

'This would be like an apprenticeship,' she said, 'where he should learn the ropes and the nuances of a complicated trade. Buying and selling, at the right price, were the vital ingredients in creating profit and sustaining an existing established business. Cyprian would receive an education, second to none, by watching the 'master' in action and learning the intricacies of the trade operated successfully.'

A relieved Albert deposited his frame into his comfortable leather captain's chair and invited Haley to sit on a nearby bench.

Again, she suggested that it was too much, too soon.

'Do you mind if I ask another intimate question please?' she said.

'Please, ask away,' was his quick reply.

'What value would you put on all of this,' she said and extended her arms.

'That depends on Anna's monthly stocktake,' he jokingly said. 'We've had a good few months, but I haven't had the time to replenish stock recently. I suppose, including the building and various quality pieces which I have at home, somewhere between one point two and one point seven million, depending on the number of bidders.'

Haley was taken aback by the casual and honest reply and the fact that he was willing to share such an amount with a young part-time employee.

Again, Haley insisted it was way too generous, and his protégé should first cut his teeth on the basics, before sharing such a large slice of a tasty pie.

Albert, while extremely relived, was impressed at Haley's mature assessment of the trade and the fact that she did not jump in agreement at his generous offering.

He realised this was another family member he now could trust, one hundred per cent.

'While I am asking awkward questions, could you possibly answer one more please?' She smiled at him, and he nodded his approval.

'What would be your most expensive, individual piece?'

Without giving her time to complete the sentence, he replied, 'A Jack B Yeats oil painting - "Late Evening Mist". It's a stunning piece and is by far my favourite. Certainly, the most expensive item.'

Haley had glanced around his gallery, but Albert added, 'It's not here. It hangs at home, pride of place - on our sitting room wall. I've seen similar pieces sell some time ago for between one hundred and twenty and one hundred and eighty thousand. Again, he added that it was not for sale.

Mr. Long swivelled his captain's chair in front of Ms. Harington. He was about to invite her into a secret part of his life that ultimately would define the character and personality of her nephew's future employer. This reminded Haley of how her grandad would position himself prior to imparting his words of wisdom. This was not to be about cloud formations, and their unique images.

There would be resonances for Haley, which she could never had predicted but would reach deep into her own experiences.

Two weeks after a young Albert Long had collected his honours business degree and tossed his 'mortar-board' into the air. He was now a fulltime employee in the family business, the exact same building in which he now was reminiscing. Both parents and son lived in the upstairs apartment. His father, an austere individual, was a shrewd business man. The antiques trade was not as glamorous back then and only the large galleries attracted the major pieces. In many ways, they were viewed as posh junk shops by the average citizen, which was never a true reflection of their standing.

Even with his degree, Albert's role in affairs, was restricted to menial tasks and all purchases being the domain of his father, Damien. However, trade was profitable and his salary reflected this. Meaning he enjoyed the limited good-life Dublin offered in the sixties.

Two years into his 'apprenticeship' Albert recalled how during breakfast, his father threw him the keys of the family, beat-up Ford Cortina in addition to a long list which had arrived by post some days earlier.

He instructed his son to drive to a 'house-clearance' sale in County Kilkenny. A large stately home had been sold and was being transformed in a modern Country-Club. All items of furniture - cutlery and assorted pieces were a 'must-sell.'

His father's departing words were 'be careful what you buy, money doesn't grow on trees.' His mother, Lucy was more circumspect as she handed him his pack lunch, flask of tea and an apple along with a warning 'No speeding and drive carefully.' The house was huge even by Dublin standards, with a large crowd viewing the vast array on display. All of the furniture was in excellent condition and also extremely expensive. The silverware and crockery were top quality and also achieved high prices. Very large paintings were secured by galleries and serious collectors. It was a long day's trading and the auctioneers were obviously anxious to finish-up and enjoy their hefty commissions.

Albert noticed a selection of smaller art pieces and suggested to one of the team, that perhaps he should group them into lots, to speed-up proceedings.

One particular lot had caught his attention. An oil painting and two seascape watercolours. The seascapes were by an artist which he was unfamiliar and the signature was blurred on both.

Not wishing to return empty handed, the hammer fell to Albert's final bid of nine hundred and eighty-five pounds - a princely sum in those days.

His parents had just finished their evening meal when he marched into the dining room to proudly display his purchases.

This was his maiden voyage on antique bidding and he carefully unwrapped his package and placed them on three chairs for viewing and approval.

'Oh, they're ever so nice' cooed Lucy, 'especially those seascapes,' searching to identify the artist's signature.

'How much were they?' asked Damien.

'Nine hundred and eighty-five,' replied Albert.

He could see the visible shock and annoyance on his father's face as he got up from the table, leaving the room quickly - muttering about sending a boy to do a man's job. His mother offered words of re-assurance as she placed a reheated plate of beef-stew on his table mat. 'They are nice pieces son. They really are.'

Albert had lost his appetite. He realised the 'Yeats' would sell but had a liking for the other two, feeling the work was particularly striking, regardless of who the painter was.

A 'sulky' air hung in the shop for the next three days or so, as his father constantly re-arranged the paintings in an attempt to attract a potential buyer. It didn't help matters when a national newspaper expressed their amazement on the exceptional prices achieved at this particular auction. His mother reassured them both that quality comes at a price and will always sell. 'Yes!' his father muttered, 'but at whose price?' Lucy barked back at him, 'give it a rest Damien. I am sick of your whinging for the past few days. There are umpteen pieces here for the past ten years or so, that we may never sell. So, please put-a-sock-in-it!'

Albert had never heard his mother make an aggressive stand like that before and obviously neither had Damien. The bell almost dropped off the front door when it slammed, as he left in a huff. The remaining duo shared a grin together, as he marched down the street like an angry sergeant major about to attack the enemy. The named signature on both seascapes did not appear in any of the limited information literature, available in those days.

Eventually his father mellowed, knowing a buyer would appear and hopefully the oil painting would cover the outlay.

About three months later, Lucy was informed of the death of an elderly relative who had resided near Wexford town, a two-hour drive from their home. It was the first occasion Albert was left on his own, in complete charge of the prestigious family business. Damien was not content and his parting words were a growling 'don't sell anything for less than what's on the price tag.' Albert purposely ignored such childish advice. 'Do you understand' his father loudly roared. Albert replied calmly, 'Yes. I am not a complete idiot and neither am I hard of hearing, so please don't bark'!

His mother smiled, as the overhead bell on the door was the recipient of anther excessive wallop when they left.

That morning was exceptionally busy in their showrooms. The phone rang almost every ten minutes. Browsers asked about, and queried many stock items. Albert was extremely pleased with one particular sale. It was a canteen of old silver cutlery and he enhanced the deal by persuading the client to include a silver tray. He had convinced him that the combination greatly enriched the purchase. It was a successful ploy a certain young inexperienced Cyprian had used to great effect, just a few months ago. The item had lain unsold for many years on their shelves. He had only polished it thoroughly the previous day and the combined sale increased the value by an extra ten pounds. An elderly fussy man had examined and queried a least fifty separate items in various sections of the store, but bought nothing. 'Jeez, he asked more questions than a quiz master' muttered Albert as he decided he deserved a well-earned brew. His kettle had just boiled when a young couple entered the store. He watched them proceed immediately to his art collection. In his discreetly placed wall mirror he saw they had picked up the two seascapes. They examined both in great detail and the lady beamed with an excited smile. Glancing around, the man placed his hand on her shoulder in calming action. 'Carpe diem', though Albert. He made his way into that general area and re-arranged some items to their correct positions. Damien hated it when browsers never replaced examined items into their original slots.

The couple, each had one of the 'infamous' seascape paintings and had even produced a magnifying glass to examine both pieces. Not wishing to intervene, Albert noticed she was particularly enthusiastic, while her partner tried to look calmer. Eventually he called out to Albert and enquired about the seascapes.

'Ah! Yes', Albert answered. He told them they were recently acquired and they certainly have attracted much interest. Unfortunately, he was unable to provide accurate information on the artist who created such mastery. The lady was about to say something. Another calming hand from her partner intervened. Albert announced that the gentleman who had just exited, was on his way to the library to do some research. It certainly was created by someone talented, as the attention to detail and brush strokes are sublime and …

'How much asked the man?'

'Seven hundred' replied Albert. This would allow him some 'wriggle-room' and even at five hundred, the remaining Yeats from his 'buy' would be a bargain.

'You have a deal' came the immediate reply.

'Again, my apologies for lack of detail as we like familiarise ourselves with quality works similar to this,' as all three walked towards the counter. 'He was my late uncle William' the lady announced. 'He was at sea all his life and only began painting when he retired. Being eccentric and unmarried, he only sold his work when the old house needed refurbishment. Unfortunately, most of his paintings were destroyed when his dilapidated studio burned down. The family are attempting to track down and retrieve as much as possible of what he had sold.' Their plan was to have them on permanent exhibition at the library in his home town in England. She was genuinely thrilled at finding two, well preserved and beautiful pieces which Albert was now carefully packing. The man had been counting out from a bundle of fifties. Albert expected a stop when he reached seven hundred, but the count continued. 'Twelve .. twelve fifty .. thirteen .. thirteen fifty .. fourteen. There we are he said, seven multiplied by two.' The packing was complete as Albert attempted to calmly write the 'bill-of-sale.'

As he escorted his clients to the door, he wished the lady well in her quest to recover as many as possible of her family heirlooms. Watching and waiting until they were out of earshot, he strolled across the shop floor with air of smug arrogance, raised both hands to the ceiling and shouted; 'YEEEEEE- HAAAAAAAAA !'

'Now, let's see what Lord Damien Know-All has to say,' as he settled into his well deserved cuppa.

Later that afternoon his parents had arrived home. 'I hope the funeral wasn't too upsetting for you, Mam,' Albert asked. 'No, she was a great age and had enjoyed life to the full until recently, so it wasn't the usual tearful affair' she replied. Damien had cast his observant eye around the store and immediately noticed two empty slots on the artwork wall. 'The seascapes' he said as Albert was rummaging through papers on the desk.

'The seascapes' he asked again in a much louder, inquisitive tone. Albert casually informed him that they were sold, and continued his 'fake' paperwork. Damien had become more agitated and asked how much they fetched. Albert replied in a slow and exaggerated voice; 'One thousand four hundred pounds.' Damien could not believe his ears, as he whispered, 'What?' 'Yes!' announced his son. 'I did tell you they were class,' as he produced the wad from under the desk.

The elderly man ran to his son and grabbed him in a bear-hug as he blurted 'Well done my boy, very well done. That's a huge result.' He took a step back, holding him by both shoulders and with tearful eyes said 'I am so proud of you.' He then grabbed him in another tight hug, praising him for his keen awareness.

Haley had listened intensely to the protracted tale and watched the expression change on Alberts face.

'That was the first time my father ever hugged me. Dads didn't do hugs. That was girlie stuff.' He called out to my mother and sang my praises on a magnificent result.'

They had made a profit of over four hundred pounds and still had a 'free' Jack B Yeats. Albert composed himself in his comfortable chair as he announced to Haley; 'that was the day, the boy became a man.' He explained how, from then on, he was an integral part of their business - being consulted on all matters and whose advice was sought on most large deals. He also noticed how Damien was more at ease with both himself and his mother. His parents began taking holidays. Damien and himself went for a few drinks each Friday evening after work. They had become pals. Life on 'planet-Long' has changed enormously, and for the better.

Haley sat in silence. There were no words for what she had just heard. Bearing an intimate piece of his inner soul, it required neither encouragement or approval.

'So, you can see why that piece of art has such meaning to me' he added. 'It's not the monetary consideration but its sentimental attachment, that is impossible to value.' Looking up at the wall behind his leather chair, 'it hung there for three years,' Albert explained. Neither family member had the appetite to complete a sale of its masterful expression. It was as if the work had become part of the family. It always attracted the eye of experienced viewers and was admired by all who walked the cluttered floors of their shop. Albert explained how Damien had gifted him the painting when he and Cathy got engaged to be married. 'The cheapskate' joked Haley in mock horror - 'You produce a handsome profit on your first venture into dealing - end up with a free Jack B Yeats masterpiece, and he gives it to you as a present!' That put the first smile on Albert's face since the conversation began. 'Yes! he agreed but attached to the back was an envelope which contained a two week, all expenses holiday in Italy. It was our honeymoon sorted, there and then.' When they returned, Damien had purchased the house in which Albert now resided, and both he and his new bride settled into the apartment upstairs. They raised their two children there and only moved into their parent's property when both passed away, within three weeks of each other. That was almost fifteen years ago.

Haley herself could feel the raw emotion. So much of what had just been related to her, mirrored her own life and particularly the unpredicted events of the past few weeks. Albert was not a complex or complicated character. She knew that this kind hearted individual had 'unburdened' a piece of his DNA which outlined his personality, and determined his future as an adult and successful business man. Somehow the story had not yet been completed and her nephew was to be part of his plan. Haley could see the many connections and realised that Cyprian would be safe and secure within the confines of "Times Long Past."

She watched Albert's handlebar moustache twitch, as he pursed his lips and rotated his wedding ring while obviously considering the happier moments of his reminisces.

'Mr Long' she quietly interrupted.

'Oh! More business if I now become Mr. Long again,' he replied.

Haley asked for his permission to make a suggestion, and he gently nodded his approval. She had no wish to upset the delicate equilibrium of his plan for the future.

'What if?' she quietly asked, 'I'm just saying, what if?' She was repeating herself and actually saying nothing, unsure how to phrase the thought she wished to convey. She took a deep breath. 'What if I were to buy your Jack B Yeats, for one hundred and fifty thousand, in cash. But on the strict proviso the painting never leaves this building - never. That price would equate to about ten percent of your companies' value - based on your earlier assessment. It will remain here, always, and I will sign a guarantee to that effect. It can become Cyprian's buy-in, for a ten percent stake in your establishment. Thirty is way too high, as he is still a boy - he needs that chunk of experience to be transformed into a man.

'As you intend moving from your present home, the funds from that sale, plus the one hundred and fifty thousand should ensure sufficient reserves to cover all the nursing costs you now endure. You had mentioned that physically, your wife's health is good, and hopefully that continues. Ultimately you, yourself may require medical care, so extra funding may be needed. Then and only then, should the Yeats be sold to provide you with sufficient funds to cater for such. It most certainly will have appreciated in value by then.' She pointed to the empty space over his chair; it reminded her of a slot in a shrine patiently waiting for the 'second-coming' - that was its home, so perhaps it should be returned there.

This time, it was Albert's turn to sit in silence as he certainly was not anticipating his visitor's suggestion to be so detailed.

Haley asked if he knew a reputable legal firm to document what had been discussed should he feel more secure with an official legally signed contract. She again reiterated she would never contemplate removing the Yeats and it would be their private agreement, which she would willingly sign up to.

Albert quickly informed her that his near neighbour, Philip, operated his law firm from three blocks down the street. He also added that Philip's son was returning home from Saudi Arabia having completed a ten-year, tax-free stint as a civil engineer. He was currently house hunting, and tentative approaches had been made to Albert. One reason being the large garden he enjoyed; he had also 'garaged' his collection of vintage motorcycles - often admiring Alberts twenty-five-year-old Mercedes Estate car.

Haley saw another suggestion in the offering, suggesting that Albert should add twenty thousand to the property sale price and include the almost vintage Merc, as a 'clincher'. The old car was the last motor purchase by his late father, and Albert had ensured it was garaged each night and regularly serviced. Haley even suggested that it was part of the property and perhaps should remain there. The new potential owner would most certainly cherish it.

Albert, realising he would be 'without-wheels', was about to interject with a query when Haley continued her thesis. 'My nephew is a sharp cookie and would realise he was not just going to fall into a shareholding, without making some contribution, and you would require a motor.'

Haley quickly added that he could secure a bank loan and provide the business with a more modern and suitable mode of transport, which also must reflect the company's standing. Advising Albert that he could let Cyprian believe it was his contribution to being accepted into the business. Albert would then have a much more comfortable vehicle for his travels - Cyprian could complete any deliveries or collections from auction rooms around the country. Pointing to his silent computer, she added that he could also update 'this piece of antiquity' and set-up that website they had discussed. 'On second thoughts,' added Haley, 'you should keep that computer, as it soon will be vintage and may create a profit in years to come.' That drew a smile to the perplexed expression on Albert's face.

He had her in his fixed gaze, unsure how to react - unable to reply. Even the loud clatter, when Anna dropped a canteen of cutlery and swore at it, was unable to destabilise the moment.

Haley again confirmed that her cash offer would be their secret arrangement, and she did not require a receipt or bill of sale. She trusted the authenticity of the wise, honest brain hidden behind that handlebar moustache.

Albert leaned forward from his relaxed pose - hands clasped, with both index fingers pointing like a spear straight at Haley. The smile from the old computer joke had disappeared, and he inhaled deeply. He now had that austere look she had often seen as a child, before her late father would administer an authoritative lecture.

She was unsure how his reaction to her uninvited suggestions would be taken - had she overstepped the mark and crossed too many boundary lines by interfering in his attempts to plan his remaining years? Speaking in a slow, deliberate and very controlled voice, he said, 'Ms. Harrington, you have a unique … devious … and most inventive …. business brain.'

His facial expression never changed.

Haley was unsure whether that was a reprimand or a compliment.

'You, my dear lady should be Minister for Finance in our Government, as you would have our fiscal manure-heap sorted out in jig-time,' he smilingly added.

Haley's heart rate just then returned to normality. She felt she had 'lost-the-run-of-herself, interfering in both her nephew's career and Albert's business arrangements. However, Albert heartily endorsed every aspect of her new-found ideas and again complimented her on the ingenuity and inventive structure she had offered.

He suddenly felt more at ease. The final pieces in his life's jigsaw had been presented to him, slotted into the remaining empty spaces and a completed picture was there for him. He insisted on a formal agreement being written up as it would clarify matters later in life should there be any family objections. It was highly unlikely, he conceded, but Haley had been correct in advising such. Again, she had requested that nothing would be mentioned until exams had been finished.

'Mr. Long, I need you here please,' Anna called.

'The day-job proper awaits,' said Haley.

Albert, uneasily, broached the production of one hundred and fifty thousand in cash.

'Leave that to me Albert. You will have your money.' Suddenly concerned for his safety, Haley asked if he ever had undesirables in his store who tried to swindle him.

Without blinking, he reached below the counter producing a sawn-off shotgun.

A shocked Haley roared, 'Sweet Jesus. Where did that come from?'

A smiling Albert, with the gun slung over his shoulder, told her it was supposed the weapon used by 'Stumpy' in the classic Western movie, Rio ...

Haley finished his sentence, 'Bravo. It was our favourite video with John Wayne - Dean Martin. James and I would watch it at least twice a year, roaring fire on a cold Winter's night, a glass of chilled...' Her voice had now faded into a saddening whisper.

Albert quickly interjected, 'The firing mechanism has been removed. But when it's pointing at some thug or would-be thief, they never seem to ask - just RUN.' Haley asked if he had done such, recently.

Sounding like an old-time Marshall, he told her, 'Not in the past ten years or so.' But he actually did, and it had the desired effect. 'Word seems to have gotten out, that there's a crazy old coot with heavy artillery in here. Sometimes the discreet threat is more potent than brute force,' he offered in sagely advice.

Seeing an opportunity, Haley asked if he dealt in precious stones and jewellery.

Albert shook his head. 'Absolutely not, that's a specialist trade which I avoid, as it can be tricky. My insurance broker, a retired police officer, advised me many years ago and I paid heed. Not all these places are legitimate trading establishments. I often have individuals showpieces here, and unless there is a genuine bill-of-sale to accompany it, I politely decline. I regularly have an offer from one particular house, with product which I know is expensive, but with no receipts to ensure authenticity, but I always pass.'

Haley enquired if this would be some shady back-street dealer and was surprised to be informed otherwise. This trader has a 'prestigious-address' just off Henry Street. Haley knew the area, it being a famous part of the city.

'Emeralds I,' he told her, adding, 'what a unique play on words.'

'Mr. Long, are you going to play Cowboys and Indians or help me here,' called an irritated Anna.

'The boss needs you,' said Haley with a smile.

'Racing hormones,' replied Albert, rubbing his pushed-out-stomach. 'We'll talk again in a few weeks or so, and let's keep thing 'stchum.'

Haley departed. 'I really do hope my nephew has his sights set on a career in the antiques trade as I would hate to untangle the last thirty minutes conversation,' she muttered quietly.

Later that afternoon, Haley had tucked the vacuum cleaner away carefully ensuring it was in the exact position as Dansie always sussed if someone had used 'her' equipment, thinking it as some kind of threat to her duties. A car door slammed, and Haley recognised Cyprian's voice as he thanked Edel for all her help.

She watched from the sitting room window as he stood outside the gate with a small box laying on both palms.

She waited for him to come in. After a few minutes, there was still no sign of him. Realising he must have used the side entrance, she walked to the kitchen. The shed door was open. Her nephew had begun neatly digging the top slice of grass from a corner of the back garden. She would not involve herself in this private ritual. Having removed a large portion of soil and spread most into the adjoining rose bed, he emptied the contents of the urn which was inside his package, into the hole. He topped up with some of the soil and carefully replaced the grass sod to ensure the lawn was even, and not out of shape. A few taps with the spade had also secured a small aluminium plaque which read, "TYSON - 2012".

He stood gazing down at the completed work for a minute or so. Haley had boiled the kettle, prepared two extra strong 'Americanos' as he opened the door. He dropped his slightly soiled shoes on the floor and stepped inside. She was expecting to meet a blubbering incoherent mess as he washed his hands in the kitchen sink. Handing him a warm mug, she quietly said, 'I see you've completed the task.'

She was surprised by the calm replies from him. He reiterated that whilst Tyson was just an animal to many, he was part of their family and had protected him, when the need arose. He also warned his aunt that it could have been her who suffered the attack. Haley asked if his own bruises were healing as they had looked nasty. He reassured her that he was on the mend and there was no need for her to be concerned. As he sipped the coffee, his demeanour changed. 'Did you know that idiot Chalky had the neck to ask a friend of Edel's if she had seen any of the 'Duffy girls' lately.'

'Did he hassle her?' asked Haley.

'NO! he wouldn't dare, as her dad is an Army Major and two of her brothers are also in the forces,' he said.

'She had told him they were both working away from home, adding that she couldn't understand what Edel saw in a shitface like him, anyway. He just stormed off.'

This bothered Haley as she realised these thugs were still on the prowl. The positive feeling of her successful morning's work had chilled slightly.

CHAPTER TWELVE

An Angelus bell rang from a nearby steeple.

The blue metallic sparkling BMW 535 was blasting loud hip-hop music, as cigarette smoke billowed from the partially opened driver's window. Down the street, muscle-bulging young men entered and exited Flexo's Gym and Fitness Centre.

A solitary figure, dressed in a yellow high-viz jacket with silver fluorescent strip, approached the stationary vehicle. A hand rapped on the driver's door. The driver sporting a black crew-cut hairstyle lowered his window completely. 'We're about to move. We're only just parked, Officer,' he said.

The left hand of the jacket shot through the open window and a Glock pistol rammed under the driver's jaw. The other hand immediately removed the car keys and threw them under a van parked directly in front. This meant the car was in lock-down mode.

A low husky voice with a clipped Cockney accent snapped, 'None of you shits move, or his foking 'ead ends up in your lap.' He pointed to a blond male in the back. 'You,' he said, addressing the front seat passenger, 'ands on the dash - now I'm only gonna say this once - you dicks 'ave been pissin' in the wrong pots of late. Jabbing the pistol further into the driver's neck, look in your wing mirror - see that rag 'anging from the fuel cap. It's laced with petrol.' An open canister of lighter fluid was emptied onto the front seat passenger's lap.

Haley had her neckerchief pulled up over her face. The sunglasses and black wool hat disguising the fact that it was a woman in conversation.

'You shits beat up a kid and attacked his girlfriend recently. If any of you ever even speak to them again or as much as look at them, you will all be singing soprano in the prison choir - gottit? Just do what you're been paid to do, and keep your snots clean,' she barked. Taking out a lighter, she flicked it on and off. 'On second thoughts I might just fry you stupid fokks 'ere and now, like that clown of a brother-in-law, of yours. Couldn't do a simple fokkin' task.' Each time she released the top of her lighter, it automatically extinguished. The two passengers were in genuine fear. But the driver had a cold icy stare and showed little emotion, even as the Glock was pushed deeper into his jaw bone.

'Brilliant, idn't it - blacked out windows, no one can see in, so no one out there gives a toss. Ere, I think we should 'ave some real smoke.' She flicked the lighter into action and tossed it onto the front passenger's lap. Of course, it had extinguished itself, but the panicked occupants' brains hadn't connected that fact, and they tried to climb out the windows which were locked. Spike was first out, as his window was open, shouting, 'I'll fucking kill you.'

You fucking bollix.' By then Haley has dashed down a side street - turned the jacket inside out - it was now grey, pocketed the neckerchief, hat and glasses and was calmly walking up the opposite side of that street.

An elderly man, out dog-walking noted, 'Would ya look at that. There was a time when young fellas would break into a car but have a look over there. Breakin' OUT of a car - amateurs, total fuckin' amateurs. Is it any wandor dis country is in de bollixed-up state 'tis in?'

Haley just smiled and continued her brisk walk home, recalling Albert's thoughts on the potency of threats rather than brute force. The two other passengers had eventually fled the vehicle, fearing it would explode.

Their leader had availed of his secure head-start, and all three disappeared into the safety of their sweaty fitness centre.

Her brisk walk home was almost a run, as she longed for the security of number fifteen. The pistol which she had stuffed down the front of her jeans was an irritation, rubbing against her lower stomach.

Back home, a long hot shower eased the tension and lowered her anxiety levels.

As she placed her underwear and shirt in the laundry basket, she knew if adrenaline had an odour, this would be it. A strong coffee laced with Remy Martin slipped down with refreshing ease.

Haley was now certain that Chalky, who she presumed was the backseat thug, and the guy in the front passenger seat would pay attention to her outburst. It was the driver, Spike, who could still be a problem. She saw the cold, steely look in his eyes even with a pistol stuck under his chin. He had little respect for man or beast - a phrase her late dad often used to describe gangsters. She had seen his brutality to her nephew and his dog, so there was the evidence of that long-forgotten saying.

When the gun was removed, his first instinct was to threaten murder, and flee, rather than assist the gang who supported him. His priority was himself, and her intimidation did not scare him.

It probably incensed him even more. Obviously, he had not connected the dog walker in the park and the potential shooter he had just encountered. For one frightening moment, Haley thought, what if he had attempted to resist her. The house phone rang. A crackly inaudible ring tone eventually cut off as she answered.

She had left her own phone on the charger and checked it for missed calls. There were two unread messages. The first from Sally, "Howdy partner, hope all is well with U. Your old shack is coming along fine. We had to make some adjustments to the kitchen units. What U had picked would not fit properly. I made an executive decision. U do trust my taste as I did employ U :). This is better stuff and will cost slightly more, but I'll work your ass off when you get back, so U can afford it:). We miss U here. Luv, Sally & Jake XX."

Haley returned an immediate reply, thanking her and giving them a free run at the refurbishment. She now had some spare cash, so additional costs would not be an unnecessary worry for her.

The second message was a long-winded text from her sister, basically confirming what Trevor had said a few days earlier. Again, she returned a reply. Hopefully it would avoid any more inaudible phone calls. Reassuring her all was well and hoping they would catch-up with Chloe soon.

The chilling words of Spike still rang in her ears. It had the same vicious, callous tone she heard when he bludgeoned Tyson. He obviously didn't do intimidation. He did revenge. That made him a far more dangerous thug than she had reckoned him to be.

She now had two pieces of human filth on her radar, and with the anger she felt there and then, she would have no hesitation in 'plugging' either.

CHAPTER THIRTEEN

~

The Thursday morning nine o clock news headlines and the weather forecast had been announced by the enthusiastic presenter on her 'oldies' radio station. As ever, Dansie was her usual punctual self when Haley opened the front door. Shaking the morning mist from her well-worn coat, hanging it on the last post of the bannister while in full cheery greeting to Haley. Haley hadn't had the chance to speak, as Dansie, attempting to look around her, queried, 'Where's me auld slobber-chops. He's always out in the hall to greet me.'

Haley escorted her into the kitchen, sat her down and prepared two strong coffees. She explained the whole saga to a shocked Dansie, from entering the park, right up to the ashes being buried. Dansie sobbed throughout, only interrupting with a 'Why would some scumbags do such a thing?' Haley had continued with her edited version of events. She was not going into the 'whys' of the story.

'And did the Guards catch them?' Dansie cried.

Haley calmly explained that it was Cyprian's pet, and it was his choice not to involve the law. There would be statements to be made - forms to completed and besides the Guards had their hands full of murders and gang problems. She advised that her nephew did not wish his parents to know the exact details as they had sufficient aggravation in their lives at the moment.

Dansie angrily insisted the Guards had to be informed as it could have been Haley that was attacked.

The sadness and anger of Dansie was obvious as Haley attempted to calm her. She insisted Cyprian had exams to concern him at the moment. He just wanted to move on with his life. She informed Dansie they would tell his parents that Tyson had a brain haemorrhage and had to be put to sleep.

Dansie agreed it was partially true and that she would not tell the full sad details.

'Our Aldo has a good pal in the cops and he's high up,' she announced, 'and he told my son he would do him a good turn anytime.'

'I think it's best to just leave it,' Haley said attempting to finalise the topic. But, Dansie felt the urge to ensure justice was done and if the law couldn't or wouldn't someone else should. Another pair of coffees were introduced, both laced with expensive Remy, as Haley felt it may ease Dansie's obvious distress. Reluctantly she allowed her to continue talking about Aldo's friend in the police force.

Time would prove it to be an extremely productive discussion.

One evening, eighteen months previous, just before Aldo was about to lock up for the night, he received a call to go to a friend's house to 'jump-start' his motor. To save time, he had taken a 'short-cut' through the Phoenix Park. Being the largest enclosed park in any European City, there was a myriad of roads transversing its one thousand eight acres. His attention was drawn to a stationary VW Passat with full headlights and hazard flashers. The occupant was a woman and a mobile phone illuminated her agitated face. Being concerned for her wellbeing as it wouldn't be a safe place to get stranded as darkness approached, Aldo parked his van in front of the VW and walked towards the car noticing the engine was switched-off. Asking if there was a problem, the lady driver reluctantly opened the window slightly and muttered that she was waiting for her sister to return her calls. A young boy's voice cried from the rear seat, 'our car is broken and I want to go home.' 'Shane, be quiet' snapped the distressed driver. Aldo informed her that he was a motor mechanic, pointing to the "Aldo's Autos" sign on the back boot of his van. 'Personally, I prefer to be called an "Automobile Engineer," he joked. The driver did not see the humour, as she anxiously tapped numbers into her mobile phone. 'I want to go home NOW!' screamed the young boy.

Reluctantly she allowed Aldo to check the problem as she complained about all the flashing lights on the dashboard. The solution was simple - as the empty fuel gauge indicated. The young boy was getting more upset.

'Shane, I need your help here, as this is mans-work' he whispered to him. The child settled down. Aldo explained the problem to her, as he collected a 'jerry-can' of fuel from his well-stocked van. Producing a funnel with well-padded tissue, he asked Shane to hold it steady while he poured two gallons of petrol into the empty fuel tank. The fussy driver asked if she could help. 'Mans-work, Mam' came the reply from the youngster. His mother lightened-up and smiled. Removing the funnel and offering Shane a fresh tissue to ensure his hands absolutely clean, he then produced a small packet of jelly sweets -'pay for your great work, buddy' said Aldo. As he was securing the can into the van, 'and don't tell Dad. Do you understand,' were the departing words as she drove away.

'And thank you very bloody much also,' muttered a disgruntled Aldo. With no thanks and no payment offered, at least that was his good deed for the day completed as he drove away from the dark, shady parkland.

A week later Danno and Aldo were busy with a difficult repair job when a uniformed officer called from the door- 'who is Aldo, around here.' 'Oh Jazsus' was Danno's response. Identifying himself, the officer enquired, 'Did you stop for a broken-down Passat in the Phoenix Park last week?' 'Yeah, I did. What a spot to run out of fuel.' he said. 'Why. Did something happen to her, or the young lad?'

'Mans-work, my arse,' laughed the Garda. 'Do you think my son could keep a secret for two days?' He then thanked Aldo for his assistance that evening, suggesting that not everyone would stop and offer help. Adding that many would see it as an opportunity to accomplish a more sinister act. He also apologised for her not paying, as he stuck a 'fifty euro note' under the wiper blade of the car they were working on. 'Makes a change from parking tickets,' joked Danno. The friendly Garda chatted with Aldo as they walked across the forecourt. Glancing around the yard, the Garda passed a comment on an unused break-down truck parked-up in a corner. Aldo explained he had taken it in as a swop for a van. The out of town owner had little use for it where he lived, and it only required a water-pump. The Garda suggested that the truck should be repaired - cleaned up - pass it's NCT and then presented to his local Garda Station. Handing Aldo his card, 'call me when it's ready and I will ensure you get any breakdown or tow-away in this area' he offered.

'One good turn, deserves another he smiled - be sure to ring me first and I'll put the word out in the office.'

Aldo could not believe his luck - eventually being paid for the night stop, and getting a contract with the police force, - guaranteed payment each month. Danno was chuffed, as that was part of the work that did not require heavy pulling and dragging, so was ideal for him. Business at "Aldo's Autos" had taken a turn for the better. Dansie confirmed that life in their house was now more comfortable with the additional income - all because her son had been a 'Good Samaritan' and starting-up that woman's car. 'That's karma' added Haley. 'No, it was a Volkswagen' replied Dansie in a corrective tone. Haley smiled to herself at the error. Dansie added 'when you do something nice for a person, something good happens for you, - when you do something bad, as she looked at Tyson's empty bean-bag, the you should be made pay for the badness.'

Getting up from the table, Haley said her larder needed restocking, and she had best attend to it, as the drizzly rain had ceased. 'That second cuppa was much nicer than the first' said Dansie with a cheeky wink. It was Haley's escape from a conversation that made much sense, but it really was too late for police intervention. However, the preparator could, and most certainly would not be ignored.

CHAPTER FOURTEEN

Another week had elapsed, with Haley getting regular up-dates from Sally on the refurbishments. Heather and Trevor were making slow progress in Africa but still had been unable to ascertain the exact location of their daughter.

The college term had finished, and exams would commence in a week's time. Cyprian was unconcerned as he felt his studies had covered the full curriculum and was quietly confident; he would be successful.

Haley took the opportunity to visit his potential employer. She was greeted by the enthusiastic proprietor who told her that he had received a positive response from the Saudi connection. Her idea of including the vintage Merc was the 'kicker' and would be the clincher. He had approached his lawyer, who was most impressed with the ingenuity of the total package. Official documents would be drawn up, and all should be ready for signature within the month. Albert also insisted that Cyprian take a holiday when his exams were completed and enjoy a summer rest - a point on which Haley was in complete agreement. The conversation was short as there were many browsers. Anna's morning sickness added to his workload. Haley even offered to help out, explaining that their pet was deceased and she now had more time on her hands. She spared him the gory details. Albert was genuinely upset at the news as he had met Tyson when Cyprian walked him at weekends.

'I suspect it's like a family bereavement to your nephew,' he quietly observed, suggesting that Tyson was probably akin to the brother he did not have. Albert apologised if he had inappropriately phrased his feelings on the matter, saying that an animal can always be replaced. He understood that losing your family pet was not a painful as the death of a loved one. Haley re-assured him that she fully understood his genuine expression of compassion. She had lost her husband, best friend and would never be replaced, while Albert was in almost in a similar position.

He had the warmth, affection and companionship of Cathy. She was now just a shadow of the best friend, business partner and lover who had raised a family with him. The dementia she endured would not kill her, but it had robbed her of emotion, memories and the power of recollection. Each visit by Albert to the care home was a painful reminder of the life they had both enjoyed. He knew she would never be coming home to him, and he sensibly had made appropriate plans to adapt his own living arrangements. They agreed to meet again in three weeks or so to finalise their agreements.

On Thursday morning, Dansie had surprised Haley by arriving thirty minutes early. She apologised, requesting to finish-up earlier than usual as she had a chore that needed attending later that morning. That was not a problem for Haley as the house required little attention anyway with just Cyprian and herself living there. However, Dansie, in her honest approach to employment, insisted on completing her hours.

'Do you know, this is a very happy, united house to live in,' she said, taking Haley by surprise. 'I'm not just saying it because Mrs. P is your sister, but there is a peace and a calm here like no other. I have never heard any shouting, screaming abuse, banging of doors in a sulk, ever. It's obvious they are a very contented family unit, and it speaks volumes for Mr. and Mrs. P.'

Haley was taken aback by the sincere tone of voice. It helped negate many of the concerns that haunted her, on Heather's child-rearing ideas. 'But there's a hole in this house,' Dansie added, looking at Tyson's empty basket. Haley had no wish to revisit that topic.

Quickly she suggested that it was her nephew's pet and was his decision. She would not even touch the old beanbag and encouraged Dansie to 'leave-well enough-alone.'

Haley used the excuse of groceries needing to be replenished to exit and leave Dansie to her chores.

She took a long walk to delay things and returned three hours later, laden down with two heavy bags of provisions. It had just begun to rain, and she dropped both bags in the hallway. 'I really should have taken Heather's car,' she admitted, 'as I'm not as strong as I used to be.'

Dansie had completed her work, donned her coat and was ready to leave.

'Can I give you a lift?' asked Haley as she shook her wet jacket, 'it's not looking too pleasant out there.'

'Oh, dear God.' Haley suddenly realised she not driven the car since she had arrived. She had not even started the engine, having been instructed to do so by Trevor.

'Would the damned thing even start?' she asked Dansie. 'Don't worry, if it won't,' replied Dansie, 'sure haven't I two mechanics getting fed and watered in our house.'

First turn of the key and the two-year-old Toyota Corolla hummed into action.

'You'll have to guide me, as this doesn't seem to have sat-nav,' said Haley.

'I'll give you directions, and all you need to do when we get there is put the car into reverse and back up all the way home,' joked Dansie. Haley had driven in Dublin on many occasions, but there seem to be constant route changes to confuse even regular road users.

Driving past the shopping centre they had visited some weeks earlier, Haley wondered if that cranky security guard had enjoyed his drink. Dansie chatted on relentlessly, giving directions as they now seemed to be entering the outer suburbs.

'Just turn right here, past that small church,' she called. It took them up a narrow lane with open fields on both sides. Old donkeys, ponies, goats, a sheep and a shabby horse grazed as the car approached a large old shed. There was a penned area with some hens and ducks adjacent.

'I'll just be a few minutes,' whispered Dansie and alighted onto the gravelled surface. Haley waited and attempted to find a music station on the radio to avoid listening to a variety of irritating chat shows.

The engine was still running when Dansie appeared at the door and beckoned her in. Turning off the engine, she could then hear the barking of dogs from the premises. Dansie introduced her to a portly lady with red chubby cheeks as Stella - her old school pal and drinking buddy. It was only then Haley realised she was at an animal rescue shelter. A range of pens housed a variety of dogs, mostly mongrels but all seemed healthy. Stella offered sympathy to her visitor on the distressing ordeal she had endured. Adding that she and her three colleagues often witness some appalling cruelty to some of the inmates. Sometimes people drop off a pet they are unable to care for and hope it can be re-homed.

The penny had dropped with Haley as to the real purpose of this particular imaginary chore Dansie had to complete. Stella produced three mugs of piping hot strong tea and offered a plate of biscuits as she explained the work they do. Adding that they never turn any animal away and are lucky that young vets from college gave their time free to the shelter. With an invite to inspect the premises, Haley reluctantly agreed. The dogs were all shapes and sizes and excitedly barked while viewing their new visitors.

It was as if they were trying to attract attention to be picked. In one particular pen, numbered fifteen, sat a lonely figure of a most unusually coloured canine. His coat was mainly red, interspersed with black and white dapples. He never barked or moved towards the protective bars on his pen, unlike every other inmate.

'How long do you retain them?' asked Haley

Stella said they were lucky in so far as most got rehoused, but those who didn't were put to sleep after six weeks as there was a constant demand for the limited space available. Haley agreed it was sad to euthanise their lives, but at least they would not be battered to death.

'That's Ali,' said Stella pointing at the multi-coloured dog. 'He wouldn't win any prizes for good looks, but there isn't a bad bone in his body. We believe he's a cross between an Irish Red Setter and a Border Collie. Now if he was human, he'd be a cross between the Pope and Saint Martin De Porres.'

'How long has he been here?' enquired Haley

'Five months,' came an immediate reply. 'None of us have the stomach to put him to sleep.'

Was it a series of coincidences - a dog named Ali after another famous fighter - housed in pen number 15 - a reference to the Saint whose shrine was illumined by that old lady's candle? Haley stooped down to the door and said, 'Hello Ali.' The dog slowly got up from his old blanket, stretched himself, ambled to the front frame, sat with a wagging tail and extended his front right paw through the bars. Haley took hold as if shaking hands.

her brain. What would her nephew think? Would the poor dog settle in? Was he really as polite as Stella convinced her? Were they just trying to offload another unwanted mutt?

Ali had sat upright on the back seat as if it was his 'position' on journeys. He obediently waited for Haley to attach his lead and insisted on watering the nearby wall before calmly walking up the front steps to the door. When his lead was removed, he waited to be called up the hall. He then sniffed his way through the downstairs area but stopped on reaching the old beanbag, sensing it was someone else's domain. Haley threw his old blanket over it, and as she included his ragdoll. Ali snuggled down in comfort. 'Good, that's part one successfully completed,' she whispered to herself.

The next two hours dragged on forever before she heard Cyps unlock the front door. Meeting him halfway down the hall, she asked, 'So how was your day?'

Sensing something was amiss, her nephew replied, 'What's wrong, Aunt Haley. I can see it in your face. Are mam and mad OK? Is it Chloe?' Haley calmly reassured him all was well. But there was something she wished him to see. Calling Ali, the dog strolled into the hall and sat upright beside her.

'Who owns him, and where did he come from?' Cyps asked in a loud voice.

Sitting at the kitchen table with two mugs of strong coffee, she explained the story in full, from starting Heather's car to eventually arriving back home. Her nephew never interrupted the chat but glanced down regularly at the dog seated by his aunt's heel. Even he felt

Stella informed them that his previous owners, an elderly couple, had downsized their home and moved into a high-rise apartment. Animals were forbidden, so reluctantly they had asked for help in rehousing their pet. They had visited and taken his favourite foods every week, but the visits were too distressing for both owners and Ali and had ceased. Stella advised he was due his walk around the grounds and suggested Haley might oblige as she had business to discuss with Dansie.

Stella attached his lead to a body harness. 'He prefers that,' she quietly informed Haley.

They both went for a stroll around the large adjoining ground, and he did his 'businesses' against the various poles which were planted for such. On their return to the kennels, Haley reached into her pocket for a tissue. She neither had tissues or car keys and concern set in as to where they were. She briskly headed for the car, with Ali keeping step, obediently, by her left heel. Peering through the driver's door, she was relieved to see they sat safely in the ignition. Ali sat at the door anxiously waiting for it to be opened. Without noticing the moment, she looked at him and said 'C'mon Ali, let's go.' He slowly stood up and continued by her side into the enclosed kennel area. Haley patted him while removing the lead. Dansie and Stella stood at the canteen door in silence, both staring at Haley.

'What!' asked Haley in a loud voice.

'I think he'd be perfect for Cyprian,' announced Dansie with an air of authority. His parents are going to be so disappointed to see Tyson's grave when they get back. Your nephew is a great animal lover, so this fella

here looks tailor-made for the job. There was alway dog in that house, and we need to fill that gap.'

Why you crafty, conniving old fox, thought Hal Ali sat by her side, and even having the lead remove never budged. Stella made no effort to retrieve it fro Haley. There was something reassuring about havin a large dog beside her as they exchanged glance Stella politely suggested that Haley might take hii for a week to see if he fitted into their family. If thing did not work out, she could return him as he woul always be welcomed back. Adding that people look fo small cuddly puppies rather than a large four-year-ol animal. Haley had been rumbled, but there was an air of integrity and trust about this ugly mutt.

She agreed, much to the delight of Stella.

'Does he have a bed or favourite toy?' asked Haley. 'We already have a comfortable beanbag at home.'

'Just his blanket and that old woollen rag doll. He never leaves that out of his sight,' Stella replied.

Ali stood patiently and quietly accompanied the two ladies to the car. On opening the back door, he quickly jumped onto the seat and sat up in the middle watching through the windscreen as they headed back home. The return trip was made almost in silence as both Haley and Dansie weren't keen on conversation in case the words would be misinterpreted. As Haley approached Dansie's bus stop, she said, 'I think everything is going to be grand.' She smiled and got out of the car.

'Bye, Dansie, see you next week,' was Haley's parting shot. By the time she had parked at the rear of number 15, a hundred crazy thoughts had stampeded through

the connection between them, as Haley quoted Dansie, 'This house always had a dog, and there is a large hole here since Tyson died.' She also confirmed the shelter would take him back if things did not work out. 'The only reason I'm here, Cyprian, was to be a dog-sitter, as you are adult enough to take care of yourself,' she said and added that if there was no minding required, she might as well take the next flight home.

'Oh, no, no, please stay here until at least mam and mad return,' he pleaded. 'We need you to be here - all of us. Keera says you are a breath of fresh air around the place. If I had my way, we'd adopt you to stay here forever. Let's give it a try and see if Ali likes it here.'

Haley had successfully cleared the most difficult obstacle on the course, as she gave Ali a reassuring pat. Cyprian decided he would take him for a walk around the neighbourhood. Haley informed him that Ali preferred the body harness attachment, rather than his neck collar. Thirty minutes later they had returned. Haley had zapped another of her sister's precooked meals.

'He doesn't strain at the lead or get upset when other dogs bark at him,' announced Cyprian. Loose barking dogs were an annoyance to Tyson in the park. Some owners had the bad habit of letting their animals loose to run freely. A habit which Haley's polite park attendant also frowned on. 'Perhaps his previous owner had sent him to canine training class,' he suggested.

Haley decided she would have an early night and adjourned to her room, leaving her nephew and Ali to acclimatise. It had indeed been another day of unexpected developments.

Seán Kelly

By Sunday, all three occupants at number fifteen were getting along splendidly. Surprisingly, Dansie had not rang to check on the new resident. Haley, reluctantly admitted to herself the wily old devil was absolutely correct and would never have inflicted a cantankerous mutt on the family.

Keera had picked up a shift at the film studios thanks to the intervention of her sister. It was in relation to set-design rather than Edel's forte, and it was a happy distraction from her studies. Her sights were aimed at interior design and Cyps had often suggested that his Mam would gladly make some introductions on her behalf.

Both girls were calling to collect him later that evening, and he was excited at showing them his new 'acquisition.' On arriving, he stopped them entering at the door saying - 'I have a big surprise to announce.'

Both girls were intrigued by his enthusiasm as he had been rather glum since returning from the crematorium.

'You're pregnant' said Edel dourly.

Cyps ignored her attempted humour and called-out - 'Ali.' His multi-coloured canine pal ambled into the hallway, sat obediently beside him and raised his right paw. The intrigue was now a dumbfounded burst of excitement, with multiple hugs for the 'big-surprise' who lapped it all up with unbelievable calm.

The acquisition story was relayed in full detail, and all agreed it had been the correct move. Somehow Ali seemed very much at home in the company of the two girls. Keera then insisted on talking him for a walk and was amused by the fact he preferred the body-harness, even though he had an expensive leather collar.

'That's his thing,' said Haley, so we best go with that flow. Edel announced excitedly that she had a DVD of "Skyfall" - the latest Bond movie.

'How did you manage that?' asked a surprised Haley, as it's not yet in the cinemas.

'You forget I'm in the movies, babe,' was the reply, in her fake Hollywood accent. Adding that one of the production assistants had worked on the film, but she was sworn to secrecy, and it had to be returned to him early the next morning. By the time Edel and Ali had returned, Haley had removed and thawed a large holder of beef stew from the freezer. It was now being microwaved and a most sociable evening was enjoyed by all - with Ali finishing off the leftovers. Edel surprised Haley later when she enquired if there were official papers for their new dog. It also caught Cyprian unaware as they had never given thought to such. Edel had suggested that if the previous owner requested the return of Ali, it would cause much distress all round - as he was most probably micro-chipped with his old details attached.

Keera reassured them that this was highly unlikely as he was a rescue dog and had been given up, to be re-homed.

Even then, it left a nagging doubt in Haley's mind. Stella seemed an honest, straight forward type of individual and had conformed with the previous owners' wishes. She went over to the beanbag and looked into Ali's alert eyes. The words of her 'extra-camp-demon-barber' echoed back to her - "I bet there are some dark mysteries hidden in there."

CHAPTER FIFTEEN

The sun shone brightly from a clear blue sky the following Tuesday morning, as Haley opened the door to the always-on-time Dansie, at nine am. She was in a chirpy mood, with no coat to plant on the bannister - just her handbag.

'Well! How is the slobber-chops behaving?' she asked with a degree of curious suspicion.

'Ali,' called Haley and the new arrival trotted down the hall, sat in his usual upright position and lifted his right paw.

'Would ya looka dah?' exclaimed Dansie in her best Dublin accent. Bending down to rub his ears, she told him he was the luckiest dog in Ireland, to end up in that particular house. Haley confirmed that he just slotted into everyday life with complete ease and that her friend Stella was indeed correct as to his kindness and attitude. Dansie never passed a comment or replied, seeing it was her underhanded ploy that matched them together initially. Ali ambled back to his old blanketed beanbag with Haley advising he was just like Tyson, in that he would not be disturbed from his comfort patch, or indeed from the diamonds hidden inside the beanbag.

As usual, it was best to let Dansie get on with her chores alone - between the vacuuming, washing machine and the oldie radio being loudly blasted.

She decided to take another visit to the City centre and kill a few hours browsing. The taxi dropped her in central O'Connell Street. Noticing a sign for Henry Street, she recalled Albert mentioning a certain jewellery house of dubious note. The area was already busy with shoppers, tourists festooned with cameras and other browsers just moving about. There were a few side streets off the main thoroughfare, and as she passed one, she noticed a large shop sign with the words "Emeralds I". The letter 'I' was embedded into a small map of Ireland, with four shamrocks denoting the four Provinces of Ireland. It was almost 10 am and whilst all other premises were open or in the process of setting out their wares, this heavily secured unit was closed. As there was nothing to view, she continued her tour of the area. Two hours of walking and an extended coffee break later, she was on the same side street. The steel door was now open to trade, but heavy steel grill bars protected the windows which displayed an array of loose gems and expensive jewellery pieces.

She heard the sound of an inner door opening and footsteps hurriedly approaching. There was a burst of Russian from within, and she just had enough time to dash across the street and hide in a shop doorway. She got a fright when she saw a tall man with long blond hair emerge from the jewellers. His head was down, his face hidden, as he spoke furiously into a mobile phone. The man was quick on his feet, and although Haley tried to keep up the pace, she soon lost him in the crowds of shoppers. She was troubled by his strong physical resemblance to Conrad Kremlin and wondered what had he been doing at the jewellers. Perhaps he'd been checking if anyone had tried to pawn the diamonds.

The thought gave her a jolt, and not for the first time she wished she had never removed the hold-all from the Mercedes.

By the time she reached home, Dansie had finished and assured Haley that her sister would be well pleased with their new pet. She added, 'Hopefully Chloe will return home them, and they can be the usual happy family unit they always were.' Haley thanked her for all her work and kind words and confirmed again that Ali was now officially part of the family.

The next morning, Haley set out for her regular extended walk accompanied by her new canine pal. As they approached the entrance to the park, a mother and her very young daughter were about to exit the park. The little girl got very excited on seeing Ali and made an attempt to rub him. Her protective mother immediately stopped her and aggressively scolded her for attempting such.

The little girl cried - 'I only want to rub him.' Haley calmly reassured her mother that he was very friendly. Ali did his greeting-trick - raising his right paw in the direction of the child who immediately bent down to catch the outstretched animal's leg.

'Come on love. We'll be late for creche' said the mother as the happy twosome walk away. As Haley attempted to enter the park, Ali sat and watched for a few seconds, as the child was being escorted down the street. It was as if something had resonated inside his brain for those few moments. He then stood up and quietly accompanied Haley on their morning ramble - always at her tempo and always by her left heel. That nagging feeling of doubt about paperwork would not go away.

The following morning Haley decided she would return to the rescue shelter and have a chat with Stella in an attempt to clarify matters.

She recalled the route and remembered to turn right after the small church. Driving up the narrow lane, Haley pulled into the animal shelter. Stella who was having a cuppa and cigarette at the front door, rushed to the motor when she recognised the occupant. 'Oh! Jesus, what happened? Is everything okay?'

A surprised Haley replied 'nothing is wrong.' 'He's an absolute star and my nephew loves him to bits - best choice ever and thank you so very much.'

Haley said that she was just wondering if there were any papers that needed signing as everything happened so quickly last week. Stella ushered her into the office where the whiff of stewed tea competed for supremacy with cigarette smoke - it was an unusual clash of aromas. Rummaging through a set of files she inquired if Haley would a like a 'cuppa.' The offer was politely refused saying she had a late breakfast.

Reading from two sheets, Stella observed that Ali had been recently vaccinated and would only require a booster shot when next at the vet. She also added that his old micro-chip had been removed and suggested that particular procedure should be updated. It was now law and was a safety feature in the unlikely event of him 'going-missing.' This was the confirmation that Haley needed to ease her now un-necessary fears. Stella photocopied the paperwork for her.

Stella told her, the previous owners, Jackie and Margo Doyle had rung at the week-end. It was the first time their names were mentioned and Stella was about to apologise for doing so, as she had learned to keep such matters 'in-house.' 'I told Mrs. Doyle that Ali had been rehomed into a lovely family and that everything was perfect with Ali and the new owners. I realised I jumped-the-gun, but I just knew he would slot right in.

The poor woman cried for about five minutes when she heard the good news. Little kiddies only like cuddly pups and not big fully-grown dogs - especially mongrels. That's the only reason he was here with us for so long. That poor family endured enough hardship, without worrying about their dog being rehomed' she sadly announced.

Haley asked if there was a specific reason why Ali preferred the shoulder-harness over his dog collar.

As Stella closed the filing cabinet door and drew a long breath, Haley realised there was something else about Ali's past that would be revealed.

Stella spoke with a mixture of sympathy and aggression as she snarled - 'the Doyles are decent people and should never have been inflicted with all the shite they suffered.'

Opening one of the large windows and lighting up a cigarette, Stella added another spoon of sugar to her mug and sighed 'I don't even know where to begin with this.' She gulped a mouthful of her brew, sucked deeply on her Marlboro Light. 'Just start at the start' Haley calmly suggested.

'Jackie and Margo Doyle had lived for seven years at number twenty-five, Gorteen Downs on the outskirts of the city. Jackie was an operator of a heavy lift multi wheeled mobile crane. It took a sharp eye, steady hand and an accurate sense of judgement to operate such a large piece of expensive equipment. This was reflected in his salary and they enjoyed a decent quality of life together. His employer was "Sky-Hi-Crane-Higher"- he liked the play on words - a small family owned business run by Villiem Hilund. He was an engineer originally from Sweden who had come to Ireland to oversee the erecting of large gantry cranes at various ports. He also saw the potential for mobile units in a developing Irish economy. He ran a profitable company and was joined by his only son, Terry.

The Doyle family were elated at the news of Margo's pregnancy even though they were both in their late forties. Five years ago, a daughter, Amy, was their pride and joy but then a routine check with their GP turned life at number twenty-five upside down. Amy had a mild form of autism and there were complications with congenital hips. This would require various surgeries which unfortunately revealed further difficulties with some of her internal organs. However, the Doyles were both determined to ensure their precious Amy would get the very best treatment.

By now she was a beautiful two-year-old - long golden blonde hair and piercing ice blue eyes. She was having mobility difficulty and balance and was not as advanced with her speech as other kiddies of similar age. Yet she knew and understood everything her parents said to her. Multiple trips to Harley Street clinics had drained their savings and they were finding it difficult to balance the household budget.

As Jackie took his break one particular day, a young dog strayed onto the site he was working on. Sensing the animal was hungry, Jackie shared his lunch with the multi-coloured animal. He returned regularly and Jackie noticed he was always had a better appetite each Monday, as he obviously wasn't being fed elsewhere.

Construction was delayed during a heavy snowfall for two days. When Jackie returned to work, his mongrel pal was curled-up under the huge machine where there was no snow. Jackie fed him most of his lunch pack and took him into the warmth of the cab. The dog slept quietly at his feet for the full eight-hour shift.

Jackie hadn't the heart to abandon him back onto the ice-cold site, so he placed him on the back seat of his car. Unsure how his wife would react to an extra house guest, he stopped and bought a large bag of dog food and a bunch of flowers. On opening the front door, Margo exclaimed - 'what's that'? They're blooms for the blossom of my life' he splurted.

'No! him' pointing at the dog.

By then Amy had wobbled her way down the hall. Hugging the dog, she turned to Jackie and uttered 'thanks Da.'

Both parents stood in shock and amazement. It was the first time their beautiful but handicapped child had expressed any form of emotion - and it was to a mongrel dog. Margo burst into tears and ran to the safety of her kitchen. Jackie leaned down to Amy and said 'he is all yours.' 'What will we call him?' Her limited vocabulary allowed her to say Ali. It was a day that enhanced all their lives for quite some time.

A neighbour suggested they get a harness similar to the one people with impaired vision use with their guide dogs. Ali instinctively knew he was a walking aid for this child and her movement and stability improved enormously over the next year.

When Margo took her daughter to a pre-school, she always seemed lost in the class and had difficulty relating to other kids. Eventually the owners requested she leave, citing that she needed a special needs facility.

The Doyles were upset but determined their daughter would be given every opportunity, regardless of cost, to enjoy her childhood.

Amy and Ali were regulars around the local area and well accepted by all. Obviously, there were local bullies, but Ali somehow sensed that fact. A snarl and gentle show of his fangs, always ended any intimidation.

A special needs educational centre was located not far from their home and Amy was enrolled. Again, she found it difficult to adjust without Ali by her side. An astute elderly teacher, suggested that Ali be allowed to stay in the class room for the four-hour sessions. The first day was complete bedlam as all twelve kids wanted to play with the new canine pupil. After that, things settled down and the teacher saw an enormous improvement in Amy's concentration levels coupled with a greater learning ability. This applied to many of the other kiddies also.

It was even suggested to other parents that they should give serious consideration to adopting a similar approach with an animal companion.

The Doyle's took caravan holidays together and Ali was a star attraction wherever they toured locally.

However, Amy's internal organs were not moving in line with her body development, and another expensive three week visit to the London clinic has decimated their merger savings. The specialist confided that his team had almost exhausted preventative surgeries and her fragile body may not be able to sustain further treatments. However, a new form of medication would enhance her quality of life - but was expensive.

Their precious little beauty would be given every chance regardless of cost.

Villiem was tragically electrocuted when his crane jib hit an electricity cable and company ownership transferred to his son. Unfortunately, Terry's panache was for fast sports cars - rally cars. His aim was to be a champion driver on the European circuits. He enjoyed limited success but company profits were being funnelled into his sporting ambitions with little financial return. The only glory was being regularly photographed. Matters were not helped by a down-turn in the construction trade. His efforts at sporting glory were eating into company funds and their extended bank overdraft.

From the Doyles' prospective, things deteriorated when Jackie was placed on a three-day week. The family still had large medical expenses, but now had a reduced income.

Attempts to refinance his mortgage, which cost one thousand five hundred and fifty euro per month were rejected. They even took an extended loan from their local Credit Union. This temporarily eased the situation, but all loans must be eventually repaid and Jackie was really coming under severe pressure from all his financial lenders.

As a family unit, they made the best of the hand they were dealt with Ali being the only real friend their daughter had. Reality set in, when blood tests showed Amy's immune system at extremely low levels. She would now be susceptible to many of the winter viruses which meant keeping the house extra warm.

Their finances were stretched to breaking point. When the local Lion's Club delivered an extra-large Christmas hamper to their house, Jackie and Margo knew they were on the official bread-line - the new poor.

Linda, Terry's wife, who was running their now struggling business, presented Jackie with a month's wages as a Christmas bonus. It was a welcome relief and eased their burden during that festive season.

On a cold January night Jackie was waked by the persistent barking of Ali outside Amy's bedroom door. 'What a fucking hour of the night he decides to have a piss' Jackie grumbled, climbing out of his restful slumber. Ali had Amy's hamper present - a Popeye the sailor blanket at his feet. Jackie rushed in to find his precious daughter motionless in her bed.

An ambulance arrived within fifteen minutes with an active resus team on hand.

Amy had lapsed into a coma and spent the next week in a high dependency unit connected to an array of drips, oxygen and attachments to noisy machines.

She eventually came-to, but was very weak. Delighted to see her parents, her first words were 'where's Ali?'

Animals were not allowed onto such Wards, but a large photo of him was eventually secured and placed over her bed. Her condition did not improve and after another coma lapse, she passed away.

Jackie and Margo were devastated, even though they both knew that the inevitable was unavoidable. It still came as a devastating wallop.

One week after the funeral, another body-blow was dealt to them. Margo had just arrived home having visited the grave. There was a loud knock on her front door. Three burly men stood menacing at her step. One produced a document stating it was Court Order eviction notice. They began emptying all their household belongings onto the front lawn. Ali had to be locked into Amy's bedroom as he was going berserk. A shocked Margo was unable to contact her husband, as the family now only had one mobile and that was in her handbag.'

'I'll have that cuppa now please,' said a distressed Haley. 'I can't believe that anyone would perform such a callous act in an official capacity and almost immediately after the funeral.' Stella presented a steaming mug of well-stewed brew to her host. Adding, 'that auld shite only happened four hundred years ago, when Oliver Cromwell was acting the thug here.' Immediately apologising, when she realised Haley was British.

'No apology needed' replied Haley. Stella continued with her sorrowful tale.

'The elderly next-door neighbour gave a distressed Margo sanctuary, as most of their belongings had been dumped outside their home. Locks were changed, with a notice pinned to the front door - "Repossessed private property - Do not enter or you will be prosecuted."

Cyril, the neighbour had ripped the piece from the door and shredded it, when the bailiffs had ended their nasty deeds.

When Jackie returned from his day's work, all their belongings were safely stored in various rooms and garages by his thoughtful neighbours.

The elderly couple housed them for the next week.

Luckily, a kind soul in the Housing Department at the local council was aware of their plight and quickly arranged their present accommodation. Unfortunately, the apartment block owners had a strict rule - "No animals." Their elderly neighbours who were both in their late eighties, cared for Ali during the next month. He only needed to be fed as his day was spent, pining at the Doyles back door. That's when Margo took the decision to attempt having him re-homed. Jackie hadn't the stomach to abandon the animal he had rescued three years earlier - who had become an integral part of their lives. His loud barking had actually saved Amy's life that cold winter's night and it was Margo who taxied him to the rescue shelter.

Haley now had the full story. She again reassured Stella that Ali would be loved and well treated by her nephew. She was sad at hearing the depressing events and regretted even asking - but at least she now knew.

'Do you think Mrs. Doyle would be annoyed if I called to her - just to give additional assurance that their pet is safe,' Haley quietly asked.

'I think that would be brilliant,' answered Stella, 'as they were both so upset parting with Ali.' She scribbled an address on a piece of paper and handed it to her.

Haley asked if their centre received any funding for their caring work. She was informed that they were on the land, rent free, and got donations from various charities and fundraisers. Most staff worked for less than a minimum wage and many helped-out free.

'Our family would like to make a contribution to your excellent project' as she produced an envelope of fifties.

'There's a lot in there' exclaimed Stella. 'One thousand,' Haley casually replied. Stella was thrilled and immediately began writing a receipt - saying everything had to be accounted for. That will help with the feed bill and medications she happily added. 'One last thing' said Haley producing an additional one hundred, 'that's for when you, Dansie and your pals all hit the pub. If I give it to her, she will just refuse - so tell them you won it on a horse and enjoy,' she winked.

The seven story 'Lego-block' type building, now home to the Doyles, was easy to spot against the Dublin skyline. There was indeed, very little green area in the vicinity of the building itself - so she could understand the 'no-pets' rule. It looked like it had been 'plonked' into the numerous small housing estates which surrounded the apartment complex.

Having parked the car, she entered the building lobby and stepped inside an elevator. She checked the scrap of paper to confirm she was heading for apartment number 515. She knocked, unsure how to approach the topic with the Doyle family. Eventually an inquisitive face peered out through the safety chain. 'I'm not interested,' snapped the curt voice.

'I'm so sorry Mrs. Doyle. I got your address from Stella. I'm Ali's new owner' Haley rapidly answered. The door slammed - the safety chain was removed and a tired Margo Doyle wept as she reopened her front door.

Haley was invited to step inside. The small living/ dining room was bright and clean. Two large bags of groceries lay unpacked on the table. An unusual floral pattern on the wallpaper added to the calm silence. Apart from a wedding photograph of a beautiful Jackie and Margo on their special day, the room was decorated with multiple framed pictures of their child. One in particular stood out - an enlarged photo of a beautiful young blonde child hugging her multi coloured canine pet - right paw in greeting mode.

Haley apologised for calling unannounced and informed Margo that their pet was safe, well cared for and would never want for anything. 'He's now part of the furniture and would always be loved as he was such a loveable animal himself' she said.

Margo had begun to repeat much of the information Stella had already imparted. Haley politely interrupted in an effort to change the topic as Margo was becoming more distressed. She expressed her shock that any Judge, with a modicum of sensitivity should never had issues an eviction decree. Margo apologetically added they were 'way-behind' on the mortgage payments. But Jackie made a point of religiously making a cash payment on the first of each month, adding that some months it was only two hundred short of what was due. It was all they could afford some months, but never missed some form of payment. A friend of Margo's advised her to ensure Jackie got a written receipt for each payment. Haley still found it impossible to comprehend why they would evict yet understanding all lending institutions need to recoup fees. Margo was more upset at the fact the eviction took place just seven days after the burial. She said they were too weak to bother attempting an argument and were drained mentally and emotionally having sustained such a personal loss.

Having to give-up their beloved pet was the last-straw for Jackie as it was, he, who had rescued him. He was now a broken man and had no interest in any of his old social habits. She was extremely concerned for his health but now knowing that Ali was happily rehomed and in a loving family environment would give him a 'lift.'

'What kind of judge would grant an eviction notice in such circumstances?' Haley angrily asked.

Margo opened a cabinet door and produced a bulging pink paper document wallet adding 'I was going to burn this lot last week as it's only a reminder of badness and nasty people.'

Haley was struck by the lack of bitterness in her words. Was it, that the loss of her child had insulated her from the distress of being evicted from her home so shortly after the funeral?

Margo took the top letter from the pile. It was addressed to both Jackie and Margo with large printed heading "Eviction Procedure." There were many paragraphs on the various payment agreements which were neglected and ignored by the tenants. The last line was to inform them that the institution were legally entitled to repossess the property.

While Margo produced a mug of coffee for her guest, Haley re-read the letter a third time. She was now completely dumbfounded.

Haley calmly said 'Margo this is NOT an official Court Order. It's been typed up and framed to look like one. It's a starchy, aggressive letter from a firm of solicitors. There is no Court stamp or judge's name attached!'

The relevance of that sentence was completely lost to Margo, as she asked 'how many sugars?'

Haley did not wish to add further distress to her as she asked if all the monthly receipts were also in the file.

'Everything's in there. We just don't have the will for another battle and only want to get on with our lives.' Margo added that her brother had a successful construction firm in Australia and offered to fly them out there. Jackie would have great wages and she could do some part-time work to keep herself occupied.

'But we'd be half way around the globe and what would we do on Sunday mornings?' she sadly admitted.

'Sunday mornings?' enquired Haley.

Margo explained that they call to the cemetery after Mass and chat to their daughter's headstone. 'Imagine two grown adults talking to a tombstone - how idiotic is that'?

The hard lump in Haley's throat, salty stinging moist eyes and runny nose could not possibly allow a coherent reply. She just nodded her head, knowing too well how they both felt.

She allowed Margo talk about the good days they all enjoyed while Amy was healthy enough to travel.

She was now composed as she politely asked if she could retain the file as she knew someone who may be of assistance. Margo had no objections adding she would be glad being rid of it and its bad memories.

Once inside the privacy of her car, Haley again read the 'Court Order.' It was nothing of the sort. It was an aggressive threat from their lending institution

- "Mercurial Financial Services" and they obviously used the opportunity to gain entrance, remove personal belongings and change the door locks. 'Fuck those evil bastards,' shouted Haley as she closed the folder.

In her annoyance, she turned onto the wrong section of motorway. She had to continue to the next exit to correct the mistake. While watching for her road sign she saw what appeared to be a builder's yard with a large crane visible. It was the base of "Sky-HI-Crane-Higher."

The three-acre site contained two large mobile cranes, a bulldozer, two small dump-trucks and forklifts. There was also a large repair garage which was not in use. Haley drove slowly to the office, passing a sign, warning 'Beware of Dog.' Opening her car door slowly, to ensure there was no dog around, she stepped up to the partly opened office entrance. The voice of an irritated woman was in a heated telephone discussion.

"I've told you ten times; he is not here. He's in still in rehab, unable to move and will NOT be out of hospital for another month, at least. Yes, I am well aware of the implications and there's no point in you bitching at me' …. I am not shouting; I'm SCREAMING as you seem to be deaf as well as irritating … Do whatever the fuck you want because that's what you are going to do anyway.' The call abruptly ended.

Haley knocked on the door and took one step inside saying she hoped there was no dog about. 'No! that was her on the phone' came the sharp reply. 'If you are selling, I'm not buying, if you collecting, the petty cash box is empty.'

'Neither,' answered Haley. 'I'm a friend of your employee, Jackie Doyle - well actually his wife, Margo.' The pretty young lady stood up from behind her desk and apologised for her 'flowery outbursts' and invited her guest to take a seat.

Haley hadn't thought this through and was unsure why she was even on the premises. It was just a reactionary follow-up to the sad conversation from twenty minutes earlier. The walls were decorated with pictures of rally cars in full flight and a handsome man being presented with many large trophies. The obvious starting point was to enquire as to her husband's health.

Fifteen minutes later she was still listening to the history of his 'near' successes. Unfortunately, his last crash was almost a fatality. His motor was a complete wreck - he had multiple fractures and it seemed like the end of the road for his sporting ambitions. The young lady, his wife, hoped it was, as the business needed his full time attention.

It was exactly as Stella had related. She also explained how she was getting 'untold-grief' from her finance company. 'Was that the 'dog,' on the phone?' Haley jokingly asked. 'Yes! That bitch with the double-barrelled name, from Mercurial Financial Services' she added.

Haley voiced an opinion that she seemed a nasty piece of work, and she was capable of underhanded methods - as the Doyles had discovered. Linda and Haley swapped introductions as they were certainly in agreement with that particular assessment of Mercurial. Linda informed her that they were being threatened with receivership, if the outstanding repayments were not forthcoming. Haley had seen the stationary units which were park-up outside and asked why they were not being used to generate income.

Linda told her that she had recently miscarried - being absent from work for two weeks, and it was Jackie who was keeping the ship afloat. Her husband, hopefully would be back in a few months, and it was difficult to get professional, capable operators for these sophisticated cranes.

Leaning forward towards her cluttered desk, she stated that whilst the business seemed profitable, the firm had lost direction. She stressed that it needed a restructure plan and all these loans had to be extended or refinanced.

'Jesus, Villiem would turn in his grave if he knew what a balls-up we'd made of his business.'

'Linda, you, and you alone must take responsibility of running this operation or they WILL appoint a receiver and all will be lost.' Haley loudly explained - 'I know how her callous, twisted mind thinks and operates.'

The business generated profits when all their plant was out on working sites but profits were being pumped into loss making sporting activities - outstanding overdrafts need to be addressed - qualified staff need be sourced to keep the unworked machinery moving - the company needed a cash injection or downsize completely.

Linda also confirmed that the tax commitments were up-to-date and that they paid off something each and every month to Mercurial Financial Services. This bore a similar resonance to the Doyle's saga and Haley was aware of how that ended.

'You do know that Margo's brother offered to fly them to Australia and guarantee permanent employment in a better climate?' she added. Haley's word had only left her lips when Linda shouted, 'Oh Jesus no! - we need him here, and need him badly.'

'I never said they were taking-up the offer. I just said it was there for them' remarked Haley.

Linda's head sank into both her hands as she rubbed her cheeks in a frustration - 'I don't know what to do anymore' she sighed.

'Yes, you do' replied a confident Haley. She did not wish to give a patronising lecture to a young woman who had hit a severely distressing patch in her life. Haley simply suggested many of the obvious solutions, which unfortunately Linda was unable to comprehend - due to the anxiety clouding her judgement.

She suggested to her, that Terry take-up a more sedate pastime and forget his rally-dreams. Linda agreed saying, 'we were always at the feast, but never dined at the top table.' That for Haley, summed it up perfectly-buckets of cash going out, and precious little coming in.

She also queried if a call to Linda's uncle, whom she worked with, could yield a positive outcome - giving him those dump trucks outside. They were clear of finance repayments and should be used as 'hello-money.' Working in tandem with his firm and contacts, would be beneficial all round.

Haley had an idea that the pregnant Anna would prefer her marine-engineer husband, to be in full time local employment, so that may be an option for later on.

She intimated that the Doyle's financial situation might be getting a boost in the near future, and perhaps it would help in their current cash-flow predicament.

Linda's face lit-up, saying sometimes you cannot see the wood from the trees. Haley asked if she could have copies of recent correspondences from the banking companies, and these were quickly presented to her.

'I have copies of everything, going back twenty years here' Linda said pointing to a large filing cabinet. 'The old man was meticulous in his record keeping, and every job he ever did was fully documented, with the receipts to verify.' She smiled as she said 'he warned me to never throw any job details away, as they may be required someday'.

Haley wondered if there was something buried in its midst that may provide 'ammunition' for her, at a later stage.

'Perhaps it's best if we keep this between ourselves for the time being - let's keep the boys out of it, until things get sorted' Haley smiled to a relieved Linda.

Looking at the paper filled desk, 'I should let you get-on with your day job, while I'll check these out' - holding up the large file of documents.

Adding, 'please speak to your hubby, and pointing at the telephone, hopefully we can keep the guard-dog at bay.' The phone rang, as if on cue. It was a client requesting a quote. As Linda politely chatted to him, Haley took the opportunity to quietly exit.

She now had two folders of separate problems, and one common denominator - Mercurial Financial Services.

As she started the car engine, her phone beeped an incoming text message - "H, same again @ 14.00. Ed J."

The dashboard showed she had over an hour to drive home, collect Ali and make it to the phone kiosk.

At 1.59 pm she rang and following the same ritual the phone rang back to her. After the usual exchange of pleasantries, Eddie told her it had been confirmed Kerri was alive. They were unsure of his physical condition, but he was now in a secure military hospital on the outskirts of Moscow. No official comments had been released from any of Government sources. It would still be an embarrassment to both countries, and very few were being made aware of activities, even at a local level.

'I hope he's OK and ye can eventually get him home,' was the only appropriate reply from Haley. Eddie said their only chance was a swop of some type, but they would need a high-ranking diplomatic spy to trade. Moscow was being ultra-careful in their relationship with the European Union and was not the potent aggressive force of old - despite what American Intelligence agencies were portraying.

The genuine intel was with Mossad who was active in ensuring security on all their borders. Their interest in Russia was that arms manufactured there were finding their way via Iran to various Islamic extremists. They also had a supporting ally in The United States of America. Europeans were dancing on a delicate tight rope between both. The emergence of many right-wing political parties being opposed to mass immigration from Africa and the Middle East seemed to fragment the comfort zone of most middle ground Governments.

'Eddie, spare me the political waffle, and please tell me where is all this going?' asked an agitated Haley.

Eddie apologised. It was his frustration at all the misinformation they had been fed over the past two years, while Russian crooks, once their allies, were freely roaming about Europe.

It took an eavesdrop on a chat in a Dutch embassy, with intel from Mossad to surreptitiously discover that one of their staff was in a secure jail. He was unsure even if the Russian Embassy in Ireland were aware of Conrad's presence there. He again warned Haley that should he catch a glimpse, and recognise her; she would certainly be in danger. 'He is now a cornered rat, and that's when they are most dangerous,' he warned.

Changing the subject, he announced that the rugby team would be in Dublin in three weeks' time. 'I would love to meet-up and have a chat if you had an hour to spare,' he asked. 'We have much catching up to do.' He added that it was safer for him to meet away from his workplace. 'We shouldn't be having these conversations,' he whispered.

Haley informed him she might have returned home by then if her house repairs were completed.

'Again, don't ring this number, but text anytime and keep me posted on your stay,' he replied.

Haley was now even more concerned, as to the fact she had a sock full of diamonds. She was spending some of the cash and had made use of the Glock. But the diamonds were untouched - not knowing if they were real or fake.

Ali had sat patiently at her feet and was anxious to exit the tight enclosure of the kiosk. 'Good boy,' she said, patting his head. 'I need a brisk walk to clear my own head.' It had been another unusual day of unexpected complications.

CHAPTER SIXTEEN

Cyprian and his colleagues were about to begin one and a half weeks of exams. The written, oral and evaluations of their efforts would determine their careers for life. Haley tried to avoid any contentious topics during the days prior to this. At least, her nephew had a unique opportunity to enter a successful business, which was just a short walk from his abode.

Without being aware of events, he had a huge head start on most of his classmates.

Haley watched him from the front room window as he departed for the first day of his sittings. She did not wish to add to the anxiety by fussing with "best wishes-keep calm-hope all goes well" phrases.

At ten o clock, the doorbell rang.

It was Edel.

She had an anxious look on her face as she plonked her large suitcase on the step.

'Haley,' she sternly asked, 'are you positive you want to go through with this?'

'Absolutely,' was the immediate reply as she led her visitor into the kitchen.

'OK, let's see how good you really are,' said Haley adding that she had found one of Heather's sports bras. 'So that's good for a start.'

One hour later, Edel had almost completed her task. 'I just need to darken your chin area a wee bit, and lift that neckerchief slightly higher,' she added.

'OK,' she said, 'that's it. Go take a look in the long hall mirror.'

Haley was amazed at the transformation.

'Jeez, I really do look like Spike's twin brother.'

'NO! Haley, PLEASE remember the low gravelly Dublin accent, as you'll get tripped up,' Edel warned. She added, 'I prefer not to know what this is about, and I still do not like it.'

Edel provided her with extra-long suede gloves. The tips were padded to ensure the hand looked that of a man. Her final touch was to apply a transfer of the three letters C C C on her left wrist just above the thumb. She now looked like a fully-fledged member of the Crew-Cut-Crew.

'Righ, I'll be bleedin' grand,' Haley croaked in her best attempt.

'Not bad at all,' replied Edel.

Twenty minutes later, Edel dropped-off her passenger, relatively close to Henry Street.

'Remember, no lady's walk, and keep the low accent,' Edel warned. 'And if something happens, you ring me immediately.'

'I'll be fine and tanks for evertin',' Haley croaked back to her, in the mock accent.' I'm jus gonna mug some ole dear and rob her handbag.'

'NOT funny,' Edel shouted, 'and be sure to text me when you get ho….'

Haley quickly closed the car door.

Good God child! You are beginning to sound like me, she thought. But then again, Edel had lived among these thugs for a while and knew what type of feral rats they all were. Haley turned and waved at her driver. Deep down, she was delighted at how much Edel had matured following her near-miss with the Chalky.

Haley strode down the busy street until she came to the side lane which housed "Emeralds I". She waited until two clients had departed and stepped inside. She took no time to inspect the interior but went straight to the middle-aged man behind the counter.

'You da gaffer,' she grunted in her lowest voice.

'Yes, I am the manager,' he warily replied reply.

Haley produced a diamond in her left palm.

'Me auntie died, like, a while ago, an I now own dis. I wanna know how much 'tis wort,' Haley grunted.

The manager was unable to hide his enthusiasm as he viewed the piece under his special eyeglass.

'Your late aunt had exquisite taste in gems and this is a most unique example of a pure quality,' he politely replied.

'Yeah, like, buh whatsa wort like, to sell?' Haley enquired.

The manager explained that such a remarkable diamond should fetch between eleven and twelve. But should there be additional pieces of similar size and quality, the value would increase substantially. He explained that a single unit would make a superb ring. But it there were three, then matching earrings would greatly enhance the totality of the sale.

'So, you're sayin de more there is a dem, de more dare wort,' Haley croaked.

'Precisely,' the manager replied. 'And are there anymore in your family's possession?'

'Aah, they might be,' came the reply.

Haley could see the manger was extremely anxious to ascertain the quantity and asked to retain the piece to assess the possibility of an immediate purchase.

'No! Dat stays wit me, but youse can take a foha of it,' she replied. Haley was having difficulty retaining the deep-throated accent, as she again held the diamond for him to photograph. The piece looked stunningly beautiful, as it sparkled on her black suede glove. She made sure the C C C transfer was clearly visible in the shot.

'Do youse have a name for dis typa diamond?' she asked.

'This is a magnificent example of a Marquise 1.75 and are rarely presented to us in such remarkable condition,' he eloquently said.

She was now certain the gems were one hundred percent genuine and had an idea of the value.

The manager was adamant that the client should return first thing in the morning with whatever else was available.

That was one risk Haley was never going to take. She explained she would ring him from the gym the next morning when the exact number of gems were clarified. Again, the manager was insistent on a personal visit, as he handed out his business card with his private mobile number written on the back.

'Righ, I may be back in de mornin, buh I'll ring youse anyway,' was the gruff reply.

'Yes, please do, or preferably visit here, and I'll guarantee you the very best price in town,' he enthusiastically offered.

Haley exited immediately. She quickly turned the corner and entered a sportswear shop. She removed the wig and spikey sideburns with great speed and stuffed them into the pockets.

She donned a white 'hoody' jacket and new trainers, dashed to the counter, and handed the assistant one hundred euro, asking for the old black jacket and boots to be placed into a carrier bag. Adding she would wear her new clothes instead.

As she casually strolled past "Emeralds I," the manager was on the telephone. His over-animated actions suggested he was in a serious discussion, and she could hazard a guess that it was in relation to her visit.

Sitting in the taxi on her way home, she reckoned the value of her gem haul would be over seventy thousand assuming his value of one thousand two hundred each was accurate.

There obviously has to be another stash of diamonds somewhere in transit, as seventy thousand would not travel very far for three criminals. Had they cashed in some of the 'skimmed' haul elsewhere or perhaps it was the loot in her suitcase?

She had plans for that, and Conrad Kremlin was certainly not included.

In the safety of her kitchen, she opened an internet search engine and typed in "marquise diamonds, 1.75".

'Dear Jesus in Heaven,' she exclaimed. The actual value of such a quality was nearer to fifteen thousand euro each. That valued the total haul at nine hundred thousand.

She had mistaken his figure of twelve, for a hundred rather, than a thousand. 'No wonder he was so anxious to have me return with some more,' Haley said with a sigh.

She now realised that unique pieces of cut diamonds like these may be easy to transport, but will draw attention when an attempt is made to cash them in.

She had shaken the tree, and it was now time to see what would fall out. There was absolutely no way she would return to his den but needed to keep him 'interested' and perhaps something unusual might show.

'I need to re-assure 'mother-hen', noted Haley as she tapped into her phone: "Hi Edel, home safe & sound, no pensioners mugged :), so all's good and tks vm again. Remember, not a word! best rgds, H."

She only then noticed not having hidden away the folders of accounts, and was concerned that Cyprian may have seen the contents. Producing her calculator, pen and paper, she began to re-arranged the assortment documents into chronological order. It may bring some focus to the various financial quagmires and perhaps an amicable agreement may be identifiable.

The Doyle family had the safety net, of beginning a new life in Australia but they really no desire to move half-way around the globe. If Jackie's employer ceased trading, the situation would just get even more complicated and troublesome for all concerned. If she could somehow join-up those difficult dots, then perhaps there was the possibility of a result.

Jackie and Margo deserved that at least, but the 'fly in that sticky jar of ointment' was the 'wicked-witch' who controlled Mercurial Financial Services.

AS she totted-up various figures, from aggressive final demands she thought to herself - 'perhaps a friendly girlie chat may help'.

Ali had settled into a comfortable daily routine and contented himself by remaining downstairs and never venturing past his comfortable blanketed bean-bag.

'Do you realise, your neutered butt is sitting on a small fortune, she questioned towards him?'

Between the sock and the suitcase there was a stash to kill-for, but Haley had no intention of dying for it. She needed to figure how best to put it to proper use, and hopefully ensure that the thugs who invaded her life got their 'come-upping's.

Haley aware that Dansie was about the ring the doorbell. 'Goodbye son and thanks for the lift.'

Once inside, Dansie was her usual talkative self, petting the dog, calling him Tyson, apologising for the error, inquiring about Mrs. H and Chloe and dragging her cleaning equipment from the cupboard.

Haleys phone rang.

Dansie shut-off the noisy vacuum cleaner, but was within earshot of Haley's conversation:

'Ah yes, and thanks for returning my call, Haley said in her most polite accent. Could you put me through to Ms Penelope Harwood-Smythe please? No, I don't have an account with your company - no, I don't wish to open an account - I just wish to speak to your manager please - no thank you, I need to speak with Ms Harwood-Smythe - It's a private matter that requires......'

'You, ignorant bitch' Haley roared, looking at the blank screen which showed 'disconnected.' Facing Dansie, Haley bellowed 'that stupid cow cut-me-off in mid-sentence.'

'The height of bad manners and impudence' Haley barked.

Dansie very casually replied, 'I'm not one bit surprised, if she works for that bully with that long-complicated name.'

'So, you have an account with that institution?' asked Haley.

'I most certainly do NOT,' replied Dansie with an air of contempt. 'So how do you know her?'

'I don't - It's Aldo.'

'So, HE has an account with them?' enquired Haley.

'NO, he has not, nor would he touch them with a barge-pole,' came the even more aggressive reply.

'Let me put the kettle on and I'll explain it you in detail,' she replied.

It turned out that year her son, Aldo, dated a beautician who was employed in a large city centre store. She had been introduced to his family, and Danno firmly believed there would be wedding bells. 'We're getting shut of him at last and it's about time he moved out,' Nanno had joked.

However, he was stood-up, for his football club dinner-dance, and found it extremely embarrassing, as she never returned his calls or text messages.

A friend of his much later, delivered a polite note from her, explaining that she had resigned her job and was now General Manger of a new, exclusive female-only fitness centre. She apologised for her behaviour and informed him that she and her new partner were setting-up home together.

'Aldo got some bleedin' shock, said Dansie, because he never suspected that she was that-way.'

'What way?' asked an agitated Haley

'Lesbian' answered Dansie. 'We never told Nano as she wouldn't understand all that.'

'Dansie, what's all this got to do with Penelope What's-her-face?'

Dansie had topped-up both mugs, with her strong brew and continued with gusto, to flesh-out her informative saga.

Three months later, on a Friday afternoon Aldo was called to remove a break-down from a bus lane.

By co-incidence it was in the vicinity of his former girlfriend's new fitness centre and as he was securing his load, he noticed a magnificent brand-new BMW sports car. An agitated lady was grabbing at the door handle.

She approached Aldo, noticing he was an auto repair man, and asked for assistance. It turns out she had locked herself out of her expensive motor - handbag, phone and keys inside. She said that having gone to collect her parking permit disc, the car automatically locked itself.

Aldo explained it was a new safety mechanism of some modern cars.

'Now, yur wan was gettin pure wicked as this stage' explained Dansie. 'Aldo would have a 'yoke' for doing such' she added, 'but didn't want Miss Hoity-Toity to see him in action.'

Aldo asked her to check the emergency kit inside the car boot for a small screw-driver and while she rummaged about, he had inserted a thin steel strip inside the window and quickly 'popped' the lock.

'He tells yur wan, - job done missus, and she was delighted' said Dansie.

'She just plonked the parking disc on the dashboard top, grabbed her keys and bag and dashed-off down the road, not even saying thanks, let alone getting paid,' added an indignant Dansie.

'In her rush, she dropped a business card with her name and photograph on the footpath, Ms Penelope Harwood-Smythe, Manager Mercurial Financial Services. Aldo watched to see where her urgent appointment was,' she continued.

Her destination was to the exclusive establishment where Aldo's 'ex' was the general manager. A friend of his happens to be a member and she had informed him that it IS strictly for a certain type of lady.

Dansie's power old recall was incredible as she continued her monologue.

'Exactly one month later, at the very same time of evening, Aldo was passing that particular address and 'yur wan' was getting of her posh car. I know because it was the last Friday of the month. My self Stella and two old school chums meet for drinks on the same day each month. Aldo is our chauffeur to the 'watering-hole', so times and dates are set-in-stone for this monthly ritual. We're actually off out tomorrow evening,' Dansie merrily added.

Haley moved to the sink and began washing her tea stained mug. 'By any chance, can you recall the name of that fitness club,' Haley casually asked.

'Dear God, no! Haley' she replied in horror. 'I wouldn't be got dead near a kip like that'. Dansie dashed to her handbag, removed her phone. 'Now! Let's see. One is for home. Two is the phone box across the street, and three must be Aldo' she announced, 'because four is for Stella.'

She pressed the button and ten seconds later her rapid-fire conversation began: "Hello son. This is yur Ma. What's the name of that place where your 'ex,' Shaniya, is now working in? What! Hold on a second - say again'. 'La Femme Discreet' shouted Dansie, so Haley would remember. 'And by the way son, don't work yur Da too hard today'. 'I need him for ten minutes of action tonight'. 'MA'! Was the audible reply as he rang off.

'I do loves winding him up' laughed Dansie.

'Ten minutes,- should I be so lucky! He was once a marathon-man - Now he's a sprinter,' she continued as they both laughed hysterically.

Later that afternoon, Haley and Ali took an extra-long stroll through the park and an extended route home.

As they approached the gate of number 15, she wondered if Ali would remember where exactly he was. The gate was open, and without invitation her canine pal wheeled-in immediately.

'Well done and good, good boy' she said, rubbing his neck.

Ali knew he was definitely home, and he was enjoying it.

As she opened the front door, the whiff of fresh food greeted them. Cyprian obviously had called to the take-away as he bellowed - 'Grub's up.'

As they tucked-in to his presentation, Cyprian said, 'Do you realise something strange - just when we think that we have rehomed a stray dog, it actually feels as if he has adopted us!'. 'The lady who controls the rescue centre says that he was the most loveable animal ever set foot in their kennels' Haley answered.

'Well! he won't be going back there,' whispered Cyprian

Haley was anxious not to get deeply involved in Ali's previous life story and quickly changed the topic.

CHAPTER SEVENTEEN

～

The following morning as Haley sat in the taxi to Flexo's Gym, she was concerned.

'Can you wait around the corner, as this won't take long' she politely asked the driver, handing him €20 to cover his delay.

A well-muscled young man was behind the counter as an array of customers filed in and out. Approaching him apprehensively, Haley asked in a flustered voice 'do you have a public phone here as I've done something terribly stupid. I've locked my handbag with mobile phone and keys into my car, and I just need to ring my partner to collect a spare set, and he will go ballistic - bitching-off about women drivers,' Haley sheepishly added.

The attendant said no, there isn't, but you may use the office phone, as he presented her the handset. He was still within earshot, as she asked him 'if he could get her an energy drink - being completely addled from the experience.' She had observed the cabinet positioned, at the far end of the long hall.

She handed him a twenty euro note adding 'and get one for yourself'. She moved away from the counter while dialling the personal-number at "Emeralds I."

It was immediately answered, and she recognised the polished voice.

Haley grunted in her low mock Dublin accent - 'I was in wit youse yesterday and youse are a robber.' 'So, you have additional pieces' the voice replied 'as the combination of many would greatly enhance the total value.' Haley interrupted quickly. 'Yeah, I do, but I won't be dealin' with youse lot.' She disconnected immediately and then redialled her own mobile number, which was on silent-mode in her pocket. This was in the event of the attendant hitting his re-dial button and getting the jewellery store. He had just arrived with two cans of Red Bull and placed the change on the counter.

Haley smilingly returned the telephone and thanked him, adding she had gotten a proper earful.' Opening her can, she took a large gulp and insisted the attendant keep the change for his polite, courteous assistance. She left quickly, and dashed around the corner to her waiting exit carriage, giving the driver her address. She most certainly did not have any desire to catch a glimpse of the thugs who had caused so much pain in her new household.

She had now shaken another few branches on the tree, and surely something of interest would drop down.

The next afternoon, Haley had found the address that Dansie had described in her conversation. The area had recently been upgraded with modern industrial buildings. One such construction was a house behind a large wall. The only entrance was a solid wooden door, without any windows or identity plate to indicate what operated inside. The heavy door reminded her of a church door. Somehow, she felt its protective force was not to retain any air of solemnity, but to repel sanctimonious invaders.

Even the intercom did not show a named occupant. Haley was certain this had to be the exclusive female-only fitness centre 'La Femme Discrete.' It was indeed a discreet parlour.

Her parked car was a short distance away, and she now had an uninterrupted view of the surrounds. At 5.25 pm, an almost new BMW sports car, reversed into the vacant slot behind her. A smartly dressed middle-aged lady stepped out, and the two sharp flashes of lights, indicated her vehicle was now locked.

She returned a few minutes later and placed a parking disc on the dashboard of her sparkling, metallic purple vehicle. She then adjusted the strap on her Gucci shoulder bag and with an air of confidence, strolled towards the area Haley had just inspected.

Standing at the large wooden door she tapped a series of numbers into the access unit and replied to the answering voice. Five seconds later she had entered the secretive confines of that mysterious building.

Haley adjusted her phone to camera-mode and photographed the vehicle, its reg plates and parking disc.

The next hour would be a boring wait. She observed numerous ladies enter and exit the building, always in haste.

At exactly 6.30 pm the wooden door which she had under constant surveillance opened, and released the driver of the expensive purple sports car.

She moved quickly to her car, discarded the parking disc, and drove away at speed. She was rapidly absorbed into the collective traffic rush.

Haley readjusted her phone to video-mode, placed it into her breast pocket allowing the device sufficient room to film and record. She walked to the heavy door and was about to push against it when the release catch sounded.

A plump middle woman was exiting, and held the door open for Haley.

'Oh, thank you. You've just saved my new nails from damage, on that damned access machine,' Haley said with a smile.

There was no reply, but she was now inside a perfectly manicured garden area. A paved path led to a large frosted-glass door. There was no name plate and thankfully there were no more access code devices.

As she stepped into the warm, tastefully decorated foyer, she was greeted with the most wonderful scented aromas. A small office area with a high counter seemed to offer protection to a long hall with four or five doors on each side. A steam filled glass door at the very end, suggested it protected a large sauna room.

A well-endowed young woman, in an undersized French-maid uniform, appeared from behind a flimsy screen. She seemed surprised to see Haley as she asked, 'Your membership number please?'

Haley suddenly re-enacted her ultra-posh accent, in an attempt to extract as much information as she possibly could from the receptionist.

'I was hoping, you could assist me in that particular department,' Haley enquired with her best air of sophisticated elegance. 'I was informed by a reliable friend that your discreet club, provides the finest of services with utmost discretion. You must confirm such, before I would even consider membership.'

'Absolutely' came the reply. 'We pride ourselves on anonymity.' Adding, 'we are the essence of discretion within these walls.'

She then asked Haley to leave, as the rooms were strictly for members only and suggested that Haley contact a full member who could 'nominate' her. Then find a 'seconder' and submit her application. If successful, then and only then, would she be allowed to enjoy the delights of their quarters.

'Thank you so much for your polite and informative introduction, and you are?'

'I'm Zara, - with a Zee,' came the reply.

'Well Zara, I so look forward to seeing more of you, and enjoying what you have to offer,' Haley cooed back to her. The receptionist gave a flirty smile saying, 'It will be nice, I promise, but you really must leave now.'

Switching off her video in the safety of her sister's car, 'JEEEEE SSSS UUUUSSS what the hell is that place all about?'

The next day Haley decided to visit some of the quality antique shops in the city. It was the perfect opportunity to check out the 'opposition' and get a feel for what type of goods were on offer.

She had booked a taxi, and it was now very late.

She couldn't hide her impatience when the taxi driver pulled up outside.

'Sorry about the delay' the driver said -'traffic is wicked downtown this morning. Cops everywhere, stopping everyone. There was a major hoist at a jewellery store, this morning' he offered.

This sent an unnecessary tremor through Haley even though she had absolutely nothing to do with it. Perhaps Conrad was attempting to top-up his funds or most likely; it would be local gangs. Either way, it would draw attention on the 'fences' who launder such loot.

As the financial district covers a fair stretch of ground, the driver asked 'Any particular address at Custom House Quay?'

'Wherever is convenient' replied Haley.

She quickly found the large glass covered building with the well-polished name-plate of "Mercurial Financial Services." The notice in the polished foyer showed it to be on the fourth floor.

Stepping out of the elevator, a further notice indicated it to be at the end of the long hallway.

She was about to knock on the entrance door when the little voice inside her head yelled 'Hell no'! girl. Just get in, and do your thing.'

It was a large open-plan office with all seventeen or so desks occupied - all by ladies.

There was just one door which showed a sign - "Manager."

One of the staff approached Haley.

'I take it Ms. Harwood-Smythe is at her desk this

morning' said Haley, nodding towards the managers door.

'I presume you have an appointment' came the curt reply. Haley recognised her accent as the individual who had disconnected her last week.

'Oh! we both go back a long way,' answered Haley as she forcibly brushed past her, and headed for the door.

Inside, the well-dressed driver of the expensive BMW sports car was finishing-up a telephone conversation.

'Ms Penelope Harwood-Smythe, we get to meet at last' gushed Haley. The manager stood up, but Haley calmly sat down, on the opposite side of her large mahogany desk.

'And you are?' questioned the surprised manager.

'My name is Harrington, no additional hyphen. We couldn't afford one,' Haley sneered.

'Do you have an account here?' the manager asked.

'Oh goodness no, and I don't think I would chance it either. No! I represent two clients of yours.'

'So, you're a solicitor' snapped Penelope.

'More of a financial advisor' replied Haley with a cocky air of arrogant aggression.

'In that case our advisors will gladly help you ….'

Haley abruptly cut her short - 'today, sweetie, I am giving, NOT, receiving advice.' Glancing around the large neat office, Haley noticed an array of photographs, all including Penelope collecting prizes. On the desk were two mahogany plaques. One mounted with an outsized golf ball and the other a similar, illuminous green tennis ball. Each included a silver pen set.

Haley enthused 'Wow! I never actually realised you were such an accomplished sports lady as well as business person. Well done you, so great for the girls!'

The manager relaxed slightly in her chair and lapped-up the false gush of compliments.

'So, what can we do for you today?' she politely asked Haley.

'Like I said, I represent two clients who've experienced some bother here, and thought perhaps both you and I could resolve these 'sticky' items, between ourselves - girl to girl?'

'The first concerns the Doyle family of Gorteen Downs.'

The manager interrupted - 'That lot! A delinquent account that was completely out of control. The bank had no option to enforce its rightful authority and have them evicted.'

'But those people spent every cent they ever had and more, trying to give their terminally ill child some degree of comfort' said Haley. 'Mrs Doyle even pawned her rings to raise cash to pay the mortgage. They at least paid something, each and every month.'

'It was always way short, and they reneged on their commitment,' the manager barked.

'But they had a very ill child and Jackie, as the only earner was reduced to a three-day week, through no fault of his,' Haley pleaded.

'NOT MY PROBLEM' came the sneering reply - 'Business is BUSINESS.'

Haley was about to erupt with the most vile, vulgar insults she could muster onto the cold, uncaring person opposite her. She had lowered her head to calm herself in an effort of self-control.

When she straightened up, the manager was standing, with both fists on the desk, and a vicious look of aggression on her now distorted face.

She snarled at Haley, 'I have just four words for you - Get-the-fuck-out,' as she made her way towards the door.

'Great, as we are now playing word games,' was Haley's reply - 'I have three words back for you'- "La Femme Discreet."

The door which was partly opened was immediately closed, as she stuttered, 'What is that? - No idea wha.. what you are on about.'

Ms Harwood-Smythe had resumed her position behind the desk. 'So, what's this Femme thing you are talking about, she nervously asked?

Pointing to the two large mounted trophies and the tennis item in particular, Haley smiled 'here's a good one, I heard recently.'

Holding out both her fists in the 'arrest-me' position, she asked -'What would you have, if you had a green ball in one hand and another green ball in the other hand?' There was a five second silence as the manager sat quietly, unable to even comprehend an answer. 'You'd have the undivided attention of a Leprechaun,' Haley announced, in a fit of false laughter.

'I think that's just pure brilliant, don't you' she added, to the sullen figure in the executive chair.

With a fake smile, Haley said, 'I do believe I've now have YOUR undivided attention.'

'I've got no earthly idea what you are raving about,' the manager answered in an agitated voice.

'Oh, dearie me - the old convenient memory-loss trick' answered Haley - 'So let me refresh your slight lapse!'

'How dare you waltz in here uninvited and accuse me of memory-loss, and whatever this femme discretion phrase means,' shouted Penelope.

Haley eased herself into a comfortable poise and calmly said - 'Let's see how I can best describe "La Femme Discreet" to the uninitiated?'

Speaking in an exaggerated slow tone, she said - 'It's a private pleasure dome, where a lady can visit for a discrete service, woman to woman.'

Adding, 'I believe that's an accurately portrayal of this particular establishment.'

The manager had taken a deep breath and exhaled slowly before being confronted by the angry figure of Haley, fists resting on the desk in the same pose she herself had adopted some minutes earlier.

'Now, YOU listen to me' snarled Haley.

Penelope attempted to interrupt the conversation.

In a louder and more aggressive tone, Haley snarled -'Shut the fuck up, and listen very carefully, you cold-hearted, callous bitch.'

The manager was shocked at the outburst and was obviously not used to being addressed in such a forthcoming tone.

Haley opened the leather document holder and produced a large envelope. She emptied a collection of prints onto her lap.

'Item one' she announced, producing a photo to Penelope - 'This is a picture of your beautiful sports car taken at 5.30 pm last Friday. See - there's the reg number.'

'Were you stalking me, as that's a criminal offence snapped the manager?'

'Oh! goodness no, I just happened to be in the area, and if I had been there at same time a month ago, I would have pictured you again,' Haley smiled.

Haley's false smile turned to an ugly growl as she ordered Penelope to remain quiet, warning her that there was much more to get through. 'Perhaps you would like to open the door, as I'm sure the office girls would love to hear what's coming next' she sarcastically said.

The smug arrogant look on the manager's face had faded as Haley produced additional pictures.

'Item two, is you tapping-in your access code.'

'Item three, is you, alighting at 6.30 pm, with a wonderful glow of satisfaction.'

'Item four, is you, discarding your parking disc onto the footpath - litter lout as well, I note. Major mistake sweetie-pie, major mistake.'

'Item five is an enlarged copy of said parking disk.'

'Item six is the charming Zara, with a ZEE, who informed me of all the discreet services available to the select ladies-only members of La Femme Discrete.'

Haley continued with her pious observation - 'do you realise if this were a men-only club, it would be called a brothel?'

'But us girls, we can call it something more exotic.'

Penelope had sunk lower into her executive chair. 'NOW!' exclaimed Haley, 'this is what WILL happen and it is NOT for negotiation, so please, do pay attention or else, I may have to post out these other two envelopes. Both contain similar wonderful snaps, although I'm unsure if hubby, or your CEO in London, will be too impressed when they both receive them. Especially your sweet innocent hubby, with his plum post in the Department of Justice. That would make for embarrassing reading in some tabloid, and most certainly would NOT help his promotional prospects.'

Penelope's ghostly pallor indicated that Haley was now in the 'driving-seat,' and she was going to give that callous bitch, full revs.

'So, let me spell-it-out for you and NO interruptions' she barked.

'You will hand back the keys of number twenty five, Gorteen Downs to Mr. and Mrs. Doyle.'

'In return, they will provide you with a bank draft for overdue remittances. YOU, personally will supply a grovelling letter of apology for the appalling behaviour of this institution and your utter lack of professional courtesy towards them. Again , not negotiable.'

Penelope had checked her computer screen, and announced, 'their monthly repayments were one thousand five hundred and fifty and they are in arrears to the tune of fourteen thousand two hundred and fifty.'

'Absolutely NOT,' corrected Haley. - 'That inflated figure includes your exorbitant interest rate of nine percent, and additional 'late-payment' charges which border on criminal extortion. My figures suggest it should be nearer nine thousand two hundred euro.'

Penelope fumed, 'are you completely mental?'

'I advised you to listen, but now I am WARNING you, to shut up and do NOT inter-fucking-rupt me again, or I will open that door so your staff can get verification of what type of pig-headed, lying crook you actually are!'

Penelope sat back in shock, and even Haley was amazed at her own 'flowery' expressions.

'By the way', Haley quietly asked - 'When was the last time you actually visited Gorteen Downs?'

Penelope stuttered 'ah, about five months ago or so.'

'Oh goodness me,' announced Haley in mock horror, as she produced the last of her photos - 'You should check on YOUR property with greater frequency. This was taken some four months ago.'

It showed a caravan, empty pallets, tyres and large bags in its driveway. 'I believe the back garden can accommodate another four or five caravans' she casually added, 'and you know what it's like trying to shift these people once they gain a foothold.'

The information also mentioned ponies and camp-fires.

'Sweet Jesus, I,, I,, Nobody told me … I… ponies?... I… I…' stuttered Penelope.

Haley promptly announced that Jackie would ensure all trespassers would be removed from HIS property, once the keys were returned to him.

She continued, 'as the house has been unoccupied for the past seven months, it requires complete redecoration, so there will be a deduction of two thousand two hundred euro to cover that expense.'

Haley confirmed that the bank draft would be made-out to Ms Penelope Harwood-Smythe directly, as SHE was the official owner, NOT Mercurial.

Haley stared at the manager with an insincere look of indignation, and calmly said - 'Penelope, you have been a naughty girl - very, very naughty girl indeed.'

Haley calmly informed Penelope of being aware of her misdemeanours with a particular construction company also.

The manger had provided full finance for the purchase of the site at Gorteen Downs, plus the construction of twenty-five dwellings. The builder had not lodged the requisite deposit to avail of such funding, as the application had been falsified, to indicate such.

This was during the 'Celtic-Tiger-Era' and there was a property boom, so profitable sale was always assured.

Haley took delight informing Penelope that her personal commission; backhander; under the counter payback; was the showhouse - free!

This was the property Jackie and Margo had purchased to be their new home.

Penelope attempted to mutter something but was promptly halted. 'It was criminal enough that you acquire a free property, but you then charge the buyers an exorbitant nine percent per annum for that particular privilege. You cheated your employers, and then 'screwed' your buyers. What a greedy thieving pig, you are.'

Haley quickly added that it was most likely, Penelope's gift was never declared as income, and obviously would have avoided paying income tax on this. 'So, there would be a hefty tax settlement, PLUS penalty charges of double the original sum,' she reminded her.

Haley then sadistically sneered 'I know of criminals who went to prison for much less. Goodness me, I shudder to think what would happen to a firmly-figured-nymph like you in there. Can you just imagine being ravaged by some big ugly butch brute, in return for protection. It doesn't bear thinking about!'

Haley was now at her most arrogant and aggressive best, as she issued Penelope her final warning.

'Now listen very carefully as this IS how things ARE going to play-out!'

'The house mortgage is being refinanced and extended by five years so forget your criminal interest rate of nine percent. We are allowing you two percent to cover inflation, even though you, personally are not a licenced lender. This reduces the Doyles monthly rate, to nine hundred and twenty euro per month, which will be paid directly to YOUR personal savings account here. Mr. Doyle commits to this, and will present you with a bank draft for seven thousand euro to cover the arrears on receipt of the house keys, and the letter-of-apology.

He will undertake to remove that unsightly encampment from his property, free of charge, although I really think YOU should be charged for that.'

Penelope snapped back, 'Is that it?'

'Oh dearie, dearie me, no!' Haley calmly replied, and burst into an old 'Carpenters' song - "We've only just begun, dah ,, dah'......... 'I'm afraid that's all I can remember' she added, 'but we have some unfinished business that MUST be sorted and is relevant to this matter. It refers to Mr. Doyle's employers - "Skye High Crane Hire." Penelope quickly interrupted shouting, 'another crock of shit account,' and delivered a five-minute rant on the companies' misgivings, refusal to comply with written agreements and un co-operative directors.'

Haley sat in silence as she readjusted the paperwork inside her leather case and pretended to be mildly interested.

Penelope was almost out of breath by the time her monologue had ended.

Haley politely smiled at her, and said 'now sweetie just relax and listen, because I have listened to YOU.'

She then calmly said, that she actually agreed with most of her tirade, and that it was an over lapse, on behalf of the present directors. The company had been, and still was, profitable and both agreed the cash flow had been decimated by Terry's panache for an expensive sporting hobby.

Penelope was jolted from her comfort zone when Haley informed her that her 'hubby' had availed of the companies' generosity on many occasions. Both of them attending rallies in far-flung mountainous regions of Europe. These additional expenses for all the 'hangers-on,' including the Harwood-Smythe's had eaten into company funds.

Haley firmly stated that all this was finished - for good.

She advised Penelope that Terry had given-up on his plans to be a champion, and would return to his full-time day job. Also informing her the company would be receiving a cash injection and that Jackie Doyle would now be a partner in the business.

Penelope sensed a reprieve as she adjusted her computer screen.

'They owe the Bank one hundered and five thousand euro she snapped, so they injection syringe best contain at least that,' she snarled.

'Oh, dearie me, Penny, you seem to believe everything on that damned screen,' replied Haley.

'It's Penelope,' the manager fumed back.

'By the time I'm finished here, it could be Prisoner 386625' came the angry retort, 'so again - Shut-the fuck up and listen, you arrogant snotty cow.'

'You see, that nasty number includes your nine percent interest plus another penal charge for late payments. Once again, may I remind you, they did not walk away and ignore you, they paid what was in the 'kitty', even though it was below the agreed terms, but to hit them with such an exorbitant interest hike while you both were enjoying the freebie as well - now that was nasty.'

Before Penelope could interject, Haley had quickly continued her dissertation.

'The purchase loans for the cranes and earth-mover will be refinanced over an additional five years. That nine percent interest rate is a 'goner,' as are the penal additional charges. The going rate for such loans is five percent and this IS what will apply. Your old 'Shylock' monthly repayments were nineteen thousand five hundred euro but with the new refinanced package, it will now be twelve thousand three hundred euro.

Continuing on, she said 'This saving, plus the newly secured contracts will certainly ensure the company's prosperity. Skye-Hi will present your company with a bank draft for sixty five thousand euro to cover the arrears, as your penal figures again border on being criminal.'

Penelope's smug few moments of a reprieve were shattered as she fumed. 'The bank won't allow this … not a chance… not the remotest chance in hell! This is blackmail.'

Haley leaned across the deck and whispered 'Not my problem. I can you recall your phrase of some ten minutes ago, "Business is BUSINESS!" I don't give a damn who you must brown-nose to sign-off on this. Tell your cronies that this is the only option and at least, they WILL get their dollars. It just takes a little longer.'

'Failing that,' Haley sneeringly added 'you will have three large cranes and a bulldozer, abandoned outside your posh office door. They will be rather difficult to move, as the four sets of keys will be at the bottom of the River Liffey. It's in your interest to ensure it goes according to plan -'my plan,' you may just salvage a tiny shred of decency, manage to keep your boney ass on that comfortable chair, and have a marriage to go home to. Just in case many of these numbers have washed-over your head, I've taken the liberty of having them typed up for you.'

Haley handed her two pages, outlining her rearranged figures.

'I'll have a professional legal company draw-up the necessary documents verifying all this, she added. 'It most certainly will NOT be that shower of cowboy thugs, you engaged to evict the Doyles, so you have four full days to 'untwist-your-knickers' and get these affairs sorted. I shall return here at precisely 11 am on Friday next with the appropriate legal documents and guaranteed bank drafts for the said amounts,' said Haley with an air of confident arrogance.

She faked a polite smile at the pale, shocked figure slumped in the leather chair, as she marched to the door.

'It's been - interesting - meeting you Penelope.'

As she opened the door, Haley loudly added, 'so until Friday next at 11 am sharp and thank you so very much again, for your most illuminating and co-operative understanding.'

On leaving, she banged the door as hard as she could.

The young lady who had attempted to block her entrance earlier, was at the water cooler, topping-up her cup.

Haley said 'I think you should bring that into your boss as she has 'come-over-all-funny', waving her hands in front of her face. Adding, 'it's a bit early for her to be having 'hot-flushes', isn't it?'

As Haley closed the main door, the last sound she heard was Penelope screaming - 'Get the fuck out of here. Get back to work and don't interrupt me again.'

Haley had the urge to run down the long corridor but she decided instead that a thankful prayer was in order to match her confident stride.

The prayer of thanks, was to Villiem Hilund's meticulous keeping of records in his day-book. His accurate accounts were the ammunition Haley required to sort out 'the wicked-witch' and take her down, a peg or two.

Only then did she realise she was actually in a lather-of sweat. Removing some tissues from her bag, she attempted to dry her brow and neck. She glanced into an adjoining mirror and realised her silk blouse was 'painted' onto her bra in a most revealing manner. 'Jeez Haley, you look like some bimbo coming from a wet t-shirt contest' she smiled to herself.

"Ground floor. Doors opening," announced the annoying, invisible voice, as she alighted into the busy foyer. 'I hope none of you lot are destined for Penelope Fanny-Face,' muttered Haley as she stepped towards the welcoming cool Dublin May air.

Her throat was dry and she badly required some liquid refreshment to settle things down. On the opposite street corner she spied a neatly decorated lounge with an array of floral hanging baskets. She had to dodge the drops of the recently watered display. 'I'm wet enough as it is' she muttered without all this.

CHAPTER EIGHTEEN

The bar was busy for that hour of the morning, mostly with young executive types in deep discussions, over their morning coffees. Two elderly punters were in loud conversation at the counter. They needed to be, as they were in completion between Johan Strauss and a large plasma screen TV, blaring out the news headlines.

A barman asked Haley, 'What's your pleasure madam?'

'Large vodka, ice, slice with a dash of 7-up, please,' came her reply, 'and would you have Grey Goose?'

As he looked towards a high plastic tray, the barman replied, 'If I did, he'd be down there among the ham sandwiches.'

Haley was not in the mood for Dublin wit. 'Whatever you've got then!'

One of the old guys at the bar was very loudly correcting a news item to his pal. 'That's more it, Joey.'

'The Gardai are appealing for witnesses,' he bellowed. 'Appeals is something that the Red Cross does, if there's a flood in Finland or a typhoon in Timbuctoo. Dats what appeals is, right!'

'What dat wan shudda said is, 'the Gardai is looking for Paddy Public to solve the case for dem, right! Because they haven't a bloody clue.'

'If it wasn't for 'a man-out-walking-his-dog' they'd never be a dead body ever found, or crime solved in this country.'

The barman presented Haley with her order, and she handed him twenty euro. Haley took a large gulp, and it slid down easily. She still felt 'sticky' from her brisk walking, as she copped the barman viewing her clinging blouse. He returned with her change, and she cheekily ensured he got a double eye-full. Another swallow and she was now totally relaxed and happy with her morning's accomplishments.

The TV was still annoyingly loud, as the reader blandly announced, 'The dead man was known to the Gardai.'

The man at the bar was still interpreting her announcements for his pal. 'That means, Joey, he had a criminal record as long as Henry Street.' They both laughed in agreement.

The reader continued, 'He was the alleged leader of a local gang, known as the Crew-Cut-Crew.' Haley was in mid-swallow when she heard this and coughed up part of an ice cube.

'You OK, luv?' enquired the barman.

'Yup, down the wrong way,' croaked Haley.

She took another large swig, gathered the change from the counter into her bag, and made a hasty exit.

She hailed a passing taxi, sat into the back seat and said, 'Fernpark Drive please.' The car radio was also relaying the latest Dublin murder. Their reporter at the scene was just regurgitating the same facts as already reported. He announced that the individual, who 'came-across' the body while walking his dog, said the corpse had severe bruising and seemed to have a bullet hole to the head. Haley felt the throb of her phone which was still on silent mode.

'Oh, shit!' Another batch of crazy paranoid notions rattled through her brain. They have tracked me.

By the time she had reached into her handbag, the paranoia had disappeared. It was Sally.

The taxi driver had switched off his radio, mumbling, 'That's enough of that auld boring shite. I hope they all blow each other up.'

Relieved it was her old friend, Haley erupted with a joyous 'Hello Sal. It's so good to hear your melodic voice.' 'Are you on magic mushrooms,' replied Sally with a laugh.

Haley received a fully detailed description of how all the new alterations had progressed. Her kitchen units were now installed, and painters were about to commence their part of the contract. Sally sheepishly informed her that they had spent slightly over budget on the project. She never mentioned the exact amount but added that it was worth every penny. Her son, who was charged with the supervision, reckoned the house would be habitable within two weeks, should Haley wish to return.

The taxi was approaching Fernpark Drive when Sally said, 'Must go - punters await, so we'll talk again soon.' She rang off. Stepping from the cab, Haley was delighted with her house news but more concerned about the murder of Spike.

It was obvious her visit, and the phone call to that jewellery store were closely connected. Somehow, she felt little remorse, as that thug got his comeuppance. He was always going to end up a violent statistic, and it just happened to be on Haley's watch.

As she entered the house, she was met by her frantic nephew. 'Did you hear the news, Aunt Haley?'

'What news?' she calmly replied.

'Spike,' Cyprian spluttered.

'Did he attack you again?' said Haley in a quizzical tone.

'NO! He's dead - murdered,' shouted Cyprian. 'It's all over the news.'

Haley's phone beeped an incoming text message.

It was from Edel, "Haley, PLEASE tell me you are OK. Luv, E."

She replied immediately, "I'm fine. No probs. Cyps is just filling me in on Spike. Talk soon and remember not a word. tks. H."

Cyprian had produced two mugs of coffee as Haley calmly asked, 'So what happened to him?'

He told her that seemingly Spike was abducted while leaving Flexo's. He was bundled into the boot of a silver Mercedes car by some burly East European guys. Chalky and Tank had attempted to intervene but were on the receiving end of a thumping, as it was Spike, they were after. When word broke, the gang were last seen heading with bags packed for the Liverpool ferry.

As Haley sipped her coffee, she casually said, 'Well, I did remind you that violent gangsters like that end up dead. They eventually step on larger toes and pay the price.' She glanced casually at her nephew and said, 'There will be few tears shed for that lot, and now you and your friends won't need to be avoiding them.'

'That's exactly what Keera said,' replied Cyprian.

Haley piously added, 'I recall our old religion teacher quoting from the Bible - 'He who lives by the sword, shall die by the sword.'

'He really must have pissed someone off, big time', said her nephew.

If only you knew, thought Haley to herself.

She needed a hot shower and change of clothes and the opportunity to think things through carefully.

Haley now knew there were crooks out there who badly needed to collect their gems and were prepared to kill to recover their booty.

The other certainty in the equation was - "Emeralds I."

She was still unsure whether it was the manager there, the African who she saw leave or some Russian mobsters. The story, as related to her nephew suggested it was the Russian connection and if so, then Conrad was lurking in the shadows.

How could she flush him out into the open? Then she wondered if she should just hand over the sock of diamonds to Eddie, as he was due in a couple of weeks' time. She realised there would be a mountain of questions and follow-up reports to be investigated. She knew it was too late for that but needed to figure out a safe course of action.

She recalled a saying of her late husband, "When you are faced with a mountain of shite, make sure you have an extra-large shovel - then hand it to someone else."

The hot shower was her first priority as her underwear and blouse were stuck to her body.

Having showered, she then decided she would take a long relaxing hot bath, recalling how refreshing her previous bathing experience was.

She found the salts and oils her nephew had produced for her and filled the tub.

Ten minutes of uninterrupted bliss had presented her with a new perspective to the conundrum she faced.

Haley now realised the full implications of her sales enquiry at "Emeralds I" and decided she should pay another visit to that area.

Next morning at 9.45 she took a window seat in a coffee shop which gave her a clear view of the jeweller's shop front. The usual array of shoppers, tourists, and workers passed her viewing position.

A postman wearing his summer shorts uniform delivered to the various clients on his round. Nodding in his direction, Haley smilingly said to the waitress serving her, 'I hope he gets the weather he's expecting.'

'That's our Ritchie,' replied the waitress, 'he's as regular as clockwork. Here with his large sack of bills at 9.50 each morning and insists on wearing those shorts from May to September.'

At 10 am the steel door frame was being removed and the man who dealt with Haley a week earlier was also collecting his assortment of post.

'Seems everyone around here has a fixed routine,' Haley said quietly.

She had ordered a refill, but none of the clients who entered the jewellery store over that two-hour period bore any resemblance to her 'quarry.'

'Perhaps that slurry-pit needs to be flushed again,' she thought.

Haley decided to take the long walk home. It would allow her uninterrupted thinking-time as recent events had moved along at a brisk pace. There was still a small fortune in diamonds hidden under the dog's sleeping quarters, and she needed to rid herself of that particular burden.

As she approached the Shelbourne Hotel, a car removal truck was about to load its cargo.

'It just stopped and won't move,' an agitated lady was explaining. 'That idiot slapped a parking ticket on me and then he rang the Gardai. I was trying to contact my husband, but he is off-air, and now it'll cost me another one hundred and fifty euro to reclaim a car that's busted and can't be driven out anyway. Where's the fucking logic in that?'

'Settle down missus, I'm just doing what was asked of me,' the young truck driver replied, trying to be as polite as possible. 'Your motor is causing a traffic back-up and has to be moved,' he calmly explained. By then, the young woman was in tears, mumbling about collecting her child from a creche and also others from playschool.

Seeing her plight, the driver calmly said, 'Sit into my passenger seat, and I'll take the car back to my garage.' The priority here is to free-up traffic. Or I'll have the Traffic-Corps on MY case also.'

He explained she would avoid the reclaim charge, and if her motor needed a simple repair job, he would sort it, there and then. If it not he would loan her a vehicle to continue with her chores.

Haley watched as a relieved lady driver was accommodated by a thoughtful, sensible recovery man. As they drove away, Haley noticed the small sticker on the side of the recovery truck - "Aldo's Autos".

'Well done lad. You ARE your mother's son,' she quietly said, 'and I may have some business to put your way very soon.'

College exams would be finished soon. The youngsters would obviously take time out for their relaxation and high-jinks holiday breaks before their arrival into the real-world of careers and bill-paying. Luckily for Cyprian, he had a genuine opportunity sitting on his doorstep. Haley now had fleshed out the business proposal she had presented to Mr. Long.

More importantly, she had to rid herself of that small sock of 'fortune' under Ali's bum.

She now had that 'extra-large-shovel,' but who could she hand it to?

On arriving home, she was greeted by a tail-wagging Ali who escorted her to the kitchen door. 'Good boy, it's business time,' she said, allowing him into the secluded back garden. 'And no peeing on Tyson's headstone,' she laughingly added.

She scrolled through her contact list, searching for Dansie's phone number. Just then, her phone rang. It was Dansie wondering if it was OK to miss the next day as Danno had been called for a back scan. He had waited two years for an appointment, and it was vital not miss out. Haley joked that perhaps the ten minutes of 'action' had taken its toll on his spine. They both enjoyed a good laugh as Haley reassured her it was not a problem and wished them well. She then requested Aldo's phone number, and it was promptly provided.

She waited until lunch time before making her call, realising he might be busy sorting the car which he had towed away earlier. A munching voice answered the phone. Haley apologised for ringing during his break and introduced herself to him. She explained the situation at "Times Long Past". The proprietor would require an appropriate vehicle to accommodate both his business and private travel arrangements.

'Gotcha,' replied Aldo. 'What you need is a comfortable large motor that acts a van but looks like a car.'

'Precisely,' said Haley, 'and I was wondering where we could secure such a vehicle?'

'By the way, I saw you in action outside the Shelbourne earlier, and you seem to be a dab hand at rescuing 'damsels-in-distress.'

Aldo loudly laughed, saying he felt sorry for her. 'It wasn't anything major,' he added, 'so perhaps we now have a new permanent customer.'

'Now,' he added, 'Getting back to your request, I think I may have the ideal animal.'

'It's an Audi Q5 commercial with automatic transmission; metallic paint; twenty inch alloys; still under a comprehensive warranty; only nine thousand miles and at two years old is in immaculate condition.'

'Whoa up, slow down lad, you completely lost me after 'ideal animal', Haley joked.

Aldo explained it was basically a big comfortable car that had the carrying capacity of a van. Being a 'commercial' meant the VAT content of the sale price could legitimately be recouped from the Revenue Commissioners.

'Sound perfect,' said Haley, and then asked how much a motor like that would cost.

Aldo advised that the book value was forty five thousand euro, but a cash offer would seal the deal, at a lesser amount, adding that the VAT content on that amount would be roughly eight thousand and would be returned into the company's bank account.

He explained the owner was an elderly florist who now had no need for such a large motor. A cash sale would allow him to purchase a smaller van, and he would be 'in-quids' as a result. Aldo had replaced a broken headlamp for him recently and knew the owner very well.

Haley suggested that he should run the idea of a cash sale, past this gentleman and see how he would react.

Aldo agreed saying it should yield a positive result.

'Your mam is taking Danno to the hospital so won't be at work tomorrow. So next Tuesday can you drop her off at our house and I'll pop-out to you for a chat?' Haley suggested.

'Done,' he replied, 'so I'll see you then.'

Haley allowed herself a smug smile of satisfaction at having completed that task. Seeing at first hand Aldo's work ethic, she knew the purchase would be in safe hands. That suitcase will certainly be much lighter by the time I'm finished, she thought.

Her phone beeped an incoming text message. It was from Heather.

"Hi sis. Phone service here isn't the best. We've heard bad vibes from that outstation where Chloe was. Seems the local tribes are at each other's throats in that jungle area. Embassy won't allow us to travel there @ mo as Trevor is on official business, not a personal safari. Wish I was home, but I need to find our baby. Hope all is OK @ 15 and Cyprian is behaving. Talk soon when we can get a proper line. Tks again for being there. Luv H xxx."

Haley suddenly felt her sister's pain and wished there was something she could do to ease the burden. Haley attempted to give herself a reassuring thought. She's a tough old boot and she'll get-by.

She replied immediately, "All well here. Cyprian was very pleased with the exam papers. Best of luck in your tracking and I know all will work out. Lots of love from all @ 15 XXX."

It was a much as she could muster in a show of strength and reassurance.

Haley had become so absorbed in all the crazy events that had invaded her life since arriving in Ireland that she had completely lost sight of her sister's anxiety.

She would have happily returned to her new life as a widow. She had all the well-meaning advice and was getting on with life without her precious James and believed she was doing a damned good job at it. She found it impossible to comprehend how both Heather and Trevor felt trying to track down their only daughter in such a hostile environment. She attempted to text some additional words of comfort but felt she could not add anything of consolation to her short reply.

'Why did that goddam house have to get flooded?' she muttered. 'All this shite could have been avoided, and I would have survived in blissful ignorance. What I didn't know would never hurt me, and it will not return my husband to me.'

Her thoughts were interrupted by the slamming of a car door. She looked out the window to see Cyprian and Keera getting out of Edel's car.

Eventually Cyprian entered the hall. Haley was positioned in the kitchen, busying herself at 'nothing.' He glided towards her. Wrapped his arms around her, kissing her on the forehead and with a huge smile announced, 'It's almost over.'

'Just one more day and it's out into the real world.'

'I'm really happy with all the papers, and my assessments were well received,' he proudly said. 'I just wish Mam and Dad were here, along with my scatty sister. I miss the noise of all them - us - being here together so I hope they can knock some sense into that sanctimonious head of hers.'

Haley decided she had to water down the recent text message from Heather.

'Oh, your Mam contacted me earlier,' she said. 'They are enjoying the break and are making head-way on locating Chloe. You know how it is out there. Communications are not the best, and information can lose something in translation, but they hope to catch up with her real soon.' Cyprian excitedly replied, 'Brilliant, that's absolutely brilliant as we haven't heard much in the past few weeks.' Haley chirped back, 'Sometimes no news is good news, as the saying goes.'

Cyprian then told her that the Duffy sisters were invited down to Kilkenny the coming Thursday. The city hosted a comedy weekend called "Cat Laughs" and tickets are always at a premium. A work colleague of Edel's was originally from there and had generously offered them free accommodation for the whole weekend.

'Sounds like fun,' Haley enthused. 'You deserve the break so off you go and enjoy the craic.'

'I can't believe how relaxed and calm the girls are over the past week or so,' her nephew observed.

'Include yourself in that, as well,' added Haley.

'I hope you didn't take offence about me wanting all of us here, as family,' said Cyprian in an apologetic tone.

'Don't be silly,' answered Haley. 'I'd be disappointed if you suggested otherwise. And I'm sure your dad will find you a secure, pensionable civil service post in some far-flung corner of the planet.'

'Not the remotest chance in hell,' he quickly replied.

'I'm a 'homer,' and realise where my bread is buttered.' He added, 'I would never put my parents through what they've endured over the past few months.'

Haley felt another pang of guilt at not relaying Heather's deep concerns at her lack of progress, but why spoil his new-found happiness. He had been through a traumatic physical assault - the family pet had been battered to death, and he had studied hard at college.

At least his reply indicated that immigration was not on his radar and the word 'homer' did not refer to a 'Simpsons' character. It seemed that her expensive plan of his integration into "Times Long Past" would yet be accomplished.

She had earlier spoken to Albert.

He confirmed his house sale would be completed by August, and he'd be ready for his move to the upstairs apartment. Albert had reassured Haley that all her relevant official paperwork would be finalised on schedule and that the Bank drafts were now in his lawyer's safe possession.

CHAPTER NINETEEN

Haley was walking Ali close by the café and park where she had found the money when she heard a shout from behind. A burly eastern-European man was trying to get her attention. He hurried over to her and looked at the dog with a vague look of disappointment. 'Is this your dog?' he asked. Ali sniffed around his legs, and he reached down to pet his head. The dog growled.

'Is he cross?'

'No' replied Haley. He's fucking vicious.'

Taking a step back, he asked 'do you walk here often?'

'Yes. Do you have a problem with that?'

The man explained that he was looking for a woman who had been spotted walking a large, black dog near the scene of an accident involving a friend of his. Haley's eyebrows lurched nervously, and she pulled Ali closer to her. The man said the woman was about her age with similar coloured hair and build.

'I'd like to talk to her about what she saw that morning,' he said.

'I'm sure the police would be interested, too' Haley nodded. She reached down and patted Ali. She wanted the man to think this was the only dog she had ever walked in her life.

'What sort of dog was this woman walking?' she asked.

'I'm not so up on dogs,' he said gruffly. 'It was big and black.'

'I don't know anything about a woman with a dog like that,' replied Haley. Ali showed his fangs and snarled. He also sensed danger and was in protective mode and his growl was louder this time.

He stared closely at her and seemed unwilling to let her off the hook so easily. There was an odour of sweat and alcohol from him.

He stood and watched her as she quickly walked away.

***

The taxi driver was more agitated than Haley as he blasted the car horn and swore at cyclists who zig-zagged their route through the busy Friday morning traffic. He still managed to deliver his client to the office entrance of Mercurial Financial Services and was rewarded with a generous tip for his promptness.

It was 10.58 as Haley opened the door to their open-plan office. Her 'water-carrier' of four days earlier, again attempted to halt her determined march to the office marked "Manager."

'I'll call you if required,' said Haley with an arrogant sneer, as she pushed open the door.

'Greetings Ms Harwood-Smythe' said Haley, with a false welcoming smile.

'Let's get on with this as I suddenly don't like the smell in my office,' came the snappy reply.

Penelope was in a foul mood and growled, 'have you got the cheques?'

The immediate reply was 'have YOU have the letter of apology?' Penelope opened a drawer and threw an envelope across the desk.

'As it's not addressed to me, you open it, as I want to see precisely what it contains' said Haley.

This only irritated the angry manager even more as she opened the envelope and produced a typed letter.

Haley took a long time reading it, adding a few 'huh's' here and there, to further annoy her. You really could have grovelled a bit more,' sighed Haley, 'but it is an apology of sorts and will suffice. Now, please replace it into a new envelope and address it your new tenants,' adding 'I take it you have visited Gorteen Downs since our last conversation.'

'YES! and that cranky old bastard next door said four horses grazed there last week, with five vans and their accumulated families parked outside,' she fumed in reply. 'And he had the brass neck to complain to the Guards.'

'Well done Cyril, you learned the script off perfectly,' thought Haley to herself.

The frustration of Penelope was obvious, as she followed the instructions, and again threw the apology envelope in Haley's direction.

'The bank drafts - do-you have them' she angrily asked?

Haley had opened her leather document folder and produced her official agreements which were drawn up by Albert's friend. Showing the manager both cheques to confirm the correct amounts on each, she ordered Penelope to sign before she would hand-over the cash. 'They have been signed by Mr. Doyle and witnessed, so we only require your scribble and the Company Stamp as verification' she added, with an air of arrogance. Penelope signed on the appropriate lines and returned one of each to her client.

'And the other two envelopes?' questioned Penelope.

Haley looked at her in mock surprise, stuttering - 'Ah... ...wha....whaa.. what are you referring to?'

'You know fucking well. You are really enjoying this, aren't you?' barked Penelope.

'Absolutely. YES,' replied Haley as she placed both signed contracts inside her brief-case. She then took the two envelopes of photos and pushed them in Penelope's direction, deliberately knocking over her opened water bottle. The contents landed onto the executive chair and emptied over the manger's lap.

'Oops, I am so clumsy at times' said Haley in a sneering mock apology.

Penelope fumed in anger. Firstly, ensuring the 'blackmail' envelopes were secure in her filing cabinet as she attempted to dry-off.

'I do hope we won't be seeing each other again, but should it happen, it most likely will be as a witness for the Criminal Assets Bureau, so I don't think I need to spell things out for you.'

The annoying employee was again at the water cooler as Haley slammed the office door.

'No more water for her' said Haley nodding towards the door. She needs some towels immediately.'

As she left the main office area, the last sound she heard was Penelope screaming 'Get the fuck out of here.'

There was no adrenalin rush on this occasion, but a sense of smug satisfaction as she strutted towards the elevator.

The seclusion of the taxi's back seat, allowed her send simultaneous texts to both Jackie and Linda, with the reassuring message - "Job done. Contracts signed. Will drop off to you later. Rgds Haley."

The two remaining residents at number fifteen, enjoyed a peaceful weekend as Haley watched Ali adjust very easily to his new home and life there. 'How could you possibly put-down such a lovable and loyal creature' she muttered.

Luckily Margo had adapted to life without her old canine pal and was more than pleased, that he had been rehomed successfully. The thought of having him return to Gorteen Downs would only reignite too many sad memories, and probably confuse the dog also. Margo and Jackie were elated to be rehomed themselves and like Haley would make alterations to their old home. New décor and discreet changes would help exorcise the ghosts of all the sad days their family had endured.

***

Sally still sent regular updates on the renovations and confirmed that the interior decorating should be completed within the week. Always adding, 'Get home quick, we miss and need you.'

Another short, crackly phone call from Heather indicated that her Dublin stay might have to be extended. Heather and Trevor were not enjoying success in tracking down their daughter.

A recent television expose on the workings on some aid agencies, had shed some of them in an unfavourable light. This added to the chaos, as do-gooder journalists attempted to dish the dirt on other do-gooders. Haley was amused at the obvious contradictions. Various governments had withheld funding in certain sectors. As a state official, Trevor's visit had become mired in this controversy, and the slow progress they made was now halted.

One way or another, her sister was not leaving Africa until she had found her only daughter - however long it took.

Haley still had unfinished business in Dublin and was also determined to see it through.

Eddie sent a less cryptic message to Haley confirming the 'stag' visit and requesting a friendly meeting with her.

Haley replied, 'Text me when you are on the way. I may need your help with a discreet matter. Will confirm later. Rgds, H.'

The youngsters had returned from their soirée in Kilkenny, and everyone had enjoyed the occasion, adding that a return next year was a must.

Haley anxiously watched for a sign or indication from her nephew of any romantic interlude during their visit. It was not forthcoming, and she certainly was not about to question him on that subject. That whole area was a quagmire of mixed emotions, and the less she involved herself the better.

All three were invited to Pinewood Studios in England for the completion of the film project. One of the production team had been impressed with Keera's input to set design in Wicklow and offered her a temporary position. She would also collect a salary during her stay. Edel felt that her future career lay in that particular field, and the years of study would eventually yield positive results. The stay would be for a week, but may drag on longer, as delays were always the order of the day in filming.

Haley timed putting out the refuse bin to coincide with the arrival of Dansie on Tuesday morning. Haley made an excuse to her about requiring Aldo's advice as she bounded up the front steps to greet the awaiting Ali.

As Haley sat into the front seat of Aldos van, he confirmed that the offer of cash caught the florist's immediate attention and a deal would be accommodated. Aldo needed to find a reliable smaller vehicle which would suit his working requirements and was confident this would not be an obstacle. Haley was delighted as she handed him a large envelope.

'What's that?' he asked in surprise.

'It's cash to complete the purchase,' came the reply, 'fifty thousand in used fifties.'

'That's way too much,' exclaimed Aldo, 'I said there would be a big change from the forty-five grand we spoke about.'

'Just listen and I will explain,' she calmly replied.

Aldo peered into the envelope of cash as Haley jokingly confirmed that it was all there.

She explained that he was to take his commission, as that was his work business because this transaction was not a charity job. She had purposely added extra. She wished Aldo to book a sun-holiday - two weeks in a nice hotel, for his parents. If she attempted to book it, Dansie would throw a 'wobbler', and it would taste all the sweeter coming from their son. She insisted it must be kept secret and nobody else be aware. Aldo told her that neither parent had a passport as they had never ventured outside the country.

'Your mam is a hard grafter and two weeks of Mediterranean sunshine would also help your dad's back condition,' she said.

'I don't know what to say Haley.' he replied with an emotional tremor in his voice.

'Don't say, just do,' said Haley with a smile.

***

Over the next three mornings, Haley sat at the same window table which allowed her an uninterrupted view of Emeralds I. It was a boring two-hour observation that yielded nothing of interest to her. By now she was on first name terms with the elderly waitress, Rita, who served her tea and toast. Rita had a strong rural accent and spoke very quickly, which Haley found difficult to fully understand at times. She explained that she was from the west coast and had 'emigrated' to Dublin more than forty-five years ago. She had never acquired the Dublin accent, and it was the one thing that still reminded her of the old home. She began her shift at 9.30 each morning, after dropping off her three grandchildren to school. She finished at 3.30 to collect and mind them until her son had completed his day's work. Her employment 'stamps' were required to qualify her for the State Pension when she would reach the eligible age of sixty-five in two years' time.

Haley smiled back at the warm rosy cheeked lady and said, 'God! That makes for a long day.'

'Needs must,' was her answer, 'but I get to see the same old faces roll by each day, and they all seem to have their regular, fixed routine. Even our postman with the hairy white legs.' They shared a laugh. 'All the young part-timers fancy him because he puts 'auld-spake' on them, with flirty witty compliments,' she added. 'It's like ground-hog-day.'

'I suppose that now includes me,' said Haley a smile, as she kept a watchful eye on her target.

Had the mobsters and the Nigerian smugglers departed and given up on tracing their lost loot? It seemed most unlikely that Conrad's gang would leave empty handed as they had the Nigerians on their tails, and if they planned an escape far away from Europe, they most certainly required funds. The shooting of Spike was sufficient evidence of that, so they had to be in the vicinity. But how could she flush them out without putting her own life in danger?

The constant messages from Eddie, warning her of such, were reminders she should not ignore. And this was with him and his colleagues being unaware of the diamond haul. The jewellery shop was the 'chain' to flush that crock of shite out into the open, and timing was all important in executing any plan to achieve this.

As Haley approached home, the postman was closing the gate, having delivered his lot to number fifteen. No flirty smile or auld-spake for this old biddy, thought Haley as he rushed busily past her, must be reserved only for pretty single teens. An array of letters and flyers lay on the hall mat as Ali ambled out to greet his 'saviour'. Haley bundled them together with the other collection that would await the householders.

She noticed one large white envelope marked for Heather's attention which had been posted with English stamps. There were no outside markings, and the delivery address was by means of an adhesive sticker. It had a similar look to the various 'small-print-pc-waffle' she regularly received from her insurance companies and such. The type of printed account material that is binned immediately.

Another 'light-bulb' moment flashed through her brain.

She boiled up the kettle and easily steamed open the loosely sealed envelope. 'If it worked in an old Hitchcock movie, had to be easy today,' muttered Haley as she removed the junk mail. The address label took a little longer, but it eventually surrendered to the steam. Ali had pawed at the kitchen door and was released into the secure back garden. As he strolled back inside, Haley had written the full postal address of Emeralds I, onto the envelope. 'Ali, you and I are like Holmes and Watson,' she chirped.

He ignored the compliment and strolled into his comfortable bed with the Popeye covering and the small woollen rag doll by his side. The old memories were still there, but he now knew for sure where home now was, and it wasn't a 'Sherlock.'

9.45 on Monday morning and Haley was escorted to her regular viewing table by Rita. 'Another dejay vu, day?' asked the waitress with a warm smile.

'Rita, for a change today, I'll have tea and toast. That French food gives me wind,' she said with a laugh.

'You had me worried for a while,' said Rita in mock horror.

'Can you do me a great big favour, on the Q T?' asked Haley, as she produced the large white 'doctored' envelope.

'For a regular polite customer, who is also a decent tipper, absolutely yes, was the positive reply.'

Haley had folded a twenty euro note between her thumb and the envelope as she handed it to Rita. She asked her to give the envelope to Ritchie when he delivered his post and say it arrived into the café in error and requesting that he deliver it to the jewellery shop. She could say that staff did not like going near that particular establishment. Rita had discreetly slipped the cash into her bib pocket and agreed with a slight wink of her left eye.

Five minutes later the hairy-legged chatty postie had arrived, and Haley watched in the mirror opposite, as Rita presented the package. Ritchie seemed very apologetic, and five minutes later he had delivered Haley's mail to her prey.

'That's done,' said Rita quietly, as she pretended to clean the side of Haley's table, 'and thank YOU very much. I don't like going near that place anyway. There was a cop's raid a few days ago - uniformed guys with guns.'

'Thank you, Rita, and not a word.' Haley smiled.

'Me lips is as sealed as a crab's arse at fifty fathoms,' replied Rita, in her best rural accent.

Haley had no wish to continue the conversation. Rita busied herself with the now packed room, as Haley had an observation to conduct and chit-chat had to be avoided.

Shortly after 10 am the proprietor arrived and began his unlocking ritual. Having removed the outer iron grill, he inserted the security key to open up the aluminium roll doors. He had picked up his postal collection, unlocked the main entrance and was now open for business. Haley wondered what his reaction would be when he opened the mail with a London post-mark. Ten minutes later, he emerged and looked anxiously up and down the street, as if he were checking for suspicious characters. The pedestrians, be they shoppers or tourists, had no interest in him or his recent postal delivery.

Instead, he was a target for the calm lady enjoying her tea and toast and his every nervous move.

When the proprietor opened the large white envelope, there was a message clipped onto a smaller brown envelope which had been thoroughly sealed. The message for him read:

"Dear Mr. Smooth talking, double dealing fence. You have been a naughty boy and unless you want your two-faced arse roasted, follow these instructions... EXACTLY ... Do NOT speak to the Nigerians (gottit!) NO TALK ... Give this package to the tall Russian with the bald head. YOU have got the blood of one poor Irish bastard on your hands, so you don't get us on your case as well.... Make sure the Russian gets this, as we are watching YOU."

This was obviously when he dashed out onto the street checking for observers.

Haley checked the camera on her phone to see if it would be possible to photograph any visitors. The reflection on the café window made this impossible.

Three of four tourists passed through the door but no one that looked like an East European. There were also no visits from the African man she had seen leaving there some weeks earlier.

About an hour later, Haley noticed a small thin man with a shaven head and a long narrow nose, who could certainly pass as East European, walk slowly past the jewellery store. He glanced through the window and kept walking. When he did this for the third time, Haley realised the messenger boy had arrived. She was tempted to vacate the security of her prime viewing position and observe whatever may be happening inside. However, he emerged very quickly, and she could see him stuff a brown envelope inside his jacket. It was similar in size, and he had to be the courier. She placed a twenty euro note under the teapot, gesticulated to Rita and quickly left in pursuit of her quarry. He walked very quickly, glancing from side to side ensuring he was not being tracked. As he approached O'Connell Street, he had his phone to his ear. He suddenly turned around and scanned the oncoming pedestrians.

Oh! I've been rumbled, thought Haley - what the hell do I do now? She casually glanced into a shop window and saw the menacing figure approach. He was angrily speaking in what she presumed was Russian as he stopped directly behind her. 'Why the fuck didn't I take the Glock?' she muttered to herself.

He slightly opened the zipper on his leather bomber jacket and reached inside. The envelope fell onto the ground and Haley knew it was hers. Suddenly realising, this could well be the end of the road for her. The agitated individual picked it up and continued his phone conversation, then suddenly turned on his heels and continued at speed in the direction of Dublin's main thoroughfare. She was safe and said a silent prayer she did not have the Glock.

A silver coloured Mercedes Jeep drew up quickly at the junction, and the courier quickly jumped in. The black-out windows didn't allow a view as to who the passengers were. But she had now seen one of the crooks, had a description of their leader and knew what type of vehicle chauffeured them around.

She had to get back home and await developments.

Her morning pot of tea with toast had taken the edge of Haley's appetite. Having taken Ali for his daily ramble she settled down on the lounge couch for an afternoon snooze. It didn't last long, as a warning bark from Ali and the doorbell took its toll.

She wasn't expecting any callers as she peered through the curtains.

A cold sweat of anxious panic descended on her when she saw a silver coloured jeep parked outside the gate.

I knew it - he saw me, she thought. They had someone follow me. Was it that country bitch in the café with her flowery chat? All the danger signals were flashing red as she dashed upstairs and retrieved the Glock. She double checked the clip to ensure it was loaded, released the safety clip and slowly walked back to the hall. The figure of a man was now knocking on the door with his fist. Her instinct was to take Ali, who was barking his head off by her side for added protection, but the thought of another dead animal was too much for her. She took him into the kitchen and closed the door.

She called from the lounge door, 'Who's there?' as she primed the gun at the figure outside the glass.

'It's Aldo here. I have that estate car outside for you to have a look at,' came the welcomed answer.

'You fucking idiot, Haley,' she whispered. Then she called, 'Just give me a minute.'

She quickly returned the gun to its secure hideaway in her bedroom, settled down Ali with a dog biscuit and calmly walked out into the street.

'It's a beauty,' she said admiringly as Aldo invited her to take a test drive.

Aldo apologised for disturbing her, as the florist had given him the motor to show off for an hour or so and acknowledged he should have sent a text first.

He innocently wanted to surprise her. Haley silently thought she could easily have blown his head off.

'This is way too good a machine for me,' admitted Haley, 'but let's go for a drive to see how it feels.'

'Aldo, where is the main train station here?' she asked.

'Heuston,' he quickly replied.

'No, not Texas,' answered Haley. 'I mean here in Dublin.'

'No, as in Kingsbridge station,' he loudly laughed, 'but you're not the first visitor to be caught out by that.'

Aldo explained that all Irish train stations were named after Irish freedom fighters who died in the 1916 Rising. 'Sorry Haley for the history lesson.' Aldo suddenly realised his passenger was British.

'Aldo, no apology required here, as our two countries have now much more in common,' she said. 'Thankfully this new generation have learned to move on and get on.' Haley was greatly impressed with the comfort and size of the motor and knew that Albert would agree.

'Can you take me to Heuston as there is a little something I need to do?' asked Haley. 'It'll only take a minute or so.'

Aldo was happy to have secured a sale and a healthy commission, so he would have driven her wherever she wished, and it was not far off their track.

'I'll just be a tick,' said Haley as the immaculate looking motor wheeled up at the main entrance.

Two minutes later, Haley was clipping on her seatbelt as they drove back to Fernpark Drive while

Aldo explained all the technical gadgets on offer inside the elegant vehicle. Haley asked if he had checked out the holiday arrangement, she previously suggested. He confirmed a local travel agent had sourced a 4star, all-inclusive package deal in mid-September at a reasonable rate. He added there would still be lots of change from the wad she had given him. Haley told him she had given him cash to purchase and arrange a holiday, and the balance was his commission - full stop.

'Just remember, Aldo, this holiday is from YOU, and my name is not to be mentioned. They'll never want to leave the house after this.'

'It's like a mad-house at times,' said Aldo with a broad grin, 'but we all get on famously, and there's never a row about anything. The only quiet evening there is on a Friday. I have my 7-a-side, Nanno has her bingo, and Da has cards in the pub. Mam has the place to herself, to watch all the 'soaps,' from seven 'till nine. The exception being the last Friday of each month when she and her pals go for a few.'

'She deserves it, and she needs to keep in contact with her old mates,' said Haley.

She gave him the full registered name and address of Albert's business, as he again confirmed the company could recoup the VAT content of the sales price.

'Just let me know when all the ducks are in a row,' requested Haley, 'and remember not a word to anyone, just yet.' They were now parked up at number fifteen. Haley thanked Aldo for his efforts.

Little did he know that he had surreptitiously provided an invaluable amount of information, which allowed her to achieve so much.

Haley skipped up the steps, well pleased at her morning's work, despite the earlier paranoia attack. She forgave herself that encounter, as to most people there would seem to be precious little difference between one large silver jeep type and another. She did not have the advantage of viewing the name badge or the motifs, but she knew Albert enjoyed comfort and quality. She was confident he would approve of the investment and the addition to company cash funds of the VAT.

She now had to wait until 4 pm to follow up on her 'brown-envelope' message. She still was confident is was that scum-bag Conrad who would open and read its contents. If her hunch was correct, he would read:

"Dear Russian Neil DIAMONDS are not forever :), make sure YOU follow these instructions precisely or you will never see the sixty, marquise 1.75 specials which I have.

"We are watching you so do not attempt to any funny stuff, or we will deal your Nigerian buddies. You've got a lot of dangerous thugs looking for you lot, and WE are the only ones who have a trace on you. Go to public phone kiosk on the corner of Bentray Park at exactly 4 pm today and wait for instructions. Otherwise we will hand you and the merchandise to the highest bidder."

She spent the next twenty minutes honing her best Cockney accent in the lowest voice tone possible. Having used it with success on her assignment sorting the Crew-Cut-Crew, she hoped it would have a similar result here.

'Oi Ali, me ole cocker, wha you been up to den, eh wha? You ain't such a bad ole geezer eh?'

The dog looked at her with complete disinterest as he pawed his rag doll into the comfort of his den. His wide yawn and curious eye contact obviously displayed the canine sign "Do Not Disturb."

Haley was now prepared to finish what she had started and it was payback time.

***

At 4 pm precisely, Haley pressed the dial button on her personal phone. She had earlier disconnected the caller ID mechanism in the event of them somehow attempting a trace on her call.

The kiosk number rang for three seconds, and a voice quickly answered, 'Yea, vare is our merchandise?'

Haley immediately recognised the voice tone as the agitated thin Russian who had collected her mail. She had listened to enough of his dialogue to be positive it was him.

'Oi squirt, where is the gaffer - the tall geezer. You're just the little shit of a mail collector. Our message said the tall guy, so we ain't dealin, gotit?'

'No, no, no, no, he busy, he werry busy,' the voice interrupted in an agitated manner.

'It's tough tit then, idden it, cause I ain't dealin with no fokin' messenger boy.'

Again, he attempted to interrupt, but Haley shouted him down.

'You've goh ten minutes to get that bald, droopy tached shit face to this phone or we will be dealin with Jungle Jonah or whoever the fok is buyin, gottit?'

She rang off as the voice attempted to say something else.

'Haley, I hope you haven't overplayed this,' she quietly muttered.

It was obvious that a 'dead man' was not going to parade around in open territory. She hoped that she had given the runner sufficient time to get his paymaster to the kiosk. He certainly had to be nearby as they would have arrived and surveyed the area well in advance.

She gave him fifteen minutes instead. It would give him extra time to make contact, or it would make him sweat it out a little longer.

This time the call was answered immediately, by a voice she recognised from days of old.

'Hello, you have my merchandise, yes,' was the agitated request.

'Well, if it ain't the invisible foking man,' Haley answered.

She was in conversation with the two-faced, thieving scum-bucket who had murdered her husband. It took every ounce of self-control to avoid erupting in profanities down the telephone line. She had a plan devised, and it must be meticulously adhered to if she was to have her revenge, and that was the only thing on her mind - revenge.

'Can you please tell me if you have all my merchandise and vot you vant,' he asked with a bloodthirsty edge of anger in his voice.

Haley now knew for certain that Conrad Kremlin was alive, and in Beltray Park where she regularly walked her dog.

He also needed his loot and was prepared to barter for its return. The Russian was obviously surprised that someone with an English accent was aware of his previous existence. He had to be sure his loot was available first, or it might be a trap to lure him into a vulnerable situation.

'Yea, we got your gear and it's hot dangerous shih, cause of its size and value,' she said in her low-voiced Cockney drawl. 'It rings too many bells when we show it, and too many shit-heads are following it; be they you, or the mob or Nigerians or some collection of rag heads from the Middle East looking for their guns,' she bellowed. 'And it'll cost too fokin much to cut it up into smaller pieces, and then loose value, so we ere, to do biz, rioh?'

'OK, if I believe you got my stuff, vot you vont, to deal,' he asked.

'All in good time, cocker,' she answered. 'You goh info we need. And we goh your goods so we need to trust each other or YOU will be fokked, good and proper, gohit?'

'Yes, but I see nothing to prove you have my goods,' he said with rising anger. 'Puh your hand under the dial box, and there is a piece of grey duct tape, the same colour as the unit. Do it now,' barked Haley.

He pealed back the tape, which was holding a very small package. This he quickly opened to reveal three sparkling diamonds. 'They only three pieces here,' he screamed.

'You fokking moron, do you think I was going to leave a full stash out ere in the open,' Haley snarled. 'You greedy bastard. You've goh nearly fifty grand worth of freebie in your shihhy paw.'

'Yes, I believe you, so vot you vont for me to get rest?' 'You first need to settle down fok-ead, cause we, still goh nine 'undred and fifty grand of heavy duty gear, and if you piss about...'

'No, no, no, whatever is needed, I do.'

'Good boy,' whispered Haley. 'And somefink else, I am only dealing with YOU, and not those muppets waiting for you to click your fingers. That little, skinny maggot almost goh lost yesterday in Henry Street, and cudda goh heself nicked by the cops with his antics. Good job the Merc jeep arrived in time, or he'd a shit heself.'

Conrad was now certain he was being watched as nobody would have been aware of yesterday's events.

'OK, I believe you, whoever you are, so vot now?' he calmly asked.

'Good boy, now listen carefully, and write it down if you must, cause I ain't repeatin it.' She was getting into full flow on the Cockney accent and was now glad she had watched all those old editions of Dirty Den and his friends in EastEnders.

'No interruptions and pay attention,' she ordered.

'On Friday evening next at 7 pm precisely, you be at Heuston rail station and enter from the main gate at the dual-carriageway. Go past the ticket windows which are on your left side and into the station proper. Be alone, on your own, by yourself - gottit? Leave the donkeys in the silver Merc. The main platforms are directly in front of you. On your immediate right are two public telephones. The nearest phone will ring at exactly five minutes past seven. Answer it. It will be me. Then YOU, and you alone, can settle our arrangement. Any sign of those gorillas or that little meerkat and I'll hang your arse out to dry. Did you get all that?'

'Yes, Friday at 7, main entrance, nearest phone on right,' he replied. 'But what if someone is on phone, or is broken?' he added.

'If someone is on the blower, shoot 'em, and if the phone is fokked, then so are you,' barked Haley as she rang off.

Her hands were sticky with perspiration as she poured herself a very large Grey Goose with the usual additions. 'Cheers Ali,' she said in her normal tone of voice, as she took a big gulp of her favourite tipple. Ali ambled to the kitchen door. He also needed some freshening, as Haley savoured a good day's innings.

Thursday morning, Dansie was her usual punctual self, and chattered away while attending the house chores. In truth, there was little to be done, as it had just been Haley and her canine friend in attendance for most of the week. On leaving, Haley asked a favour of Dansie.

Haley implied that Cyprian and some of his pals were having an evening meal and some drinks at the house the next day. She had no wish to in the middle of noisy teens, but was expecting an important phone call between 7 and 8 pm the next evening. She had already extracted information from Aldo as to normal Friday routines at his house and knew Dansie would be alone for most of the evening. She was also aware that there was a public telephone opposite their house. Dansie had mentioned this while obliging Haley with Aldo's phone number, which she had on speed dial for some unexplainable reason. Haley told her the call was about her house insurance claim and needed privacy to complete the business.

She had also overlooked the two cartons of Marlboro Lights which she'd smuggled through Customs, thanks to the antics of the 'Sisters' hen-party. These were presented to a very surprised Dansie. Haley was well aware they both enjoyed a cigarette, but Dansie never had a puff while at work. This was her considerate side, and she would never dare invade her employer's privacy.

'One for Nano, and one for yourself,' announced Haley.

'I'll have the telly turned up loud because of my hearing,' announced Dansie. 'Yea, I'm a bit deaf in one ear and hard of hearing in the other.'

'But you can go upstairs to Nanno's room.'

'It overlooks the street, but you'll have plenty of privacy as she'll be at bingo and we'll have the whole place to ourselves,' she said with a smile of agreement.

'Perfect,' said a delighted Haley, 'and thank you so very much.'

Little did Dansie realise what treachery Haley in mind with her innocent request.

But this was payback time to the lowlife who had screwed up her own idyllic life, and he was going to suffer.

CHAPTER TWENTY

Haley alighted at number 19, Celler Street at 6.50 pm
the next evening. It was best to give Dansie her ten
minutes of chat prior to soap viewing evening. Haley
was greeted with the usual broad welcoming smile as
she stepped into the warm confines of Dansie's family
home. It was a compact, tidy building with all wooden
floors on the ground floor area and the whiff of tobacco
smoke hung lightly in the air. Haley noticed the hall
and sitting room area were decorated with various
floral wallpapers. This was Nanno's idea, and she never
agreed with internal walls being painted. It came from
an era when wallpaper insulated the interiors prior to
central heating, and she was one of the 'old school.'

The droning musical introduction of Coronation
Street was beginning, as Dansie escorted her guest up
the multi-coloured carpeted stairway. They stepped up,
and Haley thought to herself, that must be the most
identifiable piece of music in Britain, after the National
Anthem.

Nanno's private den was a compact room festooned
with her life's collection of ornaments, photos and
religious artefacts. A large ashtray held its reverent

position on the dressing table beside her bed. The window was slightly open in an effort to introduce some fresh air.

'She shouldn't be smoking up here, as she could burn the place down,' said Dansie apologetically.

'Dansie, it's her private space in her house, and I am just a guest, so no problem from my side,' replied Haley.

The intro music had finished, and the dialogue had begun as Dansie left, saying she would have a brew-on for later.

'So, come on down when you are done,' offered Dansie.

Haley sat on the comfortable small chair at the window and surveyed the similar selections of buildings on the opposite side of the street. Fresh A Way was the local chipper occupying one end, and the phone kiosk was at the other end. It was her perfect vantage point being opposite the window. There were just two cars parked there as all the houses had a back street for such.

She opened her leather document holder and took out her phone, checking the time. It was 7.05 as she dialled her pre-set number. It was answered quickly with an agitated, 'Hello, yes, I am here, and my merchandise is not at phone?'

Haley had to summon her low gravely Cockney accent.

'Are you a complete fokking moron? Do you think we would leave a million worth of gems in a busy train station with about twenty CCTV cameras, plus armed coppers within spittin distance of those phone boxes?'

'OK, so vot now?'

Haley had the rat's nose almost at the steel trap, but she needed him on his own in the open.

'You ain't thinkin straight, Conrad, so listen up and pay very careful attention, cause we goh eyes on YOU.'

For a man who was travelling on under a new ID and had some other name, he never questioned her remark when he was called by his original name.

Haley was now one hundred per cent certain this was her target.

'First thing you goha do, is get your donkey's back into the silver carriage,' she barked.

'I alone, nobody inside here, only me,' he replied.

'You shouldn't trust those idiots, they are selling you out,' said Haley, 'especially that ugly shit-face now dead, Igor.'

'No, he vos good loyal friend, was Igor,' came an angry reply.

'You stupid fokking twat. He was double-dealing your diamonds around Dublin and YOU were being short-changed. I thought that was your department - short changing-skimming. Looks like you trusted him too well as he was gonna rat on you. That's why we took him out.'

'No, he dies of bad heart,' said Conrad.

'Bad heart, my sweet arse,' replied Haley. 'He was as healthy as a young bull and you bloody well know it. When did he ever complain of chest pains and didn't he ave a fokkin huge appetite?'

'No, he never sick and always eat good,' remarked a surprised Conrad.

'If you wanna go dig him up, you will see a tiny hole in his left earlobe, just like the old diamond ear-ring you wore some years ago.'

'The Irish coroner opened him and saw his heart had stopped.'

'He never bothered with a toxicity report, as he had no wounds and they wanted just to finish off a report.'

'You really do have a thing for diamonds, don't you and if you want the rest of your loot, you will do EXACTLY what I say.'

Haley had sowed a seed of doubt in his twisted mind and was sure his paranoia would kick in if she could add some more fiction to it.

There was an unease in Conrad's voice as he replied, 'Ok, vot now happens?'

'Make sure your puppets stay in that Merc jeep and don't move, especially the small skinny one with the long hooky nose.'

'He was Igor's man.'

'I suppose you didn't know that either? Did he tell about his conversation with the well-dressed Nigerian the morning he collected the package from Mr. Emerald Shit-Face? No, I imagine not. And why did you think he had his y-fronts in an angry knot, in Henry Street before you rescued him?'

There was a ten second silence at the other end of the conversation as Conrad digested the meal of innuendo he had just been fed.

'OK, I believe you. I trust vot you say, so how we do biz, me only and you,' he replied.

Haley felt a surge of adrenalin. She realised her prey was now an uncertain target as he could no longer rely on the muscle he had banked on for protection.

'Those shits in the car are gonna shaft you when you get the loot. So why share what is yours? Besides it's the info that YOU can give us, is all WE want.'

'OK, OK, now vot?'

On her test-drive and visit to the rail station, Haley had filmed the interior of the building and could visualise it's layout. She imagined, like most people in private conversation, he was facing the dialling unit.

'Now, listen, and listen good,' she ordered.

'Turn around and face the train platforms, which are on your left side.

'Ignore the two burly security guys who are on permanent stand-by there, and do not draw attention to yourself. You are now looking at the side exit beside the river where the taxis drop off their clients.

'Walk slowly out that door and take the first available taxi.

'Tell him to bring you to phone kiosk at Bentray Park, where you collected the first pieces. The trip will take fifteen minutes, so make sure you are NOT late and have no uninvited baggage, as they will probably bump you off. You have fifteen minutes, so MOVE.'

She immediately rang off, as he would only ask more annoying questions. He was now running scared, not knowing who to trust. At least the voice he had spoken with had provided him with three lumps of his stash and had information that he was unaware of. It was exactly where she wanted him - in the open and alone.

Watching from the bedroom window, she saw there was little activity on the street except for the regulars at the take-a-way.

She had timed the trip with Aldo from the station to her home which passed by Beltray. She allowed him two extra minutes to cover for Friday evening traffic.

She dialled the kiosk number. It rang and rang and rang. Afraid that some passer-by would pick up, she cut off. She allowed another two minutes and dialled it again. This time it was engaged.

'Shit, I hope it's not some longwinded gossip,' she muttered.

Three minutes later she rang, and it was immediately answered. 'There is nothing here. Where is my goods,' he shouted in anger.

'Yea, like I was goin to leave 'em pasted to the wall for that dick what was on the last call to collect. Do you think we are complete fokkin amateurs, you shit-face?'

'Tell ya whah, don't bovver. We'll deal somewhere else, as you are a fokking nutte...'

She was quickly interrupted. 'No, no, no, we do our trade, just you and me only,' he said.

'OK then,' said Haley. 'We got gear that is shit-hot and can't move easily and access to info that could be very valuable to us, so don't you go pissin about.'

'You need to get another taxi and get over to Celler Street. There is a chipper on the corner called Fresh-A-Way and phone box down the street. I won't be far away, so be there in ten minutes, gottit?'

She rang off immediately to avoid unnecessary chatter. She had dangled the worm on the hook, dropped it into the lake, and the fish had bitten. It was time to reel him in and settle an old score.

Haley reset her phone to dial the coinbox opposite her vantage point. She just hoped nobody would decide to have a long chatty gossip within the next ten minutes.

There was still little movement in the quiet neighbourhood with the odd resident exiting or entering their abode. Two drunks were winding their way from the take-a-way while having a loud argument about last evening's soccer match. Their opinions, in between munching, were audible to Haley who was some distance away. A neighbour of Dansie's shouted from his window, 'Would youse keep in down lads?'

'Mind your own bleedin business,' came the inebriated reply.

Haley was ever watchful for a silver coloured Mercedes jeep. She still had doubts about that double-dealing thug. He was now like a cornered rat, and that's when a feral rodent like him was at their most dangerous.

The noisy drunks were becoming more boisterous, and it seemed as if there would be fisty-cuffs. Haley hoped that Dansie's annoyed neighbour didn't call the Guards as this would seriously interfere with her plan.

A builder's van pulled up adjacent to the chipper, and a piece of aluminium fell from its roof.

'You fucking eegit, you didn't tie it down,' shouted the driver as his passenger reloaded the fallen object.

'So, onions on how many of the burgers,' was his request as he entered the shop.

'Jeez, talk about Send In The Clowns', muttered Haley. She picked the Glock from her case and unclipped the safety catch.

There was no silver Merc or any slow-moving vehicles on the street, but more worryingly there was no taxi and twelve minutes had passed.

Had he done a runner and waited for a more opportune time?

Had she wasted an opportunity to take him out in the park?

'Had she simply just fucked-up on a simple plan?'

The evening was setting in and visibility deteriorating. Clear identity of her target might soon be a problem.

A taxi stopped at the chipper, and a tall male figure dragged himself from the back seat. She could see he was bald, had a drooping moustache and was at least six foot three. 'It has to be him,' she whispered.

'The phone box, you idiot, NOT the chipper.'

A minute later, he emerged, and a young girl appeared and pointed to the end of the street.

He calmly made his way down the almost deserted street. 'Do you want ketchup as well as onions?' the builder's mate shouted. The tall man turned around as if he was the person being addressed. When the driver answered, he then realised it was not his conversation.

One of the drunks had begun urinating against a house wall as Haley dialled her pre-set number.

'Wha are youse looking at?' shouted the other drunk as the tall man quickly walked towards the kiosk.

'Yes! You rotten bastard,' she muttered. 'It IS you. You can shave your blonde mane, grow your Poncho Villa moustache and lose three stone weight, BUT you can't hide that leg problem.'

Ten years earlier, Conrad had broken his left leg in a parachute jump. The leg had healed, but there were severed tendons in his ankle that were beyond repair.

When walking at a normal pace or indeed running there wasn't an issue. However, when he had to walk at pace, he threw out his left slightly so his instep near his toes, hit the ground first rather that the heel. He could dress as Santa Claus and not be noticed, but when he walked at speed, it literally was his Achilles heel and could never be hidden.

She had her prey and now was certain it was the murdering scum who had planned her husband's murder. And she had him exactly where she wanted.

He was almost breathless when he picked up the receiver. 'Yes, I am here and solo,' he said. 'Where are you?'

'Watching you in your long grey rain mac,' replied Haley. 'You were late and we nearly gave up on you, thinking you might double deal again.'

'No, no, no; where do meet for biz as I need my merchandise?' he asked.

'We need info that you can get, and we need to trust you or else we will crucify you if you fokk with us,' Haley rasped at him.

'Put your left 'and under the dial box. It's all there taped inside that plastic see-through bag.

Conrad had peeled off the tape and stuffed its contents into his inside coat pocket.

'I've done my bit, now it's your turn,' said a very calm Cockney accent.

'Yes, yes, good, what you want?'

'OK,' said Haley. 'You are gonna need to write this down so 'ave you goh pen and note book?'

Conrad reached inside his jacket and opened a small notebook. He held it against the dial box.

His large body frame was now the perfect target. The only thing missing was a large X between his shoulder blades.

'OK, I write down, so tell me vot you vant me to do?'

The conversation was unexpectedly interrupted by four knocks on the bedroom door.

It was Dansie.

Haley quickly muted the phone before Dansie called out 'Haley, I have a pot brewing, as them bloody ads is on, and they drive me bananas,' she called.

Moving quickly to the door with the phone pressed into her midriff she said, 'Give me two minutes. I'll be down and thanks Dansie.'

Haley placed her mobile phone to her ear and unmuted it.

By the time she had returned to her viewing perch, the outside geography had changed.

She was just in time the see Conrad's legs being bundled into the builder's van. The two 'drunks' had sobered up, tasered the Russian and dragged him and his loot into the back of the vehicle.

'Shit and double shit again,' she shouted in anger.

Her final view of James' murderer was the tail-lights of a white van, melting into a blood-red Dublin sunset. She clipped the safety catch onto the Glock and replaced it into her document folder. She felt beads of sweat on her brow as she drew a large intake of breath, exhaled slowly, and closed the window. What just happened and was she really going to kill Conrad?

Haley found the toilet and ran the cold water tap onto both wrists for a minute or so. Her heart was racing and obviously her blood pressure was at a very high level. She had never killed a living thing in her life, but squeezing that trigger seemed so very easy and natural, just three minutes earlier. Having splashed cold water onto her face, she dried herself off, brushed her hair and headed downstairs to enjoy a mug of Dansie's strong tea.

CHAPTER TWENTY-ONE

Over the next week, Haley received multiple text messages. Cyprian informed her that they might extend their stay in London as filming was delayed because of bad light, but they were all having a fab time.

She winked at Ali and in a fake gangster accent drawl said, 'Well kiddo, it's you and me holdin' the fort.'

***

Linda had sent her a message outlining their conversation agreement at the refinancing package, and confirming Terri's rehabilitation was ahead of schedule. She said both she and her husband were delighted to have Jackie Doyle onboard as a partner-director.

As Haley had suggested, Linda's uncle was more than helpful and they were all, well pleased to be working as a team. The excess parking facility at the "Sky Hi" yard was of particular importance. It would save his units the time and expense, of travelling across town.

Haley's suggestion of gifting the two old dumpers was the icing on the cake to conclude the deal.

The was no contact from Eddie, and Haley doubted if his Dublin visit was on the cards. She would prefer if he didn't call as it was best for her to leave things as they were.

The last text from Sally read:

"Dear soon-to-be-fired staff member, get your cellulite arse back over here asap. My present husband is driving me crackers enquiring about you, as your house is now like the day it was first built. Again, sorry we went slightly over budget, but it's worth every penny.

We need you back here as we really do miss you, dear friend. We also need a new house-warming piss-up. Hope all is ok at your end (and I don't mean the cellulite) and come back here. It's your home. Luv, Sally and soon to be divorced hubby:)."

Haley laughed at Sally's crazy humour as she wondered how much over budget did her son actually go.

She was still quids-in following her investments, so it really didn't matter. For that moment she wished she could get to the airport and get back home. A lot had happened, and she had discovered hidden emotions she never knew existed inside her psyche.

She called to Albert's shop. Her signature was required to verify her agreement on the Jack B Yeats purchase.

On entering his Aladdin's Cave of treasures, her eye was immediately drawn to a stunning oil painting which hung directly over the counter area.

Albert quietly approached her and surprised Haley with, 'And are you impressed with your new acquisition?'

'That really is a stunning piece of art,' said Haley in total agreement. 'Really stunning.'

Haley explained the vacant position at "Skye Hi" and Albert was in agreement that it was an ideal employment opportunity for Anna's husband. He would not inform her just yet, and only only reveal the good news on one of her 'down days' as it would cheer her. 'You should impart positive news, on days when the manure and fan are about to collide,' he said with a cheeky grin.

Haley's phone rang. Albert suggested she go to the quiet corner at the enclosed office area for privacy.

She did not recognise the number or the long area code, and was concerned it may be from some Russian or Nigerian undesirables. It was her sister.

'Hi, Haley, everything OK back home?' she anxiously asked.

'Yupp, all's good here. Cyprian was well pleased with his exam efforts, and he's enjoying a break in London with the Duffy sisters. And how are things with you lot?'

Before she the chance to finish the sentence, her sister sobbed, 'It's a shit heap, and we're running into brick walls; shady shysters in officialdom here. Trevor had to give some overfed warlord fifty fucking dollars cash to use his personal satellite phone so I could ring you. And before you ask, NO, we haven't caught up with Chloe yet, as that area is a war zone. Militia with jeeps and heavy machine guns everywhere. James can't get any straight answers, insisting we go through all diplomatic channels. Diplomacy equals talking PC bullshit to freeloaders, who only see you as a cash-machine tourist or if you have twenty tonnes of food stuffs or medicine. Why we bother sending billions out here is beyond comprehension', she roared without drawing breath.

Haley quickly interrupted.

'Heather, Heather, please do calm down - PLEASE. That phone guy can hear everything you say', she pleaded.

'I don't give a shit', was the sharp reply. 'He doesn't speak English, and the only language he understands is dollars'.

'Heather, I know you are upset, but you need to settle down as that will not help any of you'.

'Sis, I do love you, and I'm glad you are at home minding things for us, and it's much appreciated by Trevor and me. We may have to stay a bit longer out here, as I want to find and talk to my baby. She's an adult and if she has some crazy shit-head notion of remaining out here and helping a society who don't give a damn out OUR society or culture, fine. But WE need to know and hear it from her. The umbilical cord was cut over eighteen years ago, and she can make her own choices, BUT I need to find her first', she cried.

Haley had never heard her sister so emotional, ever, and it saddened her greatly. She was speaking as an upset mother as also as a mature adult. Her assessment of things accurately reflected both emotions, but it had seriously delayed Haley's departure plans.

'Little H, I'm here for you for as long as it takes, so you go do what needs to be done and don't worry about things here'.

'Thanks Haley, I'll contact you whenev........'

The connection had broken.

Haley hit her off button and returned the phone to her handbag. She sat with head in both hands, just like at her Mass service some weeks ago, feeling her sister's anguish. Albert sensed her distress and allowed her time. Haley also realised that Trevor was keeping up appearances, but would be a burning cauldron of anger inside. It would be his polite diplomatic way of attempting to calm his wife. Haley certainly did not relish the thought of an extra couple of months away from her own surrounds, but reluctantly had given a commitment and would stand by it.

Albert eventually approached his new business partner, and politely asked if everything was OK.

Haley faked a smile and enquired if there were some documents that required signing. Two sets of the purchase were produced with Albert handing one to Haley which she stuffed into her shoulder-bag.

The store had six or seven potential clients as Haley excused herself and confirmed that Cyprian would be in contact with him when his vacation was ended.

The walk back to number fifteen was slower than usual. She was greeted by Ali at mid hall and as he bent down, rubbing his welcoming head, said, 'Looks like I'm gonna be a while longer than expected.'

Ali raised his snout and licked her face. 'Heh, stop that,' she said, laughing. 'I don't know where it's been last.'

'Just when one door opens, another slams shut,' she muttered emptying the remains of a Grey Goose bottle into a glass tumbler. The usual toppings were added, and she plonked her weary frame onto the comfortable couch in the living-room.

'Just what else can go wrong here?' she sighed as the tumbler's contents were quickly emptied.

***

Haley and Ali had returned to Ferndale Drive, from their morning walk as a church bell called the faithful to Sunday Mass. Haley wondered should she go. Perhaps to just sit in the sanctity of the atmosphere for the forty minutes it lasts, and maybe that gentle old soul who offered her comfort on that fateful morning was still alive. The thought of another boring sermon on forgiveness from the pulpit was off-putting.

Her phone rang. She retrieved it from the battery charger, praying it was not another dreary, bad-news rant from her sister.

It was Eddie, with a cheery, 'Good morning Haley, are we Ok for that coffee?'

'So, you did make it, and how's the hangover?' she replied.

'I took it easy as my liver ain't as great as it was twenty years ago,' he joked.

'Where exactly are you?' she asked.

'Outside your door,' he quickly answered.

Haley glanced through the window at the figure she had not seen in over twelve months.

She immediately opened the door and watched him gently limp up the steps, asking, 'What happened you?'

'A seventeen stone winger, half my age, crash

tackled me into the advertising hoarding,' he jokingly replied as they hugged.

'You should take up something more sedate like fly-fishing,' said Haley with a cheeky grin.

They entered the kitchen as Haley presented two mugs of her extra strong coffee. Eddie reached inside his jacket and took out a large pink envelope.

'A wedding invite?' said Haley in surprise.

'No, not yet,' Eddie quietly replied.

Haley did not recognise the scrawly small handwriting on the front - "Mrs. Haley Harington".

She opened the envelope to reveal a large floral designed 'thank-you' card. Haley was apprehensive as to what it was all about.

The card read:

"Dear Mrs. Harington, I am reliably informed that you are the reason I am able to write this note from the safety and comfort of my hospital bed in England. I have little recollection of what actually happened over two years ago. I just remember, as we crashed, James opened the door on my side of the chopper and pushed me out. Luckily some trees broke my fall before I hit the rocks below. After that, most is a blank except for the appalling pain and primitive conditions at that camp. You lost your husband and best friend, while I lost a trusted colleague and workmate. He saved my life, as you also have, by rescuing me from that gulag. The medics here say I should make a reasonable recovery as they must reset some bones and I require much therapy. But at least, I am alive and now safe. And it's down to you both of you that I am.

I hope I soon get the chance to say thanks in person. With much love and gratitude. Kerri Mc Connell."

Haley was stunned as she placed both hands across the table, lay her head between them and cried bitterly.

Her sobs were loud and the tears flowed freely for at least two minutes. Eddie did not even reach out to hold her hands. He allowed her the opportunity to grieve and hopefully empty the painful anguish bottled up inside her fragile frame. If he did touch her hand, he had no words which would offer some semblance of comfort.

After a while, he peeled four tissues from a nearby box and pressed them into her trembling grip.

Haley dried her runny nose and cleared the remaining tears. She had not wept like that since the phone call that brought her the shocking news of her husband's death. Even at the burial ceremony, her family and friends were amazed at her composure on such a sad day. She was all-cried out in the safety and sanctuary of her home for that occasion.

There were still no words spoken at the kitchen table as Haley eventually raised her head. Eddie watched as her facial expression changed from a sad demeanour to a cold, steely look of anger.

With her hands clasped, but both index fingers pointing at Eddie, she gave him an icy stare. Calmly and very slowly she said, 'Eddie, for ten glorious seconds, I had that rotten scum-bucket in the sights of my Glock 22.

'I could have popped three into his right lung.

But if I had, I would not be reading this note now.'

Eddie was stunned and once again speechless at hearing these words from that timid placid widow.

He quickly gathered his thoughts and spoke at a rapid pace.

'Haley, I did NOT hear that, and please don't say it again. I have a report to write up, and I'll be keeping it as short as possible, so the less I know, the better for all of us. I have no earthly idea how you gathered all this intel or who you had working with you, but you somehow managed what a collection of specialised units, were incapable of. So please don't say any more, as we are so pleased to have our man back home safe, but perhaps not too sound, at the moment. It's little comfort to you personally, but at least the truth has been uncovered, and it's all down to you.'

'Eddie, I had some help from you lot as well,' Haley replied, 'and I never guessed the drunks or van guys were your crew.'

Eddie explained they weren't. They were Irish Special Branch who volunteered to get involved, as it was on their patch. They also ensured safe passage to Newry where MI5 took over, and three hours after the lift, Conrad was in a secure, padded cell near Birmingham.

Seemingly he went berserk when he came to, and had to be strapped down. He was photographed with a newspaper under his chin, to verify the date and this was delivered to the Russian Embassy. They rubbished the fact, saying that the individual had died some two years earlier. When he was photographed again with his false passports and a million pounds worth of quality diamonds, their attitude changed immediately. A swop for Kerri was arranged, and within four days he was safely home.

The Irish lads then picked up the occupants of the silver Mercedes jeep, which was easy, thanks to your accurate description. This was only completed when Kerri was safely home. They handcuffed them together, parked the car outside the Russian Embassy in Dublin and deposited the keys through the security gates. What happened them nobody knew or cared.

'I can tell that Conrad will suffer the most excruciating torture imaginable before they dump him in some cold Siberian gulag,' Eddie added.

'We also managed to extract some young bimbo of a reporter, who was attempting an expose on mail-order brides. She was flying solo and should have known better, but at least that do-gooder is now safely home with Mummy and Poppa,' he confirmed.

Haley thought of Chloe, and her simplistic save the planet efforts and wished for her sister's sake, someone could do something similar.

'So, what happens now, Eddie? Will you take back his donation to the animal shelter?' she asked with a sarcastic grin.

Eddie laughed, and was glad of the opportunity to do so. 'No, he'll have a completely new ID and background detail and will be offered a new future at a safe desk job, wherever he wishes, on planet Earth. We DO look after our own Haley - it may not seem that way to the whingey know-alls in the loony-left, but we DO.'

Haley smiled in agreement.

'Oh! I almost forgot; I've got something for you, too,' she said jumping up from the table.

She opened a cupboard and produced a gift-wrapped box the size of a shoe box.

'Do I open it now?' he politely asked, as he shook the package, adding, with a wry smile, 'ist's certainly not a Glock 22.'

No, thought Haley, that's lying at the bottom of the River Liffey.

'Of course,' she answered.

He unwrapped his present. The box had layers of bubble-wrap inside. 'The Mistress of Mystery,' he quietly said as he rummaged about. Deep inside was a much smaller jeweller's box.

Eddie's mouth opened in genuine amazement as he viewed the largest diamond engagement ring he had ever seen.

'Dear God, Hale..Haley .. I don't ..can't .. I can't accept this, its … its …'

'It's an engagement ring, you muppet,' said Haley with a mischievous grin. 'When your wonky leg is better and you can kneel, I reckon the lovely Sinead will not be able to say no to your proposal.'

'I've been saving-up, myself for the past six months to…'

Haley quickly interrupted him. 'Put the saving to the deposit on your new home instead.'

Eddie was genuinely overcome with emotion and attempted to stutter some form of additional thanks when there was a blast of car air-horns outside.

'That'll be my collection of drunks,' admitted Eddie, looking at his watch. Haley was glad as the conversation had run its course, and there was nothing else to say. As she escorted him to the front door, she added, 'Make sure it is well insured.'

Eddie looked at her.

He knew.

Before opening the door, he gently cupped both hands against her cheeks and kiss on her forehead, adding, 'Thank you Haley for everything and I do hope you will be at our wedding as you are among the top of my list.'

'We'll see, Eddie. I'm not sure I wish to relive old memories anymore, we'll see.'

Another blast of air horn awaited him, as he opened the door. 'Idiots,' he said. They had parked five houses down the road on the opposite side.

'And to think some of you lot are in charge of Homeland security,' joked Haley as he hobbled down the steps.

She was just about to shut the door when she saw Cyprian running up the street from the opposite side.

'Who was he and who are they?' he asked in an anxious tone.

'He's a family friend and a workmate of your late uncle, and they are twenty-one hangovers on the way to the Liverpool ferry,' she told him.

'Look out Vomit Comet,' he said with a laugh.

Cyprian was all excited as he dumped his backpack at the stairs. 'Have I got super news for YOU. You will not believe what has just happened - I still don't believe it myself,' he enthused.

'Tell me quickly, before you explode,' answered Haley as she was expecting some juicy romantic revelation that occurred during their stay in London.

But no! It wasn't.

Cyprian said that he had just bumped into Mr. Long while coming through the park.

He then explained in minute detail every aspect of the employment offer and enthused that he would be a shareholder on a healthy salary. All he had to do was provide a suitable vehicle, as would be required by the company. He was blissfully unaware of Haley's involvement, and she listened in fake joy at his wonderful news. He had suggested searching the internet for a suitable large motor to accommodate the requirements. Haley had to intervene and recommend that they should let Dansie's family take care of that. She calmly advised him to leave that to her, and for him to firstly secure a driver's license.

In his excitement, he had never thought things through, but Haley knew she could handle the situation when he eventually calmed down.

'Your mam and dad are going to be so proud of you Cyps; there really will be. You deserve this because YOU earned it by gaining the respect of that honest businessman. Respect is something no amount of money can buy; it must be earned,' she announced with an authoritative air.

'Oh! Aunt Haley, there is something else that needs urgent mentioning,' he said.

'Sweet Jesus in Heaven, now what?' she whispered to herself.

'Is there something wrong with your phone,' he asked.

Haley checked. She had turned it off in confused error when Eddie rang. She switched in on. There were three missed calls from a number she did not recognise. 'What's up?'

'Mam rang you first, and then she rang me,' he replied. 'The two will be home in a week's time.'

'I thought your dad was committed for three full months,' Haley said.

'He is and he WILL,' replied Cyprian. 'It's mam and Chloe. They'll be home as soon as they can arrange flights,' he roared with delight.

Haley ran to him and they embraced. She scolded him over his ham-acting.

Cyprian said he was unaware of all the details, but his parents eventually found the site and Chloe begged to be brought home as she had enough of the hypocritical bullshit she had endured and wanted out, as soon as possible. Seemingly she had seen some horrific brutality and some of the charity 'luvvies' are not what they seem. She said it was dreadful the way women and young girls were treated by their own elders.

'We'll probably hear all the gory details when she returns, BUT she is never going back. She intends to return to college and finish what she started there and get into a proper life career,' he added.

'Just like you, young man,' said Haley encouragingly.

'Isn't it amazing how things turn out?' he said,

reaching for the remote control of the wi-fi radio. Haley had turned it off when Eddie arrived as Dansie always had it set on a high volume.

'Hah!' said Haley with a broad smile.

'There's one I haven't heard for a while.'

The presenter played the Aretha Franklin and The Eurhythmics hit - Sisters Are Doin' It For Themselves.

She laughed, saying, 'A hell of a lot has happened since I last heard that song!'

THE END

ABOUT THE AUTHOR

Waterford man Seán Kelly is no stranger to the literary/ arts world having multiple publications in Irish print media over the past twelve years. He has also scripted comedy for theatre and performed on stage. He also scripted a 'joke book' for his local hospice. The Dog-Sit Affair is his first novel.

PLEASE REVIEW

Dear Reader,

If you enjoyed reading this book, would you kindly post a short review of the publication on Amazon or whatever book seller site you purchased from. Your feedback will make all the difference to getting the word out about this book.

To leave a review on Amazon, type in the book title and go to the book page. Please scroll to the bottom of the page to where it says 'Write a Review' and then submit your review.

Thank you in advance for your kindness.